The

MORNING
FLOWER

Also by Amanda Hocking

The

MORNING
FLOWER

Amanda Hocking

WEDNESDAY BOOKS
NEW YORK

First published in the United States by Wednesday Books, an imprint of St. Martin's Publishing Group

THE MORNING FLOWER. Copyright © 2020 by Amanda Hocking. All rights reserved. Printed in the United States of America. For information, address St. Martin's Publishing Group, 120 Broadway, New York, NY 10271.

www.wednesdaybooks.com

Designed by Devan Norman

The Library of Congress Cataloging-in-Publication Data is available upon request.

ISBN 978-1-250-20428-8 (trade paperback)
ISBN 978-1-250-20429-5 (ebook)

Our books may be purchased in bulk for promotional, educational, or business use. Please contact your local bookseller or the Macmillan Corporate and Premium Sales Department at 1-800-221-7945, extension 5442, or by email at MacmillanSpecialMarkets@macmillan.com.

First Edition: 2020

10 9 8 7 6 5 4 3 2 1

The

MORNING
FLOWER

1

The Road

"Are we crazy?" It wasn't the first time I had asked that, and I doubted it would be the last time before we got to where we were going.

We still had another twelve hours on the road, if the GPS was to be believed. Over the past day, the two of us had been alternating as drivers in the Jeep so we could stop as little as possible. Going from Oregon to Louisiana left me with plenty of time to worry that we were being ridiculous and doing the wrong thing.

Pan was driving this shift, absently drumming his fingers on the steering wheel to "Radar Love," and he glanced over at me. We'd recently switched seats at the Texas border, so he was still bright-eyed and chipper, and that helped him respond to my boomeranging anxiety with amused patience.

"All right, Ulla, let's go over the facts again."

"Okay." I sat in the passenger seat, with my legs crossed underneath me and my Moleskine composition notebook open on my lap. All of my notes, everything I knew about my parents, the hidden First City, the cult of the Älvolk, the missing amnesiac Eliana, and the tall and handsome Jem-Kruk amounted to little more than a dozen pages.

"Are you worried about Eliana's safety?" Pan asked.

"Yeah, of course I am! She's sick, and I don't know how well she can defend herself."

"Do you know where she is?"

"Not exactly. Jem-Kruk left a note saying to come find her, and I think he's connected to the Älvolk, and they are believed to reside in the First City. And there was also something strange that his friend Sumi said: 'Remember to find the woman in the long white dress.' Whatever that means."

"Do you know where the First City is?" he asked.

"Not any more than a few rumors. But if anyone knows where it would be, it's the Omte tribe. They've sent missions trying to find it and the Lost Bridge of Dimma."

"So, if we want to find Eliana, then we're doing the right thing. Actually, we're doing about the only thing I can think of to help her, since we have to find her first," Pan reasoned.

"But we don't know Eliana that well. Her twin sister alleged that she took her home to help her, and both you and I had to take time off from our internships," I said, playing devil's advocate.

"Well, I'm not an intern," Pan corrected me. "Working at the Inhemsk Project is my full-time job. And I also work part-time as a peurojen."

I groaned. "That's even worse!"

"I talked to Sylvi before we left, and everything's fine," he assured me with a laugh. "She's letting me take a sabbatical."

We both worked at the Inhemsk Project, which was an effort undertaken to help trolls of mixed blood find their place in our kingdoms. Though primarily funded by the Vittra and run by the prestigious Mimirin Talo institute, it was open to all five tribes, with the objective of bolstering our dwindling populations and reconnecting trolls with their heritage and their families.

Sylvi was the head of the Inhemsk, making her our boss. Pan worked in the office, directly under her, searching family records for trolls of mixed blood, and I spent my internship down in the archives, helping translate old documents. That didn't give me a lot of time to spend with Sylvi, but it was more than enough for me to discern that she did not like me, and she didn't really seem to like anyone at all.

"Really?" I asked in surprise. "She didn't strike me as the understanding type."

"She's not, but she does care about the truth." Pan looked over at me. He was still smiling, but his dark eyes had gone serious. "What's going on with you? Did Elof ever let you know what is going with those weird results he got with your blood test?"

Elof Dómari—the docent at the Mimirin who specialized in troglecology (the study of troll-specific biology, including genealogy and genetic psychokinesis)—had taken blood from both Eliana and me so he could analyze it for ancestry. It was standard practice for the Inhemsk Project, a routine test to help decipher where exactly orphans and abandoned babies fit in and where they had come from.

Usually the test came back a few days later with a simple

answer. Pan had told me he'd found out within two days that he was a KanHu half-TOMB (a troll of mixed blood with Kanin and human parentage).

But my results had come back strangely inconclusive. Elof was certain that one of my parents was Omte, but the other one . . . all he could say for sure was that it didn't match any human or troll sample recorded at the Mimirin.

That was nothing compared to Eliana's experience. During the draw, her blood was visibly different—dark and iridescent. The whole incident had been traumatic for her, and it ended with a terrified Eliana running off.

"I don't know," I admitted. "Whatever is going on with Eliana, that's of interest to the Inhemsk. But my thing, it's probably a mistake. Miscalibrated lab equipment or something. I doubt that my blood has anything that would interest Sylvi."

"Have you set up another test with Elof?" Pan asked. "You know, to rule out if it was a faulty reading."

I shook my head. "There wasn't really time. Everything has been so chaotic and busy. And after Illaria took Eliana, I wanted to make sure she was safe before I worried about stuff that can wait."

"Good on you," he said, sounding mildly impressed. "The forty-one hours I waited for my results made me absolutely stir-crazy."

"But didn't you already know what the test was going to say? I mean, your mom told you all about your dad, right?" I asked.

"Exactly. I only 'knew' what my mom had told me, and her claims sounded pretty far-fetched. I'm the secret love child of a human and a troll king—and he happened to fall ill and die right after I was born," he said. "I wanted to believe her, but until Elof confirmed it, I didn't actually know."

"Did it change how you feel?" I asked quietly. "About yourself, I mean. Knowing for certain who you are?"

He rubbed the back of his neck. "It's hard to explain. It didn't really change anything, but it changed . . . the color of everything. Before, I saw the world in a shade of wondering and questioning. But now it's a bit clearer. I can see things more as they *are* instead of only as what they *might* mean."

"Yeah." I nodded slowly. "Yeah. I think I know exactly what you mean."

"I did struggle for a bit after. It was a relief, but not in the way I thought it would be. And then with the Kanin royalty too afraid or too stuck up to even acknowledge my existence . . ." He trailed off. "I didn't really know how I fit into anything."

"I'm glad you figured it out," I said.

He gave a self-deprecating laugh. "I wouldn't say I've figured it out yet. And it took some time to work through it. Actually, the friend that we'll be staying with—"

"Rikky?" I supplied.

"Yeah, Rikky helped me deal with all my stuff after I got to Merellä."

Before we'd left Merellä, back when Pan and I were still in the planning stages for our road trip/possible rescue mission, we'd discussed affordable options. Pan and I both had savings accounts, but neither of them were exactly overflowing. Pan mentioned that his friend Rikky moved back to Fulaträsk last year. So he'd called and arranged for us to stay there for a couple weeks.

"Did you become friends through the Inhemsk Project?" I asked.

"Yeah, but that basically describes literally everyone I've hung out with over the past two years. I guess I don't really have much of a social life outside work."

I scowled. "Now I feel even worse for dragging you away."

"No, don't. It only goes to show that I needed the break. And I want to help you," he said, then added, "and Eliana."

"Well, thank you. I'm really glad you're here." I reached over and put my hand on his arm, gently touching his bare skin.

He glanced down at my hand, at the unexpected touch, and embarrassment rolled over me in a hot, sickly wave. It took all my restraint not to jerk my hand away, and instead I pulled it back in a normal, casual manner.

"Are we close?" I asked loudly, and I turned my face away so he wouldn't see the reddening of my cheeks.

"Are we close to the Omte city?" Pan asked, sounding confused. "We still have over a thousand kilometers to go."

"Yeah." Then I shook my head. "No. I mean, can we stop at a gas station soon?"

"Yeah, of course," he said, then we lapsed into an awkward silence.

2

swamped

In the dream, we were flying under an endless sky. Stars stretched on infinitely, and they were falling around us like rain. Dazzling, glittering stars, and I stared through them all, with Pan by my side. Far behind me—so far I couldn't see her, but I knew she was there—was Hanna, and I could faintly hear her calling for me. Shouting my name, over and over.

The stars kept falling, until they were all gone and the sky was black. I couldn't see anything, so there was nothing but the crystal-clear sound of Eliana's voice: "The sun sets in the green sky when the good morning becomes the violent night."

And then it was gone, and Pan's hand was on my shoulder, shaking me gently awake. "Ulla. We're here."

I sat up, blinking away my dream. The sun hadn't gone down yet, but it was close, bathing the car in a fiery orange light. The Jeep was parked on a gravel road at the edge of a swamp, and tall reeds and giant cypress trees surrounded us. Right in front of the car, a long, rickety dock stretched out toward a ramshackle house on stilts.

"Are you sure this is it?" I asked.

"According to the directions, yeah." Pan grabbed his knapsack out of the back seat, and then he got out of the car, letting in the hot, thick air and a medley of amphibian and insect songs.

I got out as well and stretched out the kinks in my neck and back. That's when I noticed the leathery alligator head mounted on the post at the end of the dock, above a sign that had No Trespassing written in big red letters.

"Are you sure this is safe?" I asked.

"This?" He tapped the top of the alligator head and smiled. "Rikky calls this an Omte welcome mat."

"I suppose it's about time I learned about my heritage," I muttered as we began the long walk down the dock.

My skin was still cool from the car's AC, and the humidity clung to me. All around us the swamp stirred with life. Creatures chirped and splashed beneath the warped boards, and a pair of large vultures circled overhead.

The animal life was abundant and obvious, but this dock and dirt road were the only signs of troll (or human) life that I could see.

"This is Fulaträsk?" I asked dubiously as I looked around.

"Not quite. Rikky lives outside of the town, more in between the trolls and the humans. It's more convenient that way."

From the outside, the "house" looked like a dilapidated, windowless shack. Most of it appeared to be constructed with unpainted gray weathered plywood, patched up with sheet metal and broken pallets, and in the center of that was a rusted front door.

Pan raised his fist to knock, but before he could, the door swung open. A woman stood before us, grinning broadly. Her dark auburn hair was pulled up into a messy bun, and she wore paint-splattered overalls over a striped bralette. It was hard to tell how old she was exactly—her face was youthful, with full cheeks and dewy skin, but something about her pale brown eyes made me guess late twenties or maybe early thirties.

"Pan!" She held her arms out wide, and he didn't hesitate to go in for a hug. "It's sooo good to see you! How long has it been?"

"About a year. I think." He pulled away from her, then motioned to me. "This is my friend Ulla. Ulla, this is Rikky."

"Hi, nice to meet you," I said with a smile, doing my best to hide my astonishment that Rikky was a rather beautiful woman.

"Likewise," she agreed with a smile, but she appraised me with a sharp eye.

The water to the left of me suddenly erupted as a hefty beak snapped at the air, lunging toward my bare feet.

"Oy!" Rikky shouted at it and clapped her hands together. "Drake, it's not feeding time yet and you know it!"

Drake was a mossy green reptile, with mud and plants clinging to his bony shell. He looked like a stubby cross between a dinosaur and a bulldog, but I guessed he was some type of snapping turtle.

"Don't mind him," Rikky said, and she stepped aside, putting herself between us and the monster turtle as she held the front door open. "He's an old grump, and I'm sure you've had a long trip and wanna get settled in."

"Thank you for letting us stay here," I said as I slid inside her tiny home.

While the exterior really screamed "swamp shanty," the interior décor felt much more stylish—lots of vintage and upcycled pieces (old boat parts converted into a whitewashed flower planter, a light fixture made of fishing line with dyed feathers and glittering bits of broken bottles become a DIY chandelier.)

From the outside, it had looked like there weren't any windows, but that wasn't exactly the case. There was a small octagonal porthole in the tiny bathroom—along with a rain shower that was literally outside on a deck. And the ceiling—aside from the rusty metal joints and edging—was all skylight. Really, it was multiple panes of glass—mostly clear, but some were green, and one was a tinted car windshield—stitched together like a puzzle.

If I had to guess, I would say that Rikky had built this house with her own two hands.

That made it even more impressive that it looked as nice as it did. It was very small—one main room with a kitchen (a counter of sheet metal with a hot plate, icebox, and a metal tub for a sink), a couch overflowing with pillows and throw blankets, a coffee table made from an old cellar door, and piles of books and plants on every available shelf.

In one corner was a giant antique birdcage sitting on a stand, but inside, instead of feathers there was fur. A chubby gray squirrel was sleeping in a round fleece pet bed, and Rikky told me offhandedly that that was Wade, who she hoped would be well enough to be introduced back to the wild soon.

In addition to the main room, there was the bathroom (antique porcelain sink and a composting toilet inside, the shower outside on a deck about the size of a postage stamp), a small master bedroom, and Rikky's screened-in porch/workshop that also included a daybed, so she said it technically counted as a guest room.

"I know it's not as fancy as what you're used to in Merellä," Rikky said, once she'd finished giving us the brief tour of her home.

"Honestly, Rikky, you know it's better than my place," Pan said.

She laughed loudly, then in a flash of embarrassment covered her mouth with her hand. "Oh, no, Pan. You can't possibly still live above the tannery?"

He shrugged and stifled his own laughter. "I can't find a place cheaper that's any better than what I've got."

"Oh, yeah," she said. "There's plenty of things I miss about living in Merellä, but how damn expensive everything is isn't one of them."

Pan sat down on the couch, and Rikky grabbed a throw pillow and tossed it on the floor near his feet. She sat on it, leaning up against the couch—and almost leaning on him. I didn't know what to do, so I sat on an old steamer trunk across from them.

"This place here"—Rikky paused, gesturing vaguely at our surroundings—"costs me two hundred dollars for the *entire* year!"

I gasped. "That's unbelievable!"

"There are some major trade-offs living in Merellä," Pan said.

"I love it out here." She turned her attention to me and brushed her bangs out of her eyes. "I don't want to give you the wrong idea about the Omte. We're not all backwater Neanderthals."

"No, I didn't think that," I said, but truthfully, I didn't really know what to think.

"Did you grow up around any Omte?" she asked.

"Sorta. Iskyla is home to all sorts of trolls that don't fit in anywhere else, so that means we had a large population of TOMBs and half-TOMBs," I said. "But since it's a Kanin city, I'd say that was the predominant culture around me."

"That's gotta be hard," Rikky said. "I grew up in Sintvaan, this little podunk Omte village. I knew I was Omte—my mom raised me, so I knew all about our culture. But she didn't know anything about my dad. Which was how I got involved in the Inhemsk."

"Were they able to help you find your dad?" I asked.

"Yeah, they did." She leaned against the couch, resting her arm on the cushion so her hand rested casually on Pan's knee. "I got to meet all my Trylle family, which has been cool, but weird. There really are so many differences, since the Trylle live much more like the humans. They use *so* much technology." She rolled her eyes.

"Ulla's actually been with the Trylle for the past five years," Pan said gently, and Rikky blanched.

"I didn't mean anything," she said hurriedly.

I laughed, brushing it off. "No, it's true, but I've come around to their ways. It's been such an adjustment living where Wi-Fi isn't viewed as a basic necessity."

"We do have Wi-Fi here, and I know some Omte that

are a little addicted to their social media and crushed-candy games. But it is always an adjustment moving to a new city. The weather, the neighbors, the food," she said. "Which reminds me. Are you guys hungry?"

Pan patted his stomach, flat under his slim T-shirt. "I could eat."

"Yeah, I'm definitely craving something more than gas-station food," I added.

Trolls' sensitive stomachs and particular dietary needs made traveling and dabbling in human cuisine tricky. We'd mostly been eating some fruit and vegetables we bought at a roadside stand in Texas.

"Excellent. I thought, to help you get in touch with your Omte roots, I'd cook you guys one of our most common meals—pepper-and-bullhead kebabs with a chadron thistle salad."

"That sounds awesome," I lied with a forced smile. "Thanks."

"Why don't you two relax, freshen up, get settled in, and I'll get the grill going," she suggested.

"Thanks, Rikky." Pan slowly got to his feet and stretched. "What is the plan for sleeping arrangements?"

"I don't have a ton of room here. I thought one of you could take the daybed in my workroom, and the other could take the couch." Rikky stopped short and her eyes bounced between the two of us. "Unless you're sharing a bed—"

"No," Pan answered quickly.

"The daybed sounds great for me," I said, calling dibs on what I thought would be the worst place to sleep, thereby giving Pan the better bed.

"Perfect." She smiled. "I thought we'd relax tonight, since it's so late. And then first thing tomorrow I'll take you down to the Omte offices to talk to the records officer."

"That sounds great," I said.

Later on that night, after we'd choked down extra-salty chewy fish kebabs that left my stomach burning and cramping, and after I'd excused myself for the night, I lay on the lumpy bed under a thin sheet, staring at the moon reflecting on the swamp. The screens that surrounded the porch managed to keep the mosquitoes out, but they did nothing to dampen the sound of their buzzing, along with the sound of all the other bugs carrying on outside.

As loud as the wildlife was out here, it didn't drown out the sounds of laughter and chatting as Pan and Rikky stayed up late, reminiscing.

I wondered dimly if this was mad. If I was doing the right thing. But mostly I wondered where Eliana was, and I hoped that she was okay.

3

postkontor

I didn't think I'd ever fall asleep, but apparently I had, because I woke up to Rikky knocking on the flimsy storm door that separated the workroom/guest room from the rest of the house.

"Are you awake?" Rikky poked her head in.

I ran my hands through my tangles of hair and squinted into the bright morning light that flooded the room. The tools and paint cans stacked on the workbench cast long, cool shadows on the warped floorboards.

"Uh, yeah, I think so."

"I called down to the records office already, and I got us a meeting in an hour." Her long hair hung in a loose braid over her shoulder, and the mason jar in her hands clinked with ice cubes and dark sun tea. "Do you think you can be ready by then?"

I nodded and sat up. "Yeah, of course. What time is it?"

She glanced at her watch. "Almost seven. I've got some tea chilling in the icebox if you want any. I'm not much of a breakfast-eater myself, but Pan is scrounging something up," Rikky said with a meaningful laugh. "You know how he hates to miss breakfast."

"Thanks, the tea will be fine," I said, and she finally left me to get ready.

I pulled a change of clothes out of my duffel bag and wondered dourly what time she'd gotten up. She and Pan had still been up talking when I finally passed out around midnight.

Had they even slept at all?

Not that it was any of my business. Not really. Pan and I were only friends, but I'd thought maybe there was something more to it.

But now I didn't know. Maybe I'd misinterpreted his kindness for something else. . . . Not that any of this even mattered. I had more important things to worry about than some silly crush on a cute guy.

I wasn't sure of the Omte's thoughts on formality or how high-ranked the records officer was, so I decided to play it safe with a business-casual look—a maxi skirt and a dark peasant blouse with light makeup.

Once I was ready, I went to the main room. Pan stood over the hot plate, the pan sizzling and snapping as he scrambled something in it. His dark curly hair was still wet from a shower, and he wore jeans with a white tank top, revealing the tattoo on his bicep. It was a large clock, drawn with raw Nordic edges, and the numbers were actually various runes. The hour was pointed at the rune Raido—an *R*-like symbol that stood for "journey"—and the minute hand pointed at the Kaun rune—an < meaning "knowledge."

He'd been whistling an old Nina Simone song, but he stopped when I came in and greeted me with a big smile. "Good morning! Are you hungry? I was trying to make a root vegetable frittata with vulture eggs, but it's definitely turned into more of a breakfast hash."

"No, thanks," I declined, in part because it smelled like burnt leather.

"Suit yourself." He turned back to his cooking, then pointed over his shoulder with a spatula. "I left the tea on the table, and there's mugs by the sink."

"You really made yourself at home," I commented as I poured iced sun tea into an old Dat Dog plastic tumbler.

He shrugged. "I try to make myself useful. Rikky's outside feeding the various wildlife she's adopted."

"That explains all the splashing and hooting I heard while I was getting dressed," I muttered.

"Yeah, she apparently rehabbed a couple turtles and vultures and I don't know what else. Now they hang around, so she feeds them and makes sure they're doing okay," he explained.

"That's very nice of her." I sipped my bitter tea and looked up through the skylights at the trees blotting out the bright blue sky. "So, are we heading out when you're done eating?"

"If you're not eating, you can probably head out once Rikky is done," he said.

I looked at him in surprise. "You're not coming with us?"

"Yeah, I talked about it with Rikky, and we thought a two-pronged approach would be best." Pan clicked off the hot plate and dumped his mushy vegetable/egg scramble into a bowl. "Since you'll have someone at the Postkontor to help you look into info on your parents, I thought Rikky and I would focus on trying to find out more about Áibmoráigi and where Eliana went."

Áibmoráigi is the oldest troll establishment on earth, so it's sometimes called the First City, but its exact location has been lost for over a thousand years. Various trolls have tried to find it over the years, all unsuccessfully, and stories of it blurred the lines of fact and legend.

"And since the only info I have about my maybe-birth-mother is that she was last seen in Áibmoráigi, you're thinking that our investigations will dovetail," I inferred.

Pan gave me a lopsided smile. "That is the hope anyway."

A few minutes later, Rikky and I headed out on the air-boat she kept off the back of her dock, which she assured me was the best way to navigate the swamp that encompassed Fulaträsk. The trip took twenty minutes. It was loud, but surprisingly smooth, with me gripping the bench unneces-sarily tightly as she weaved us through the trees.

In Fulaträsk, the office where all the records were stored was called the Postkontor, and it was a squat stone build-ing sitting atop a small hill. Mossy vines grew up the side, and the vulture gargoyle perched on the stone shingles of the roof made it look like a mausoleum.

Inside, it was cool and damp, and it smelled vaguely of wet paper, which could not be a good sign for a place that stored records. The Gothic flourishes of the exterior con-tinued on the inside, juxtaposing with practical touches like fluorescent lighting, file cabinets, and dividers to create small office cubicles in the large space.

A woman stepped out from behind a divider, moving

slowly because of her stocky legs and a belly that appeared to be swollen with a late-term pregnancy. Her long dark hair was pulled back into a ponytail, and her attire was a lot less than business casual, with a loose flannel shirt left unbuttoned over an alligator T-shirt and a pair of leggings.

"Can I help you?" she asked.

"I called this morning about an Omte orphan looking for her parents," Rikky said uncertainly.

"Oh, right, of course." She walked over to us. "You must be Rikky Dysta."

"I am, and this is Ulla Tulin. She's the one that needs your help."

"Hi, I'm Bekk Vallin." She shook my hand brusquely. "Why don't you have a seat and I'll see what I can help you with?." She pointed to the right, toward a small sitting area, where bland pleather furniture was surrounded by several wilting potted plants.

"Is it okay if I head out now?" Rikky asked me while Bekk grabbed a pad of paper and a pen off a nearby desk.

I nodded. "Yeah. I can handle this."

"Great. Just call me or Pan when you're ready to be picked up." Rikky gave me a small wave and left.

After I sat down, Bekk chose the chair across from me. Once she got settled in, with her pen in hand, she rested her serious brown eyes on me. "So, tell me everything you know about your birth mother."

And then I launched into the fragmented story of my parents, which was really a story of myself. What little I knew or suspected about my parents came from what I had stumbled upon or guessed at.

I told her Mr. Tulin's version of the night a woman abandoned me at a tiny inn in a frozen troll village, and I glossed over my lonely childhood. I'd gotten to the part where I finally hitched a ride with a traveler who came through when I was fourteen and how she took me to the Trylle capital.

"Why did you decide to go with that troll?" Bekk interjected. "You lived and worked in an inn. There had to be other tourists who came through that you could've left with."

I shrugged. "I don't know. I really left about as soon as I felt old enough to, and she was nice, and it seemed like she understood what it was like to not fit in, since she was a blond Kanin."

"Really?" Bekk looked up sharply. "I used to know a blond Kanin. She fought in the Invasion of Doldastam."

Her expression was hard for me to read, and I hesitated before answering.

The Invasion of Doldastam had only been five years ago, a bloody conflict that had ended the Kanin Civil War. But while the war had started as an internal conflict within the Kanin, all the other tribes had eventually been pulled in by varying degrees, and only the Omte had backed the losing side. Once it was all over, treaties had been signed and a peace declared, but I had to imagine that the war was still a sore spot for many of the trolls who fought in it.

I finally decided to answer with the truth. Bekk was here to help me, and I didn't want to withhold anything from her. Even seemingly insignificant things might help me find my parents.

"Bryn Aven," I said.

Her eyes widened, and she leaned back. "I know Bryn." Then she shook her head. "Well, I did know her. We fought beside each other, when our Queens forged an unworthy alliance."

"It was a complicated time," I replied carefully.

Bekk nodded once. "It was." She blinked, then looked back up at me with a strained smile. "Were you connected with Bryn in any other way?"

"Not that I know of. We only met because she was in Iskyla looking for someone else."

"And then you became friends?" Her thick eyebrows arched high, and I tried not to squirm under her scrutiny.

My mouth suddenly felt dry, and I swallowed hard before cautiously admitting, "Yeah. We're friends."

After the longest ten seconds of my life, Bekk said, "Good. Any friend of Bryn's is a friend of mine."

"Great!" I said, probably too forcefully, but the relief hit me like a wake. "I mean, yeah. Bryn's great."

Bekk set aside her pad of paper and settled deep into the chair, her left hand absently rubbing her round belly, and she propped her feet up on the coffee table.

"Bryn's the only reason the Queen Regent Bodil is still alive," she said, then quickly added, "Officially, everyone will deny it. You won't be able to find any documents here about the secret meeting Bryn had with the Queen, before the war, warning her of the dangers of a compromised ally." Bekk pointed toward the file cabinets and bookshelves. "But I know, and Bryn knows, and most importantly, the Queen knows."

"What do you mean by that?" I asked uncertainly.

"The name you gave me . . ." She paused to glance over at the notes she'd taken while I'd been telling her my life story. "Orra Fågel. She's a cousin to the Queen Regent. I can give you the records we have here, but I can also tell you that all the information available to the public about *anyone* connected to the royal family will be highly sanitized and censored."

I frowned, but I tried to remain optimistic. "Any information at all, no matter how minute, would really be so helpful. I need *something* to go on."

"No, that's not what I meant," she said with a sly smile. "I don't have much to offer you here, but the Queen definitely does. And she owes Bryn—and me, honestly—a lot, but she's done very little to repay us so far. Talking to a friend and helping her find her family, well, that sounds like a small step in the right direction."

4

Friends

I spent the rest of the morning going through the scant records that the Omte had on Orra Fågel, but it was just as
Bekk had warned me—there wasn't a lot there. Birthday *1
September 1969*, full name *Orra Fågel*, her high school di-
ploma, and a long list of relatives, both parents and four older
brothers, all dead. They didn't even have her death certificate
here. Bekk explained that most royal certificates were kept at
the palace, although even she had to admit that the cousin of
the Queen Regent barely counted as royalty.

"Plus, it usually goes the other way," Bekk said. She
closed the drawer of a long filing cabinet, after a fruitless
search through death certificates.

"What are you talking about?" I asked.

"Usually it's a non-royal bragging about alleged distant
relations to the crown," she elaborated. "A third cousin telling everyone how their dad's death certificate *should* be kept
at the palace with other royalty, but it's not included, and the
crown doesn't acknowledge them.

"But this is someone who should be overlooked—no offense." Bekk glanced at me, and I shrugged. "And she's all locked up in the palace."

"That is weird," I realized.

"Kinda." She grimaced and put her hand on the small of her back. "But Bodil is rather paranoid, even by Omte standards. In her defense, having your most trusted adviser betray you and commit treason will have that effect on you. She really cleaned house after the war, changed up a lot of the staff, relocated records, and reduced public access to information."

Even with the concerns about the Queen's anxiety/paranoia, Bekk was able to deliver on her promise to get me a meeting with her. Before I left for the day, she managed to get through to the Queen Regent's secretary and set up a meeting for the next day at ten A.M.

I had taken up enough of Bekk's time—and I'd already exhausted all resources in the records office—by noon, so I called Pan, and he and Rikky zoomed over on the airboat to pick me up. On the way to her house, Rikky stood at the back of the boat, steering with a lever as we whipped through the trees. I didn't feel stable standing up, so I sat on the wooden bench seat next to Pan.

"How were your adventures today?" I asked Pan, nearly shouting to be heard over the large caged propeller—or fan, as Rikky called it—that powered the boat through the swamp.

"I don't know if they were adventures, but I think we had a productive day," he said.

"Yeah? Did you find anything about the First City or Eliana yet?"

He let out a short, tired laugh and ran a hand through his windblown hair. "Not quite yet, no. But I did spend the day knee-deep in musty books reading up on strange superstitions and ancient obsessions."

"That sounds intense," I said.

"You have no idea." He leaned closer to me, so he wouldn't have to shout so much over the fan. To steady himself, he put his right arm behind my back, his hand on the bench on the other side of me so his fingertips grazed my thigh. "They were doing all these weird old rituals you'd associate with the Dark Ages, like seriously demented things. And it's not even that long ago. Some of it took place in the 1800s, but most of the worst stuff was in the 1960s and '70s."

As he spoke, he moved in closer. My blouse had ridden up some, exposing the skin of the small of my back, and his forearm gently pressed against my bare skin. I tried to focus on what he was saying—it was important and very interesting to me—but when his warm skin touched mine (not an exciting place, sure, but a private one that rarely had skin-to-skin contact with anyone else), it made my skin shiver all down my spine, and my stomach filled with delighted heat. Even though I so badly wanted to listen to him, all I could think about was how his arm felt strong and warm, and how he smelled like summer sun and cedar and something sweet but earthly, like fresh herbs and lemonade. Suddenly the boat lurched to the side. Pan's arm slid around my waist, catching me just in time to keep me from flying out into the murky swamp. Water splashed up over us, soaking my "nice" clothes.

"Sorry about that!" Rikky shouted from where she stood

behind us. "Animals can jump out of nowhere out here, so it's best to hang on."

I dutifully sat up straighter and hung on to the bench. As much as I enjoyed flirting (or even attempted flirting) with Pan, I valued not flopping around in dirty water or being eaten by alligators even more.

When we got back to Rikky's I called dibs on the shower, which would have been enjoyable if not for the major moral dilemma that arose when I came face-to-face with a spider.

Behind the showerhead, in the corner underneath the rusting eaves, was a fat garden spider in a huge web. My stance on most living things was one of "live and let live." And I was determined to abide by that despite my very real fear that the spider would leap into my face and bite me.

This led to a terrifying, lukewarm, seven-minute shower. The one good thing was that I was so focused on the spider that I didn't have any time to worry about whether or not anyone could see me naked through the shower curtain.

When I finished, I found Pan and Rikky sitting in the main room. A ceiling fan made from old car parts languidly cooled the room, and Fleetwood Mac played on the record player. Both of them were lounging on the couch and drinking dark liquid out of green mason jars.

"Ulla! Come join us!" Rikky exclaimed as she saw me. "Have a drink!"

Before I could respond, she flitted over to the table and poured a glass from a big jug. She thrust it at me, and I tentatively took it from her. "What is it?

"Omte sangria," she said with a laugh.

Pan rolled his eyes. "It's blackberry wine and *eldvatten*,

which is a fancy name for Omte moonshine. It's good, but pace yourself."

I sniffed my drink, and the smell was a tart mixture of Jolly Rancher candy and kerosene, so I decided that I'd work up to it.

"We were talking about all the disturbing crap we learned today, including living sacrifices and *helifiske.* " Rikky did exaggerated air quotes around the final word.

"*Helifiske?*" I repeated. "I don't think I've heard of that before."

Rikky sat on the couch next to Pan and pulled her feet up under her. "Before today, neither had I. But you may know it by the more anglicized name—sacred recruitment."

That clicked with me because I'd only learned of it recently. Calder had gotten a book for me about the followers of the Älvolk—the legendary guardians who protected the Lost Bridge of Dimma—and it had mentioned something. The book was mostly a series of commandments and a few simple parables and poems, and there were key phrases repeated throughout. Lots of references to blood, "magick," supremacy, and getting to a magical land of riches and reward.

One of the ways to gain access to this utopia was to commit acts of service. Most of them were simple and made sense, like setting aside pursuits of gold and following the orders of the Älvolk leaders. But there was also talk of "payments in blood and flesh," as well as the importance of "sacred recruitment" and "*blodseider magick*"—but neither of the terms had been specifically defined in the text.

"If you're ready to get into it all, you might as well sit

down and make yourself comfortable." Pan motioned to a pile of cushions and ikat pillows on the floor, between the record player and the birdcage that housed the sleeping squirrel.

I peeked in the cage, checking out the fat gray ball of fluff, before settling down on the cushions. "Okay. I think I'm ready."

"It's sex," Rikky said bluntly, then laughed at the shock on my face. "*Helifiske*. It's the sacred act of using sex to seduce prospective converts into joining the cult. Or, I'm sorry—they prefer to be called Freyarian Älvolk or Guardians of the Lost Bridge of Dimma."

"There is a lot more to it than that," Pan admonished her. "Yeah, *helifiske* is a part of the teachings of the Freyarian Älvolk, but it is more than a recruitment. I read about a lot of rituals that mentioned sacrifice and sex with *blodseider magick*, but most of them had nothing to do with attracting new members or proselytizing of any kind."

"What were the points of the rituals, then?" I asked.

I decided it was finally time to sample the "sangria," sipping it slowly and inconspicuously. That turned out to be a very smart move, since it tasted like battery acid mixed with sugar. I managed to keep my expression neutral as it burned down my throat, and I forced myself to focus on Pan's explanation.

"I don't know exactly," he admitted. "Pleasure? Power? Delusions?"

"It all starts with Frey," Rikky interjected. "The Älvolk in general buy into the whole Alfheim creation myth. You know, the one that says 'god' or 'gods'—depending how closely you follow the orthodoxy—all live in Alfheim. They either came from Alfheim and created the earth, or they lived on earth and created Alfheim as a paradise for the gods and heroes."

Pan took a long drink of his sangria while Rikky was talking, and he shook his head as he swallowed. "No, no, that's not quite what the Älvolk believe. I don't think they know who or what created Alfheim and the earth and universe. They think that Alfheim is a better place to live with a higher quality of inhabitants. Whether Alfheim is another kingdom, continent, planet, or maybe entirely made up is anybody's guess."

"So maybe a real place or maybe a paradise of the gods?" Rikky asked with a teasing smile.

"Okay, it's basically the same thing, but I want to be precise with my language. It's one thing to believe a place is a utopia, and it's another to believe that it's an afterlife that you must do good deeds to gain entrance to," Pan clarified.

She held up her hand. "You're right, you're right."

"So how do the Älvolk and the *helifiske* fit into finding Eliana and the First City?" I asked.

"Áibmoráigi was built near the Lost Bridge of Dimma to guard and conceal it," Pan said.

"Other stories say that the bridge was supposed to be a secret, and that trolls built the First City too close to it," Rikky added. "And that's why they 'lost' the bridge, to protect it."

"No matter how you slice it, the First City and the Älvolk are connected," Pan said. "Many of the legends diverge at certain points, but there is a lot that is similar. Trolls and humans lived separately for a long time—with the trolls alluded to as being on Alfheim, and the humans on earth. There was a bridge between the two worlds, although the exact descriptions of what the bridge looked like or how far it spanned are usually vague and frequently contradict each other."

"Yeah, I read on Trollipedia that some historians thought that tales of the bridge were created to explain natural phenomena like the aurora borealis because of how often the bridge was described as bright lights that were gone in a matter of seconds," Rikky said. "But then I read several passages today that described it as a dark tunnel that took forty years to pass through."

"It could even be that they're talking about two separate things but the folklore got all mixed up together," Pan said. "But the main point is that there was some mystical bridge that connected the troll world and the human world.

"And also, just to be clear, they don't use the words *troll* and *human*," he went on. "Those from Alfheim are *álfar*, and those on earth are called *ekkálfar*, so really the bridge connected the *álfar* world and the *ekkálfar* world.

"A city sprang up around where the bridge met the earth, like many ports that eventually grew into bustling centers of culture and life," Pan said. "And that's exactly what Áibmoráigi did, eventually becoming the First City and the birthplace of troll society."

"But then something happened." Rikky's thick eyebrows bunched together, and she stared up at the skylights for a moment. "There isn't a clear record of what transpired, but something changed."

"The most consistent explanation that I've heard is that

old nursery rhyme," Pan said. "The one with a bird and a fish and a bunny and, I don't know, some kind of big cat or something. And they're all pals until this giant worm, of all things"—he rolled his eyes at that—"messes everything up. It's basically a Norse Tower of Babel."

"Tower of what?" Rikky asked.

"My bad." He laughed to himself. "I forgot you guys grew up so isolated from humans. I doubt that there's a lot of copies of the Old Testament floating around in nightstands around here."

"Anyway, it was all sunshine and Towers of Babel," Rikky said helpfully to move the story along.

"But other than the giant worm stirring up trouble, I haven't got a clue about what caused the rift between Alfheim and earth, but for some reason the *álfar* decided they no longer wanted to keep the Lost Bridge open," Pan said.

"They didn't call it the Lost Bridge back then, though," Rikky said. "They hadn't lost it yet, so it was called Bifröst."

"And it became 'lost' when the *álfar* tried to destroy it, but it couldn't be destroyed," Pan went on. "The best they could hope for was hiding it away. That's where the Älvolk came in. They were the *álfar* who stayed behind to guard the bridge and keep anyone from crossing it."

"Okay," I said. "But you said this was all because of Frey, and so far he hasn't come up."

"Oh, we're getting to that now." Rikky sat up straighter. "He was an *álfar*, and he decided to stay on earth after the bridge closed. His followers say he stayed because he was fond of everyone on earth and he wanted to help us get back where we belong. His detractors argue he stayed because his trollian abilities like telekinesis and persuasion made him like a god among the humans."

"You studied Norse, right?" Pan looked to me. "How much do you know about Frey?"

I shook my head. "I haven't studied the myths that much. Just the language. All I really know about Frey is that he's the god of love ... or fertility? I think?"

"More like the god of sex," Pan said.

Rikky lifted her glass and winked. "And wine."

"A regular party god, then?" I said, and she snickered.

"As you can imagine, a secret group of monk-like guardians had a difficult time keeping up their numbers," Rikky said. "A bunch of old dudes living a life of sacrifice and solitude protecting something that nobody really knows about didn't attract a lot of members.

"Then, suddenly, old writings of Frey's surfaced, where he details his life of debauchery." Rikky did jazz hands to show her faux-surprise. "And now these texts instructing 'ritual orgies' as a means of getting to paradise are no longer viewed as crude stories but instead as literal instructions on how to open the bridge and get to Alfheim."

"That's how the Freyarian Älvolk began," Pan said. "When the Älvolk tilted away from a simple life of service to a really twisted, zealous doctrine. But this was way back in the late 1800s. The Freyarian cult rose and fell through the years, until a particularly resilient sect took hold in a Trylle community in Northern California in the 1970s. This latest wave differentiated itself from the past iterations by having an overt mission to convert trolls and prepare for the discovery and reopening of the bridge.

"This is also the group that took the calls for blood and flesh to the most literal and most disturbing degree," he continued and grimaced.

"The records we were reading, a lot of them were partially censored." Rikky shivered involuntarily. "They were deemed too graphic for public consumption."

"So, if the Lost Bridge even really exists—if it is a tangible place that we can get to and not an allusion to the northern lights—it's currently being guarded by a group of psychotic monk warriors?" I asked.

"Yep. And that's the good news," Pan said.

Rikky scoffed. "How is *that* the good news?"

"Because at least we were able to find out more about the Älvolk. We learned something new," he reasoned. "The bad news is that we don't even know where the First City is. The location of that has been hidden for centuries, and the bridge has been lost for much longer than that. And we still don't know if the bridge is even real or just a myth about the northern lights."

"Yeah, that is bad news," I agreed and gulped down my sangria.

5

sangria

It was later, although I didn't know the time. The sun had gone down, and the bugs had come up. The three of us had gone out to the dock after our discussion, when Pan declared that he was hungry. Rikky had suggested cooking on her charcoal grill, so we all sat out in rusty lawn chairs. After we ate, we tossed the excess vegetables at Drake the alligator snapping turtle—all while sipping on Omte sangria.

We stayed out there, talking and laughing and drinking, until the air was alive with mosquitoes, then we escaped back into the house, into "my" room, where the screens kept the bugs out but let the evening breeze in. Rikky moved around some of her half-finished projects—a torn-apart box fan, a sanded old nightstand, a stack of driftwood meticulously arranged so it was starting to take shape as reptilian sculpture.

I offered to help, but Rikky waved me off, so I lounged back on the daybed. Pan moved aside a pillow, then lifted my legs so he could sit under them. Rikky talked to herself as she rearranged, muttering her plans for this or that.

In fact, Rikky had done most of the talking all night, mostly regaling me with tales of life growing up Omte. It involved an awful lot of brawls, cookouts, and various adventures in foraging—each story usually featured at least two of those elements. The Omte community seemed a lot more involved with each other and more neighborly than I was used to—albeit more assertive. I couldn't say if that was because of the warmer climate vs. the subarctic one, or if it was something else.

Rikky straightened up and let out a pained groan. "Oh, my." She put her hand to her forehead. "That sangria must've been stronger than I thought it was, and now with that little bit of work, I am winded." A small laugh escaped through her strained smile. "I hope neither of you would mind too much if I went to bed early."

"No, no, of course not," Pan assured her.

"All right, thank you." She smiled at him, still strained and uneasy, and when she walked past us, she roughly tousled his hair. "I'm leaving the stereo on because I don't want to deal with it, but feel free to turn it off."

"Nah, it's cool. Everybody loves ABBA," Pan said with a big goofy grin, then looked over at me. "Right?"

"Yeah, it's great," I agreed, but Rikky was already in the main room, the storm door swinging shut behind her.

The walls and door were thin enough that the music easily drifted through—although admittedly the disco pop was playing very loudly inside the living room. Still, when I spoke, I made sure to keep my voice low so as not to bother Rikky.

"How are you feeling?" I asked.

"Good, good." He laughed and rested his hand on my

calf. "But I don't think I even finished one glass of that, and I think Rikky had, like, three."

I laughed dubiously. "Did she really?"

That only made him laugh harder, putting one hand on his chest and nodding vigorously. The whole daybed was shaking, but I didn't really mind, because I slid closer to him, so my thighs now rested on his.

"I can't believe she stayed up as long as she did," he agreed once his laughter subsided. "I said she should slow down, but she does what she wants."

Over the course of a couple hours, I had slowly drunk from my one glass, and I was still feeling it. The alcohol left my stomach hot and tingly, and my head was light and floaty, the words slipping from my lips with an ease I wasn't used to.

"Thank you for coming here with me," I told him emphatically, and I put my hand over his—his skin felt so much cooler than mine; how could he stay so cool when my whole body flushed with heat?

"As I've already told you, like, a thousand times—you're welcome." And that really had to have been at least the tenth time he'd said that.

"I'm really glad that I don't have to do this all by myself. And I don't just mean because I don't know where I'd be staying," I said, and he laughed again—a quiet, warm rumble. "This is a whole lot to sort through, and I don't know how I can make it up to you for enduring this."

"Enduring this?" He laughed and shook his head. "Yeah, it's so brutal. I'm researching a history that really intrigues me, while hanging out in the beautiful—albeit wild—

wetlands, and I get to hang out with a very cool girl while doing it."

"Aw . . ." I started to say, when something hit me. "Wait. You do mean me, right?"

"Yeah, of course I mean you." He rested his head on the back of the daybed and looked at me. "You always gotta make me say how I think you're funny and smart and beautiful. Who else would I be talking about?"

"I don't know." I lowered my eyes and I was thankful for the dimness of the room hiding the blush on my cheeks. The only lights in the room were a kerosene lamp hanging from the ceiling and a few citronella candles.

I wasn't looking at him, but I could feel his eyes, studying me.

"You thought I was talking about Rikky," he realized quietly.

"Maybe." I shrugged. "I don't exactly know what your relationship is with her."

"She is my ex-girlfriend," he admitted slowly.

"How long did you date?"

"A little under a year."

"Wow. So, it was a serious thing?" I asked carefully, and he nodded. "Why wouldn't you tell me? You didn't even say that she was a girl."

"I don't know. It was a dumb thing to do, not telling you, but I didn't know what to say about it."

Pan fell silent, long enough that I looked up at him to make sure he hadn't passed out, and he was staring off into the night. I sat up, pulling my legs off his lap and hugging my knees to my chest.

"Okay, so I don't know how to explain it to you without putting it all out there, so here goes." He took a fortifying breath. "I like you. And I think you might like me."

He looked at me out of the corner of his eye, then quickly looked back at the swamp. "And I feel like we're in this weird spot where we're not an item but we're . . . I don't know. We're not really *nothing* either. And life happened, and the stuff we're doing to find Eliana and to find your parents, that obviously—and it should—take precedence, but then it makes our non-thing-*thing* even more confusing to me, and I guess I don't really know how to act or what the proper etiquette is in this situation."

"I don't really know either," I admitted. "But I think being honest and not keeping things from each other is a really good start."

"Smart." He looked at me with a relieved smile. "See? That right there is exactly why I like you."

I laughed and leaned in closer to him, but I kept my arms around my legs, holding them to me. "So, if we're being open and honest, is it okay if I ask you about Rikky?"

"What do you wanna know?"

I shrugged. "Nothing too personal. Just the normal basic stuff. How'd you meet, why'd you break up? I mean, I assume it was mostly amicable, since you two are still so friendly."

"Yeah, I mean, it really was," he said. "Everything I told you about her was true. We met through the Inhemsk Project. I was going through a rough patch, and we grew closer and we started dating."

He rubbed his jaw, waiting a beat before continuing. "We had fun, but we moved in together pretty fast, because she didn't have a place to stay in Merellä. But the truth is that she didn't really want to stay in the city, not after she connected with her Trylle family.

"She stayed about as long as she could handle it," he went on. "But I cared too much about the work I do, and I didn't want to give up my life in Merellä. And that's what it all came down to. She wanted to go, and I wanted to stay. So, she went, and I stayed."

I waited a moment before asking, "Do you regret it?"

"No." He shook his head. "I never have. When we first split, we both left the door open—if either of us changed our minds, we could pick it back up. But neither of us knocked on that door. Not in all the months and months since she moved here. So, I guess neither of us regretted it."

He groaned and rubbed his hands over his face. "Is anything I'm saying making sense or is this the incoherent ramblings of a semi-drunk man?"

I laughed. "No, I get it. I think." Then I yawned loudly.

"It's been a long day. We should both get some rest. We've got another busy day tomorrow." He stood up and stretched. "You're having brunch with a Queen."

"It's not brunch. Just a meeting. But yeah." I took a deep breath. "I should rest up."

He looked at me a moment longer, like he was thinking of something more, but instead he said good night and headed into the main room, turning off the stereo before crashing on the couch.

crowns

To get to the palace, we had to go through Fulaträsk. Rik-ky's place was way outside of the city limits, which was why a human-maintained road went right up to her dock, and the Postkontor office I had gone to the day before was on the outskirts, so I hadn't yet seen the city proper.

Fulaträsk was sort of like a backwoods Venice mixed with an Ewok village, where everything was only accessible by water or wooden bridges—some of which connected the treetop homes and shops together.

The Omte didn't have the psychokinetic powers that the other tribes did, and they didn't have the strength to rely solely on magic cloaking the city, the way Merellä did with the Ögonen, or even to lesser degrees like the Kanin, Trylle, Vittra, and Skojare did with their larger cities.

That left the Omte utilizing more basic forms of camou-flage. They lived far from humans in an overgrown, virtually uninhabitable swamp. The homes were hidden high up in the tops of the massive cypress trees, and the buildings on the ground tended to be masked with mud and overgrown vines.

The other part of their defense were the archers. Rikky pointed them out, or I wouldn't have noticed them otherwise. They were perfectly camouflaged and hidden behind blinds in the trees. Rikky wasn't sure how many there were in total, but she said they had archers guarding the city limits at all hours of the day and night.

Sometimes I wondered if it was worth it, the lengths we went to in order to live separately from the humans. Yes, historically humans reacted very badly when they discovered a troll in their midst, leading to whole troll villages being destroyed back in the Dark Ages. And there were also situations where the humans were justified in hating us, especially considering the practice of changelings was really an extended con involving kidnapping, robbery, and fraud.

Tribes defended the practice of changelings by insisting that it was our only means of survival and an act of desperation that the humans had driven us to. They outnumbered us thirty thousand to one, and they monopolized so many resources—and not only gems and gold, but also medicine, land, and knowledge. Humans tended to rush straight to violence and war when they encountered something they didn't understand, especially when that something had terrifying superpowers.

In Salem, they slaughtered innocent young women *suspected* of having a mere fraction of the power that the current Trylle Queen actually possessed. Admittedly, that was back in the seventeenth century, but I didn't know if that type of hysteria was something humanity could ever really grow out of.

Either way, I couldn't really fault the tribes for trying to live as far away as possible from humans—while still trying to reap the benefits of what they had to offer, like health care and Wi-Fi and Swarovski crystals.

All of that is to say how pleasantly surprised I was by the beauty of Fulaträsk—at least the parts that I could see. Last night, Rikky had gone to great lengths to tell me of the emphasis that the Omte put on functionality and practicality.

"Beauty serves no purpose for us," Rikky had said, and even then—when I was under the fog of the Omte sangria—I wondered if that was easier for her to say because she was conventionally attractive. That was definitely not a prominent feature among the tribe, with so many ogres and the frequent facial and body asymmetry. Me—with my left eye slightly larger than my right, my shoulders too broad for a woman my height, my stomach doughy and my thighs thick, my full lips making a lovely smile, my boobs large and almost perky, my legs long, and my skin smooth—no part of my appearance was spectacular, but it wasn't awful. I was neither a beauty queen nor a monster. Just average. An ordinary Omte.

Rikky was driving me to the appointment to meet the Queen, and she went slowly to prevent backsplash from messing up my nice indigo crocheted sundress. Pan stayed back at her place, sleeping off his hangover. With the speed she was going, Rikky thought it would take nearly forty-five minutes to get to the palace, and that gave me plenty of time to admire the hidden city.

The sky was completely devoid of clouds, and the sunlight shone brightly through the canopy, highlighting the sprawling tree-house city. They were clearly giant tree houses—they had to be, to house the large ogre families I saw hanging out on the balconies, watching as we weaved through the trees.

The unwieldy size appeared to be the only thing they had in common with the luxurious human tree houses I'd seen on TV. At least from the exterior, they appeared to be constructed with many of the same materials that Rikky had used on her house—repurposed barn wood, faded driftwood, mossy branches, and the occasional panel of gray-blue rippling sheet metal.

Somewhat ironically, it was precisely the nature of the materials that made the houses seem *so* beautiful. The way they were built of discarded bits of wood and upcycled windowpanes, with vines and moss growing over it all, these fabricated structures seemed to merge back into nature. They had a lovely fairy-tale quality.

Finally, I spotted the palace in the middle of a clearing. Much like the Postkontor, it was a short square block of a building, albeit significantly larger. The royal residence sat on a low hill, nearly flush with the water. Moss covered the stone walls all the way up to the rather Gothic-looking vulture statues on the eaves.

The palace blended nicely with the surroundings, and from the outside it looked about how I'd come to envisage the Omte and their kingdom: deceptively imposing and decaying beautifully. Even with my expectations, the large front doors of the palace—twenty-foot-tall iron double doors—were far more rusted than I would've thought appropriate for a palace.

Only one guard waited at the door, but he'd let only me in, since Rikky's name wasn't on the list to see the Queen. We parted ways, and the guard led me inside, where it looked more like a crypt than the home of the royal family.

The humidity and dank smell of the swamp permeated the place. The large main hall was dimly lit with iron chandeliers, so I couldn't say for sure, but everything appeared to be covered in a thin layer of moss or slime. When I passed under an arch, I had to duck out of the way of a spiderweb.

Finally, the guard showed me down a narrow corridor and into an office of sorts. It was slightly brighter than the rest of the place, thanks to a large stained-glass window letting sunlight in. However, the picture depicted in glass dampened the effect—a big black vulture stained with bright red blood. All the black and crimson created a very ominous glow.

The guard left me alone, presumably to tell the Queen Regent of my arrival, but I couldn't really be sure, since he didn't say anything at all before leaving. There was a sitting area—black velvet furniture (a poor choice of fabric for such a damp climate), with black marble end tables.

One wall was lined with bookshelves brimming with Omte "treasures." Mostly they were gaudy, jewel-encrusted fantasy statues that looked like they'd be expensive at a Renaissance fair. Lots of detailed dragons guarding brightly colored orbs, and dark birds perched on topaz-encrusted trees, but there were others, like a couple amber crystal snails and sapphire spider figurines.

On another wall was a huge portrait—nearly floor-to-ceiling and almost as wide as the wall, so it had to be around nine-by-six feet. The large crown of twisted bronze on the man's head meant he was probably the Omte King. The size of the painting may have exaggerated his build, but he looked massive. A big lumbering figure with hair of light bronze-brown, but there was something oddly cheery about his broad face. Maybe it was the slight smile on his full lips, nearly hidden in his bushy beard.

A short time later—just long enough for me to start wondering if I should sit down or go look for the guard—the Queen arrived. Or at least I assumed she was the Queen. I wasn't immediately sure, based on her attire.

She wore a pantsuit made of black velvet—which again seemed like exactly the wrong fabric for an environment where there is an above-average chance of sitting on a slug or in vulture poop—and she'd accessorized it with big bold pieces of costume jewelry with amber gems and black metals. The whole outfit seemed perfect for a supernatural lawyer in one of those teen soap operas that Hanna loved so much.

The only real indication I had that this woman was the Queen was the brass crown that sat crookedly on her dark hair. It was the same one from the painting, except it was bent now, and it appeared much larger on her smaller head.

"Hello!" I blurted awkwardly and did a clumsy curtsy. "Thank you for meeting me. Your Majesty." I ended my stammering with a quick bow, and I realized too late that I hadn't had enough experience with royalty to know how to behave around them.

In the very, very limited interactions I'd had, I was always with somebody who knew exactly what to do, like

Finn or Bryn; even in Merellä, when I met with higher-ups, I had Pan or Dagny with me.

Not that it should matter. One of the main tenets that Finn pushed on all of us—me, the kids, even Mia—was to always be prepared.

"Yes, well, sorry to have kept you waiting." Her words were short and rapid, and not exactly unkind—just quick and disinterested. "Have a seat, won't you?"

"Yes, of course." I cleared my throat. "Thank you."

"If I understood correctly, you're a friend of Rebekka Vallin's?" She sat down, crossing one leg over the other, and toyed with the numerous rings on her fingers.

"Rebekka?" I repeated, and it took a few seconds for it to click. "You must mean Bekk! Yes, but I would say she's more of a friend of a friend."

She arched an eyebrow, her dark eyes studying me. "They must be very good friends, for her to cash in a favor with the Queen."

"I believe they are," I replied uncertainly.

"So." Bodil gave me a tight smile. "What is it that you wanted to talk about?"

"Orra Fågel." As I said her name, the Queen subtly recoiled. She may have been trying to hide it, but she visibly pulled back, her jaw tensing, the veins standing out in her throat, and she lowered her eyes. "She was your cousin, if I'm not mistaken."

"Why do you want to know about her?" she asked coolly.

"I think she might be my mother."

She said nothing for a moment, then she licked her thin lips and looked closer at me. "You know that as my cousin—a mere distant relative of the Queen Regent—Orra and any of her possible heirs have no claim to any of this. Nothing from my estate or that of the kingdom. All of this"—she motioned to the space around us—"belonged to my late husband, King Thor, the Third of His Name. Before him, it was his father's. After Thor passed, it all went to our son, the Crown Prince. This is not mine, and it will certainly never be yours."

"I suspected as much," I said honestly. "I didn't come here for money or titles. I'm not entitled to any of it, and I don't want to be. I only want to know who my parents are and find out about my family."

I had spent so much of my nineteen years wondering about my parents, imagining what they were like or making up stories about why they had to leave me the way they did. In the long, lonely days of my childhood, the stories were all I had, really.

The Tulins were kind enough to me, but they didn't really love me. Nobody had, not until I moved in with the Holmeses, where the kids would throw their arms around my neck before telling me they loved me.

Even though I now had so much more love and happiness in my life, the stories from childhood still haunted me. *Who were my parents, and why did they leave me?* The question left an aching hole inside of me that would never mend until I found the answer.

"That is an admirable pursuit, but unfortunately, I don't think I can be of any help," Bodil replied evenly. "Orra died many years ago, and as far as I know, she had no children."

"I did find a telegram about her." I reached into the pocket of my dress, where I had carefully stashed a photocopy I'd made of the paper I found back at the Mimirin.

I held it out to her, and she stared at it for a few moments before finally taking it from me.

NorAm Telegram

```
province of fulaträsk 2 dec 1998
c/o p.o. box 117 Catania springs, La 70750
after much discussion we have decided that an
intervention must be undertaken. a peaceful resolution
is only possible with an intermediary. orra fägel has
been dispatched to the first city as an emissary for
the kingdom.
                        h. t. otäck, adviser to the king
```

On the same paper, beneath the typed message was a quick handwritten one:

Orra has not yet returned. What is the status of her whereabouts?

H.R.M. Bodil Freya Fägel, Consort to the King
8/Nov/1999

She read it impassively. "Where did you get this?"

"I found it among the Omte records at the Mimirin," I told her.

The Queen Regent pursed her lips and set the paper aside—on her end table, as opposed to handing it back to me. "I suppose there's no point in lying, is there?"

expectations

Queen Bodil sat beside me, and she exhaled deeply through her nose. Her makeup was quite heavy—thick coal-black eyeliner and false lashes, stenciled eyebrows and burgundy lipstick. All of that made her expression harder to read, especially considering how fiercely she tried to remain stoic.

She wasn't beautiful, exactly, but her features were dramatic and striking. A long aquiline nose, protruding dark eyes, a wide mouth with thin lips above a sharp chin, large hands with broad shoulders. The Queen Regent was an imposing presence.

So I waited for her to speak, even as the silence dragged on for what felt like an endless amount of time. I didn't want to scare her off with too many questions, so I thought it would be better to wait until she opened up on her own.

"Why do you think Orra might be your mother?" Bodil asked at length.

"It's not much," I admitted before explaining how she matched up with the few clues I had.

All I knew from Mr. Tulin was that the woman who had left me with him was called Orra, she appeared to be Omte and carried an Omte dagger, and she looked to be in her twenties or thirties in the fall of 1999. Orra Fågel matched all of that, with the added fact that she went missing shortly after I was dropped off at the Tulins' doorstep.

"It may not be a lot, but I haven't found a better match than her," I finished.

"What is it that you hope to find?" she asked pointedly. "You had access to that note, so I presume you had access to Orra's other records, and you saw that her whole family is dead. Her parents, and all three—no, wait, there were four boys—they're all dead. Even my mother—Orra's aunt—is long deceased. Orra herself hasn't been seen in nearly twenty years."

I gulped, trying to swallow down the painful lump in my throat, but I kept my expression neutral. She wasn't saying anything I hadn't already read, but it still hurt to hear it spelled out so harshly.

"If she is my mother, I would like to learn about her as much as I can, or at least find out what happened to her," I said, speaking slowly and deliberately to hold back the tears. "And I would like to find my father. He might still be alive."

"Orra and I weren't particularly close, but we were family," the Queen said. "I believe she would've confided in me if she'd had a baby."

"I was abandoned in an isolated arctic town when I was only a few days old. Whatever happened, whoever my mother was, she wanted to keep me hidden—maybe because she was embarrassed, or scared, or something else entirely. But if she hid a newborn baby, I seriously doubt she was shouting her pregnancy from the rooftops," I argued coolly.

"Perhaps." The Queen lifted one shoulder in an indifferent shrug. "But wants and needs change when situations change. What seems joyous one day can seem overwhelming the next."

"Did Orra ever mention that she wanted children?" I asked.

Bodil snorted. "Hardly. She frequently announced her disdain for the whole idea. All of her brothers were dead and buried by the time she was twenty-one, and growing up around all that death soured her on the idea of bringing more innocent lives into the world."

"That sounds like a good reason to leave a baby for adoption and hide her pregnancy," I pointed out.

"It also sounds like a good reason not to get pregnant in the first place," she snapped back. "But what's more significant is that Orra didn't have much of a social life or a need for one. She threw herself into her work as a palace guard, and . . . you were born in October 1999, correct?"

I nodded. "The beginning of October."

"Then it can't possibly be her," the Queen said with a click of her tongue. "In the summer and fall, she was on a mission with my husband—well, my betrothed back then. If she was pregnant, that's not something she would've been able to hide from Thor."

I sat up straighter. "Is that the mission she didn't come back from?" I pointed to the telegram beside her. "The one you asked about in the telegram?"

Her large hands were clasped together, and she met my gaze evenly. "Yes. That's the one."

"But your husband, he came back?" I pressed.

"Yes, he did." She glanced back at the paper and the date scrawled on it. "He was home when I sent this message. Orra had been on a mission, and she was due to come back shortly after him, but she never did."

"They were searching for the Lost Bridge of Dimma," I said.

She nodded. "And they thought they'd found it for a while." A strange, sad smile formed on her burgundy lips, and she stared at the floor. "I suppose they did actually find it—it just wasn't what they thought it'd be.

"There's no real harm in telling you this now, since the kingdom gave up its nonsensical quest for the bridge long ago," she said with a weary sigh. "The quest for the Lost Bridge had been sold to the late King Thor by his adviser Helge Otäck, who turned out to be as stupid as he was corrupt. But we didn't know that then, of course, so Thor had believed him when he told him that across the bridge they would find treasures and gems and untold riches, and all that would be the Omte's for the taking—if they could only find it.

"So Thor went after the bridge, and he took some of his guards along with him to help him in the search," Bodil explained. "When they got close, the Älvolk became involved, which is what Helge's telegram was about. Things were tense over there, so I sent my cousin Orra, who also happened to be one of the guards at the palace.

"Shortly after Orra got there, they discovered the truth, and what the Älvolk were trying to hide," she went on. "The bridge existed, but it went to nowhere. It was nothing but an arched structure, a monument to fallen warriors and long-dead heroes. There were no treasures, no riches, nothing of interest.

"The King came back first, leaving behind his guards—including Orra—to make a polite departure from the Älvolk," Bodil said. "The others followed within a week, but Orra never did. I tried to find out what happened to her, but I was never able to."

"So, they were there for a long while, months or more," I said. "Where did they stay? Were they in Áibmoráigi?"

"I don't know precisely where they stayed," she said. "They traveled to Sweden, and Thor first went to the Trylle-Skojare city of Isarna. Eventually Thor and his team moved out from there and went to stay with the Älvolk, which was when Orra arrived. The King was there to be closer to the bridge, I presumed."

"Do you have any idea where that would be?" I pressed.

"No, why would I?" she asked, narrowing her eyes at me. "I never went there, because there is nothing there. Thor left empty-handed, angry that he'd wasted a year of our lives and gold from our vault, and he vowed to never let our kingdom waste another minute or cent on *nothing*."

"If you never went there, how did you investigate what happened to Orra?" I asked. "She was last seen in Sweden, right?"

"Thor went back, and his guards went with him," she explained. "I stayed here, with Helge, to help rule in his stead."

"You were Queen then?" I asked. "Did you marry between when he first came back and when he went to find Orra?"

Bodil tried to keep her face blank, but the corner of her mouth twitched subtly. "No. Thor and I didn't wed until 2006. He had a few things he wanted to do before he settled down, like going on this guests fool's errand after the Lost Bridge. After finding nothing on enough of these ideas, he decided it was better to stay at home."

"And you stayed behind, to help keep the kingdom in order," I said, and she nodded. "And you're sure that he never found anything?"

"I'm sure because Thor was sure," she replied. "Thor was many things—crass, stubborn, passionate—but he was not a liar, and he wasn't a stupid troll. If he says there was nothing, I believe him."

I sank back in my seat. "Right, of course. I'm sorry. I never intended to disparage the King."

"His memory is not so easily disparaged," she insisted. "He stuck to his word, and he promised the Älvolk that he would keep the location of their bridge a secret, lest it be overcome with fortune-seekers and tourists. It is nothing, but it is *their* private nothing.

"Thor kept his word," she said. "All I know of the location is that it's across the ocean and nearly as far north as the land will go." She shifted in her seat. "But I thought you came here to find out about Orra. This feels more like an interrogation about my late husband."

"I'm sorry," I said again. "I only wanted to find out what happened to her, and things may have gotten a little sidetracked."

"Unfortunately, I don't think there's much I can tell you that you don't already know," Bodil said. "Orra went on a mission, and she never came back. The King led an investigation, but he never found her. As her only living family, I declared her dead years after her disappearance to pay respect to her memory. That's all there is to it, really."

"What about the others who went on the mission? Could any of them possibly have insight into her final days?" I asked.

"No," she replied with severe finality. "The King questioned them at the time, and they knew nothing more than what I've said. I would suggest that you talk to them and find out for yourself, but they're all gone."

"Gone where?" I asked.

"Died," she clarified flatly. "Ødis Haugen was killed in a hunting accident, Dorri Avdod died after extended illness last fall, Tarben Gribb and Helge Otäck died in the Invasion of Doldastam five years ago, and King Thor Elak died in an incident at the Ugly Vulture nine years ago."

"So that's it, then," I realized.

"Yes, sadly, it is. And there's nothing more I can tell you."

8

snails

I sank deeper into the cushions of Rikky's couch, staring up at the slow rotation of the car-door fan blades. Pan was down at the Inhemsk Project local office, which was basically a janitor's closet with some file cabinets and a perpetually irritated clerk, if both Rikkys and Pan's claims were to be believed. There wasn't really enough room for two, so he went there alone to try to find out more about Áibmoráigi and Orra Fågel, and Rikky had gone to her part-time job as a nursing assistant at the Omte clinic.

My meeting with Bodil ended way before Rikky had gotten done with work. When she had dropped me off, she said she'd be back around eleven to get me. Waiting at the palace was far easier and safer than me attempting to navigate the wild swamp on my own, so that's what I did.

I had assumed that the Omte palace would have a library or a museum. The Trylle palace even had a small gift shop that sold gilded stationery, jewelry with their vine insignia, and various other emerald trinkets. But there was nothing at the Omte palace. The Queen directed me to wait in the front hall.

I passed the time by counting the snails crawling on the palace walls. Before visiting here, I never would've guessed that this was something I would be doing, and I never would've fathomed that if I did, I'd make it into the upper double digits. To their credit, though, the snails were truly spectacular. They were semitransparent and shimmery, with vibrant swirls of purple, blue, and red wrapping around their shells.

The only thing that drew my attention from my new-found hobby of snail-watching was a strange sound coming from deeper inside the palace. It was like muffled shouting . . . or maybe yodeling? I was alone—the guard had gone to his post, and the Queen had gone off to wherever she goes—so I walked down the hall, past the narrow corridor that led to the Queen's sitting room, until the hall ended in a set of dark wooden doors.

Despite the heft of the doors, they pushed open rather easily. The brass doorknobs were dull, worn down, and apparently no longer lockable. I peered into the empty ballroom to see the nine-year-old Crown Prince Furston running around, wearing nothing but a burnt-orange cap and a pair of boxer briefs.

Or at least I assumed it was the Crown Prince, because I didn't know what other little boy would be running around the palace half nude.

He had his back to me, his long unkempt curls flying behind him as he brandished a large stick, carrying it around like a trident. Flying above him and keeping pace was a huge bearded vulture with rusty white and black feathers, but I couldn't tell if the bird was chasing the boy or escaping from him.

Furston's cracking tenor made it difficult to understand the words he was singing, but I think it was some type of nursery rhyme. It was catchy and cheery, but something about the way he sang it, with his vulnerable vibrato, made it strangely haunting.

Sing, sing the heroes,
The worm is full of flowers,
Hush hush the morning light
Down falls the darkest night
And now the end is ours

"Miss," the guard's voice boomed behind me, and I jumped a little before quickly turning to face him. "I believe your ride is here."

"Sorry, I wasn't snooping," I apologized hurriedly. "I heard a noise—"

"Miss, I don't really care one way or another," he interrupted me. "I'm only here to escort you."

"Right. Thank you," I mumbled and followed him back to the main hall.

He paused near the front door to pluck a snail off the wall and plop it into his mouth with a loud crunch. After that, he ushered me out and onto Rikky's airboat. As the boat took off, I leaned back into the seat, relishing the way the wind felt after the dank, stale air of the palace.

The ride back to her house went surprisingly fast. Once

we got there, Rikky went about tending to her animals. I offered to help, but she told me to relax and poured me a glass of cold water.

"Are you sure you don't want my help?" I asked her again. I was lounging on the couch, under the slowly spinning metal blades, and she'd come back in to feed Wade the squirrel.

"Nah, I got it covered." She opened the door to the cage, and the gray fur ball scampered up her arm and perched on her shoulders. "You look like you've had a long day."

"Are you talking to me or the squirrel?" I asked.

Rikky laughed, tossing back her head as she did, and Wade nibbled on her chandelier earrings. "You, Ulla."

"No, it wasn't a long day. Just . . ." I trailed off, not knowing how to say how I felt without coming off as ungrateful about meeting with the Queen.

"But you didn't find out what you hoped to find out," Rikky supplied for me.

"The Queen didn't have very much information to share with me," I answered diplomatically.

"What were you hoping she'd be able to give you?" Rikky worked as she talked, refilling food and water and tossing soiled shavings into a compost bag.

"I mean, I had *hoped* to get all the answers to all my questions," I said with a dry laugh. "I thought she'd at least point me in the direction of *something*. Yeah, I didn't really think I'd stroll up and she'd introduce me to my parents when I got there, but I did think she would have something more substantial than . . . nothing."

Rikky went over to the sink, speaking louder to be heard over the sound of her washing her hands. "Did she give a reason why she couldn't let you know anything?"

"Basically that there's nobody left alive to tell me anything," I said. "Not about Orra, not about Áibmoráigi, not about anything I asked about."

"That's not true." Rikky put one hand on her hip and looked down at me.

"Yeah, I figured that, but that's what she told me."

"No, I mean, there's a guy that hangs out at this bar, the Ugly Vulture. He's not there a lot, maybe once a month, max, probably less than that. But he's always talking up the ladies. I'm not gonna lie—I let him buy me a drink a couple times." She pressed her lips into a thin smile, then rolled her eyes. "He wasn't really my type—too old, and sort of intense. But he offered, and a free drink's a free drink.

"Anyway," she went on with a self-deprecating laugh, "he's not shy *at all* but never shared anything about himself. So, one night, he's talking me up, and I egged him on, ordering him enough shots to loosen his lips. He ends up telling me that he's an Älvolk and he's from the First City.

"I thought then—and I still think now—that he was full of crap and trying to impress me so he could get laid," Rikky said. "That's why I didn't say anything sooner. But he never says anything about it when he's sober, so I think *maybe* there's a kernel of truth buried there. And if the Queen is giving you the runaround, he's probably better than nothing."

I sat up straighter on the couch. "Do you think he'd talk to me?"

"I think he'll talk to any attractive female, and you're plenty attractive."

My cheeks burned at the subtle compliment. "Thanks. I think."

"Oh, whatever." Rikky had her back to me as she filled a mason jar with raspberry lemonade from the icebox—then topped it off with a splash of vodka from the bottle she stashed on a shelf. "You're young with great skin, unique eyes, and a nice pair of boobs. That's hot enough for most folks out there."

"I don't know about that." I tried to skirt around the topic as much as I could. "Do you think this guy would be at the bar tonight?"

"What's today?" She took a sip of her drink and peered over at the Moomin calendar tacked up on her wall. "Tuesday? Oh, nope. Not today. The Ugly Vulture is always closed on Tuesdays. That's when they have gator wrestling."

"When would be a good time to go?" I asked.

"Any other night is as good as the next," Rikky said with a shrug. "But if you really wanna find out more about him, you should talk to that Vallin girl."

"Bekk Vallin from the Postkontor?" I asked, and I realized that this was the second time today she'd come up in conversation.

"That's her." Rikky nodded. "I don't know her, but Fulaträsk isn't that big a place, so I know *of* her, and everybody talks. Around six, seven months ago I heard around town that she was socializing with him, but the rumors fizzled out almost as fast as they started—until a few months later when her big old baby bump shows up."

"You think that guy is having a baby with Bekk?"

"Maybe. It's rumors on top of rumors, so it all should be taken with a grain of salt," Rikky clarified.

"I planned on heading to the Postkontor tomorrow. I'll ask about him, see what she says," I said. "What's his name?"

"Indu." She paused, thinking. "Indu Mattison."

Roaming

The Jeep was the only place I really had privacy, thanks to Rikky's paper-thin walls. While Rikky and Pan were cleaning up after supper, I took out the composting, then snuck down to the vehicle, which was parked near the dock.

I sat in the driver's seat with the window open, letting the warm breeze blow over me. On my phone, I pulled up my messenger and scrolled through my contacts until I finally landed on Bryn Aven.

Me: Hey, Bryn. It was great seeing you a few weeks ago. We really need to catch up when you have a chance. But until then, I was wondering if I could ask you about something.

Bryn: Yeah, it was good to see you too. I have some downtime now. What do you need?

Me: Do you remember someone named Bekk or Rebekka Vallin?

Bryn: Yes, I do. We knew each other during the war, but I haven't talked to her much since.

Me: Do you trust her?

Bryn: I did five years ago, but a lot could've changed since then. Why do you ask?

Me: She works at the Omte records office, and she's helping me find my parents. After I mentioned I knew you, she got me a meeting with the Queen Regent.

Bryn: So you met Bodil? What'd you think of her?

Me: She wasn't what I expected, but I don't really know what I expected for an Omte Queen. You've met her before?

Bryn: A few times now. I asked for her help before the war, but I've had limited interactions with her at big royal social events, like King Linus's wedding a year ago, and a few weeks ago at Linus's jubilee.

Me: What are your thoughts on her?

Bryn: Hard to say. I haven't been able to figure out if she's dense and mean, or if it's all an act and she's a diabolical genius. I'm leaning toward dumb and cruel, though.

Me: That is what I was afraid of.

Bryn: Did you meet the prince?

Me: I didn't meet him, but I saw a kid running around in his underwear with a stick scepter. I'm pretty sure it was him.

Bryn: LOL. He's a real piece of work. The Omte have a very particular way of doing things.

Me: Don't we all?

Bryn: That's true. I have to run. It's Ridley's mom's birthday dinner tonight. But you can message me anytime if you have more questions.

Me: Thank you. Have fun with your family!

I slumped low in the seat and scrolled through my phone, checking my various messages. It was mostly junk mail, but there were half a dozen from Hanna—all basically demanding to know exactly what was going on and what I planned to do about Eliana. As if I had managed to figure out and solve the whole thing in the few days since I saw her last.

There was one email from Dagny, written with all the emotion and flair I'd come to expect from her:

To Ulla Tulin—

I have learned nothing new about Eliana or her whereabouts. Elof is continuing to research your blood.

Do let me know if you find anything that you think would be valuable to me or Elof.

I assume you are otherwise fine.

Best—
Dagny Lilja Kasten
Lab Assistant to Docent Elof Dómari
Troglecology Dept. at the Mimirin
Merellä, the Kingdom of Vittra

I replied to her right away. It was easy because I had nothing to tell her, and I knew she wouldn't immediately bombard me with a hundred replies demanding answers I almost certainly wouldn't have.

The Jeep was running so I could charge my phone while messaging Bryn. (The roaming drained the battery like nothing else.) Since the car was already running, I clicked on the radio. I had to surf through a mixture of country, blues, angry jazz, and more country before landing on some nice mellow pop.

Humming along to the music, I leaned my head against the headrest and closed my eyes. The stress of the last few days weighed heavily on me, and I had no idea how I was going to figure it all out.

I tried to think back to what Finn had taught me about meditation. He insisted that was the only way he could handle his demanding job, six children, and his mother moving back in with them. Breathe in through the nose, hold for three seconds, exhale through the mouth for six, and remember that I am a rock, I am the river, I am the storm before the rains.

The door to the Jeep creaked, and my eyes snapped open. I looked over to see Pan leaning inside.

"Is this seat taken?" he asked with a crooked smile.

"No, of course not. Come on in." I sat up straighter and turned down the Ed Sheeran song on the radio.

Once he'd settled into the seat beside me, he asked, "How are you doing?"

I shrugged. "Good, I guess. How 'bout you?"

"I'm good," he allowed. "But I'm not the one hiding out in the driveway."

"It's not really a driveway, and I'm not really hiding out," I argued, but Pan merely arched his eyebrows, resting his dark eyes on me. "I was texting an old friend to see if she could help me sort some of this out. But unfortunately, there's not much to be sorted out."

"What do you mean?" Pan tilted his seat way back, like mine, and he put one arm behind his head.

"Not everything has an answer." I shook my head. "Ugh. That sounds so pretentious. I'm just trying to prepare myself in case I don't ever find out everything I want to know."

"Well, yeah." He laughed. "Nobody ever gets everything they want. Did you think that was an option?"

"No, no, no . . ." I sighed. "I mean, you get it. You never met your dad, right?"

"No, we lived near him when I was a baby, and he held

me and visited us. But I don't remember it, obviously, and my mom didn't take any pictures." He paused and exhaled loudly. "It's almost like it never happened at all."

"How do you . . ." I spoke slowly, choosing my words very carefully. "How do you accept that? That you'll never really know your dad? Sorry for being so blunt. I'm trying to figure out how to deal with the very real possibility that I might never find my mom or dad."

"For me personally, the truth is that I don't," he admitted in a thick, low voice. "I don't rage about it every minute of the day, but sometimes, yeah, I still get angry about it. And if I let myself dwell on all the things that were taken from me, all the moments lost, I can be really angry for . . . for a while.

"But then I try to remind myself of the stuff I do have and then focus on all the things I want to do," he went on. "I can be sad and mourn the past, but I can't *live* there, and most importantly, I don't want to."

I smiled at him. "Thanks. I'll try to remember that."

"Are you gonna hang out in the car for a while?" Pan asked.

"I don't know," I said hesitantly.

"The fireflies are starting to come out." He pointed through the windshield at the infrequent little pops of light against the dusky pink sky and inky black water.

"Oh?" I glanced around in confusion. "They're nice, but I have seen fireflies before."

"Rikky said she's going to feed Bitta the three-legged alligator once the fireflies are out. She says he always comes out around then, and she tosses him raw chicken off the back dock, if you wanna watch."

"Oh, yeah, I absolutely wanna see that," I said. "Is she doing that now?"

He nodded excitedly. "Yeah, about now."

"Then we should go."

10

maternal

The airboat stalled out after lurching to the side. Pan had turned too sharply, barely swerving in time to miss a spindly cypress tree. I clung to the seat as the boat pitched to one side, and for a frightening moment I thought it was going to flip completely over, but thankfully it righted itself and lurched to a stop.

"Oh, my *gaad*." I laughed and looked back at Pan.

He stood with one hand white-knuckled on the gear stick, and a nervous grin slowly spread across his face. "So maybe driving the airboat is harder than Rikky made it seem."

She'd had to work again that day, and the easiest solution for us getting around the swamp was to leave us the airboat. She'd given Pan a quick lesson in the morning, and he drove her to work and dropped her off. That had gone without incident, and now it was just me and Pan, speeding to the Postkontor office.

"Are you sure you can manage it?" I asked, only half teasing.

"Yeah." He nodded as he got us moving again. "I'll take it a little slower." Another quick bump. "Or maybe a lot slower."

"I don't mind getting there late. I just wanna get there, and preferably, not get drenched in swamp water."

"I'll see what I can do," he said.

It was definitely a longer—and much bumpier—ride than it was with Rikky, but we made it to the office. Pan parked the airboat right on the muddy embankment, securing it with a rope tied to a post, and we walked up the mossy stone path to the door.

"This place looks and smells like a cellar," Pan muttered as we stopped inside, and I laughed because I couldn't argue.

"Hello?" I said into the empty waiting area.

There was the loud crack of a chair, immediately followed by Bekk announcing, "I'm on my way." A minute later, she rounded the cubicle barrier and smiled. "Hey, how are you doing? How was the meeting with the Queen Regent?"

It hadn't been awful, but Bodil hadn't been exactly forthcoming. That was to be expected of the Omte, though, and I didn't want Bekk to feel like her effort wasn't appreciated. So I exaggerated slightly with, "It was good. Thank you again for setting it up."

"Great." As she walked over to us, slowly, she glanced at Pan. "What can I do for the two of you today?"

"This is Pan Soriano. He works with the Inhemsk Project."

She eyed him more seriously. "Inhemsk? I've worked with them before."

"We've probably spoken on the phone once or twice," he admitted.

She gave him an apologetic smile. "I hope I wasn't too rude. The rules around here can be very restrictive about what information we can share."

"No, don't worry about it. I know how limiting bureaucracy can be."

"It sure can," she agreed. "What brings you here?"

"We had some things we wanted to talk to you about," I said.

For a brief second her eyes flashed wide with surprise, but she blinked it away and smiled at us. "Sure, of course. Do you mind if we sit down and chat?" She nodded toward the seating area and rubbed her belly. "I can't stay on my feet that long anymore."

"Yeah, definitely." I stepped to the side to let her by.

She sat down in a chair, and while she adjusted a thin throw pillow behind her back, Pan and I sat down across from her on the couch.

"You know that I came here because I'm trying to find my mother," I began. "My biggest contender at the moment is Orra Fågel, and her trail dries up in Áibmoráigi nearly twenty years ago. I was hoping that Bodil would know more about her, or at least give me a better idea of where the First City or the Lost Bridge were."

"And did she?" Bekk asked.

I shook my head. "No. She didn't have much to say about any of that."

"I don't know how much help I can be," she said, sounding rather apologetic. "I already showed you as much as I could when you were here before, and I doubt that I know more than the Queen does about any of that."

"Well, we came here with different questions this time," I said.

"I've been looking into the history of Áibmoráigi, which has led me to reading a lot about the Älvolk," Pan said. "How much do you know about the Älvolk?"

Bekk's eyes were downcast, her expression blank, when she answered, "Not much." Then she added, "Less than you, now, I'm sure."

"I don't want to pry into your personal life," I said gently, and I hadn't even finished my request before she sighed, like she knew what was coming. "But I've heard you have had a relationship with someone who claims to be a member of the Älvolk."

She didn't say anything at first. But when I said, "I believe his name is Indu Mattison," she lifted her head. Her brown eyes were dark and calm, and she rubbed her belly again.

"Yeah, I know him," she admitted finally. "Or at least I know him as well as anyone can know someone like him. With Indu, you can never really be sure if anything he says is true, and even then I can't say whether he's lying or delusional."

"So, you don't believe he's an Älvolk?" I asked.

"No, he might very well be an Älvolk," she corrected me matter-of-factly. "His sole purpose in life might really be to guard the Lost Bridge and ensure the prophetic duties of the Älvolk. Every word he said might be the complete truth."

"But?" I pressed when she didn't elaborate.

"But . . ." She exhaled through her nose. "He promises a life of happiness and health, but then he leaves you entirely on your own to figure out how to achieve this magical life." A pained smile passed over her lips. "He wasn't around a lot—always stopping in Fulaträsk on his way to some other, unknown destination—but he seemed like he really believed in something, that he wanted a better world for all of us. We saw each other a handful of times over a few months, and then I told him I was pregnant—and that was it. Then he was gone."

I grimaced. "I'm sorry. That sounds very difficult to go through."

"Thanks, but I wasn't looking for sympathy," Bekk replied flatly. "I made my choices."

"We're not here to make judgments or dig through your private life," Pan reiterated in his gentle, soothing voice. "All we wanna know is if you have any way of contacting Indu Mattison."

"He really isn't the kind of guy that leaves a forwarding address," she said with an empty laugh.

"So far, the only thing we really have to go on is that he likes to hang around the Ugly Vulture," I said. "So really, anything at all would be immensely helpful."

Bekk stared into the corner of the room, her jaw visibly tensing under her olive skin. Her dark brown hair was pulled up in a messy bun, and she absently toyed with a loose lock of it.

"You'll be asking around town, then." Her voice was emotionless, making it hard to tell if it was meant to be a question or just a realization.

"That will be our next step in trying to find him," Pan confirmed.

"There's something else you're going to find out." She looked down at her belly. "My little girl isn't the only baby that Indu has fathered around here."

I exchanged a look with Pan and asked, "Really?"

Bekk nodded. "By my count, he's had at least three babies born in Fulaträsk alone."

11

serial

"What?" Pan said, managing to find his voice while I stared at Bekk in shock.

"But he doesn't . . ." I tilted my head, trying to wrap my head around it. "He has multiple children here, but he doesn't live here? Why does he keep coming to Fulaträsk?"

Bekk let out a deep breath. "That is *why*. He thinks trolls are going extinct, and the only way to fight it off is to have babies with powerful trolls, and the Omte are nothing if not strong."

Pan made a strange sound—a click of surprise—and leaned back on the couch. "Did you . . ." He stopped himself and cleared his throat. "No, I'm sorry. I don't have any right to ask you about that."

"I didn't realize what his . . . intentions were until after I was pregnant," she explained wearily. "Once I was, however, his true feelings became crystal clear. His peculiarities aside, I did want a baby. So it worked out in the end."

"Yeah," I said lamely. "I'm glad it worked out for you."

After a beat, she quietly said, "I have a list. I don't know much about Indu, but I wanted to know as much as I could about the family of my daughter. That includes her half-sisters."

"A list?" I asked.

"I made it with information from the census." She pushed herself up to her feet, then walked around the cubicle wall.

I followed her and saw her taking a file out of the top drawer of her desk. It was a slightly battered, avocado-green file about a quarter of an inch thick and bound together with a rubber band.

"Here." Bekk held it out toward me. "You can go ahead and have a look. I have to use the restroom."

I took the file back over to the couch and sat down beside Pan. There were multiple stacks, separated by paper clips and labeled with names in brightly colored Post-it notes. *Holt*; *Torsun*; *Sundt*; *Lund*. I separated the piles, handing two to Pan so we could get through the info.

Speed-reading wasn't necessary, though. Once I read through the Omte legalese, there wasn't much info, and it was easy to glean the basic facts.

Meri Torsun gave birth to a premature baby way back in 1994, in the Omte village of Mörkaston in Nevada. The baby didn't live long, but Indu Mattison was listed as the father in the official documentation. Meri herself died of cirrhosis three years later.

Thora Lund—the only non-Omte member in the file—was born to Ebba Lund and Indu Mattison in Förening in 1997, but only a few months later she died, her cause of death listed as "complications due to birth defect." On the last page of her stack, a handwritten note stated, *Ebba moved to the human town of Winona a year after Thora's death.*

More recently, Karrin Sundt had a baby named Alva. This was thirteen years ago, in the faraway Omte village of Sintvann. But within a year, both baby Alva and Karrin were dead—their deaths listed as SIDS and suicide, respectively.

The final baby, Tindra Holt, proved to be an anomaly. Unlike the others, Tindra survived infancy. She was over two years old when she drowned in a "freak accident," if the *Fulaträsk Tribune* newspaper clipping was to be believed.

Her mother Eyrun remained in Fulaträsk even after Tindra's death in 2014, and according to a marriage certificate and another clipping, she'd gotten married and had two more kids with her husband.

What really stood out about Eyrun, though, was that out of the eight trolls—four mothers and their babies—she was the only one alive who still lived with trolls.

"What is going on here?" Pan muttered when he reached the end. "Am I reading this correctly? Because it really sounds like this guy keeps going around, making babies, and then . . . they all die."

I nodded once. "Yeah, I think you're reading it right."

He tented his hands together, staring down at the file, his brow furrowed and his gaze pensive. "I honestly don't know if this guy can help us at all. But . . . I wanna know what's going on here." He looked at me. "And it would probably be good if we figured it out while your friend Bekk is still pregnant."

12

Long Days

"Long days call for tall drinks," Rikky declared after she got home from work. She was short on details about what made her day so long—other than vague comments about a couple kids who had broken each other's arms wrestling—but she claimed the length of our day was written on our faces.

That made sense, since we had spent the morning at the Postkontor trying to understand Indu Mattison and the trail of dead children he had left behind him. I wanted to ask Bekk more questions about all of that, but it felt hugely inappropriate to ask a pregnant woman, *Hey, are you worried your baby is going to die like all the others?*

"Maybe it's because he's not Omte?" Pan had wondered once we were back at Rikky's and free to talk without worrying about Bekk overhearing. He sat back on the couch, which was still in the slightly disheveled state of pillows and blankets he had left it in this morning.

Wade was up, exploring his larged domed birdcage, so I poked my fingers through the bars to scratch his nose and slipped him a treat. I glanced over my shoulder at Pan. "What makes you say he isn't Omte?"

"Aren't the Älvolk supposed to be something else?" he asked. "They're trolls, sure, but they're not really from any of the tribes. By our best records, they were once known as *álfar.*"

"But the *álfar* lived in Alfheim," I reminded him. "The *ekkálfar* are on earth."

"Yeah, but we don't really even know what that means or how the various *álfar* differentiate from each other. *Álfar* could be their way of saying 'Alfheimian,' and *ekkálfar* is their word for 'Canadian' or 'Omte' or even 'earthling.' "

"Whoa. Wait." I faced Pan and hugged my arms across my chest. "If we're earthlings, does that make the *álfar* extraterrestrial?"

Pan thought for a moment before answering. "In the most literal sense, I would say . . . yes?" He shook his head. "If they even exist, and if the legends have any truth—which are two really big *ifs*—then they came from somewhere else. Whether it's another dimension or afterlife or another planet, it still means they're not from this world. *This* earth."

"But that's . . . ridiculous." I sat on the floor. I wasn't paying enough attention, so I missed the cushion and sat on the hard floor with a painful grunt, but I barely even registered it.

"Is it, though?" he asked thoughtfully. "To suggest that we're somehow connected or possibly related to other-worldly beings sounds far-fetched. But we're an ancient race of supernatural beings with a variety of psychokinetic powers, so who are we to throw stones?"

"Do you think Indu is from Alfheim?" I asked.

"Maybe. Or maybe he's someone who worships old stories about long-dead *álfar*." He shrugged. "I don't know if we'll ever find out the difference."

I chewed my lip. "Of course, we can find out. We can check the blood."

"The blood?" Pan straightened, his eyes narrowing.

"I saw Eliana's blood," I reminded him. "It wasn't like mine or even any animal's I've ever seen. It's darker than normal, like a deep burgundy, and thick like syrup. There was a strangely beautiful shimmer to it, even though it was still blood and therefore super-disgusting."

Pan leaned forward, resting his elbows on his legs, and stared off into space as he considered this. "What does your blood look like?"

"Red, wet, I don't know. I honestly have never really studied my blood."

"It doesn't look anything like Eliana's?"

I had shaken my head. "No, nothing like that. Hers was . . . dramatically different."

He'd rubbed the back of his neck. "I don't know. There's a lot of things I could speculate on . . . but honestly, we don't have a lot to go on until we find Indu Mattison."

It was shortly after that that we picked Rikky up from work. As soon as we got home, Rikky piled her hair up and ducked into her bedroom without saying anything after her brief but incisive commentary about our "long day."

"Is she okay?" I whispered to Pan after she'd been in her room for several minutes.

He shrugged and talked to her door. "Rikky? Is everything all right?"

"What?" she shouted, her words only slightly muffled by the walls. A few seconds later, she poked her head out—carefully hiding her bare shoulders behind the door. "I'm changing real quick. Do you guys need more time to get ready?"

"Ready for what?" Pan asked.

"The bar," she said, like it should be super-obvious. "You guys are looking for Indu, and we're all in dire need of a good time. Ergo, the Ugly Vulture."

"Oh, right." I said, pretending I understood that the singular mention of the bar the day before meant that we'd made concrete plans.

"Oh, okay." Pan sounded taken aback, and he ran his hand through his hair. "Are we going now? It seems a little early." His dark eyes bounced up to the sunny skies above the skylight.

"The Vulture isn't the kind of place you'd like after dark. Or at least it's not the kind of place *I* like." Rikky laughed loudly—a short burst of a self-satisfied cackle—then she ducked back into her bedroom, this time leaving the door open slightly so she could talk more freely. "They have pretty tasty bar food too, so we can grab supper there if you want."

Pan looked to me, and I shrugged, so he answered, "Yeah, sounds good."

"I guess I'll go get ready, then," I said, already backing away to the "guest room" three-season porch to try to figure out what to wear to a roughneck Omte bar.

By the time I decided—a knee-length slip dress in a brassy dandelion color paired with nearly all the black and gold jewelry I had (the legends of trinkets completely mesmerizing trolls are only *slight* exaggerations, and my trio of necklaces, two rows of earrings, and chunky faux-diamond rings would definitely make me more eye-catching and enchanting)—Rikky and Pan were talking and laughing loudly over the Rolling Stones playing on the record player.

The burgundy liquid sloshing in Rikky's glass looked an awful lot like the Omte sangria she'd made the other day, and she either didn't notice or didn't mind the few droplets that spilled onto the floor as she danced around the living room. Pan was sitting on the couch, laughing at something she said, and he turned back to look at me when he heard the door close.

His eyes widened slightly, and his smiled faltered, but he quickly corrected it with, "Looks like you're all ready to go."

Rikky spun around in surprise—she'd been so focused on Pan that she hadn't noticed me—and she laughed and threw a hand to her chest. "Ulla! Come join us for pregaming!"

"Rikky's always been big on pregaming," Pan said with a smile, but it was forced and thin, and his voice had a subtle weariness underneath his usual jovial lightness.

"It's a matter of practicality," she insisted with a dramatic head bob that made her plastic earrings rattle. "They'd charge four times as much for a drink half this size." She held up her glass as evidence. "My mama always told me: get a buzz before the bar."

"This is the same woman who told you to treat a toothache with a drop of honey in a big mug of *eldvatten*?" Pan asked dryly.

"The honey was optional. The *eldvatten* was really the key part," Rikky clarified and took a quick drink. "She had a lot of good advice." Then she looked over at me. "So, did you want a drink?"

I shook my head. "I'll wait until we're there."

"I'll finish my drink, then." As she eagerly downed it, Pan went over and grabbed the keys from off the hook by the door.

"I'm driving," he announced.

"Come on, Panny!" She grabbed his hand for the keys, but he turned and faced her.

"You know I hated that nickname then, and I definitely hate it now," he said coolly.

Hurt flashed across her face, but she hurried to smile through it, even as she dropped his hand and offered an apology. "You're right. I just forgot, Pan. I'm sorry."

"It's fine. Let's go have a good night."

We loaded up into the boat, with Rikky much more subdued than she had been in the house. That made for a long, quiet ride to the bar, but at least Pan had gotten a better handle on driving. Rikky shouted back directions until we finally arrived at a shanty-style marina that spidered out from several gigantic tree trunks.

I'd never seen the giant sequoias and redwoods of California, but I thought the thick, towering cypress trees had to be comparable. I couldn't imagine any tree larger.

Around the trunks, curved staircases had been built, leading up to a sprawling tree house spreading out through the branches. Even before Pan parked the boat, when the fan was still on, I could hear the music and yelling. The sun hadn't even set yet, but the place was packed with rowdy Omte.

13

Red Room

Inside the Ugly Vulture, patrons crowded around the bar—including several ogres lumbering around and ducking under the thick branches that held up the ceiling ten feet above. The space itself was divided into half a dozen large rooms—evidence of various expansions through the years, leading to a definite design clash between the rooms.

Overgrown vines both inside and out, with branches cutting through rooms with full plumes of leaves, gave it a jungle feel, and the sawdust on the floor and broken beer bottles felt much more rowdy-tavern.

All of it was held together with rusty nails and water-damaged boards. In most ways, the architecture seemed to mainly be a by-product of opportunity and necessity—like the chicken wire over the windows or the dance floor made of old tires. The different themes in the rooms made for a jarring mash-up: *Indiana Jones and the Biker Bar.*

And that didn't even touch on the disturbing amount of dead birds. Rikky had explained it to me like this: "The way the Egyptians worshipped cats, the Omte revere vultures, particularly their precious bearded vultures." There were stuffed birds *everywhere*—on walls, on light fixtures, even perched on the liquor casks. It was honestly a little unnerving, so I decided the best course of action was to avoid looking at them, and I followed Pan and Rikky through the crowd.

Rikky grabbed us a table near the back of one of the cleaner rooms. I didn't see any broken bottles on the floor here, but the wooden floorboards did have a suspiciously large splotch of dark red liquid slowly drying.

The walls were painted a deep violet-red, and dim fairy lights were strung through the branches along the ceiling. Here there were fewer actual birds; it was more of a vulture motif, with black feathers and shimmery black stencils of birds on the wall. Black bows with beautifully feathered arrows were a surprisingly elegant touch of weapons-as-décor.

We settled in, and as Rikky flagged down a waiter, I made a startling observation—there were a lot of attractive trolls here. Even the ogres, purportedly hideous disfigured giants, were relatively ordinary-looking, though they were definitely huge.

Sure, some had an asymmetric quality to them, with a few having exaggerated proportions. But most were no more asymmetric than I was, with many even less so.

All my life, I'd been hearing about how all the Omte were so ugly, and I'd been repeatedly told that I should feel "lucky" for being attractive "by Omte standards." I'd always thought it was a shitty backhanded compliment to begin with, but now I was seeing that it wasn't even true. I wasn't "hot" for an Omte—I was average at best.

It was the strangest feeling. I should've been saddened to learn I was even less attractive than I thought I was, that there were plenty of prettier girls than me, like Rikky and Bekk, but it was actually a relief.

Even in school, I had been taught that Omte were dumb, ugly, and violent. These were "facts" that had been repeated to me over and over. By teachers, by peers, by nearly every piece of troll literature I'd ever read. I'd been led to believe a negative stereotype about the Omte, my tribe, myself.

And now I had to wonder, how many other things had I learned about the Omte that weren't true? About other tribes? About humans?

"Ulla?" Pan was saying. I'd been so lost in thought I didn't notice that a waiter had stopped at our table—a lanky ogre with long hair pulled back into a ponytail.

"Sorry, what?" I asked.

"What'd you want to drink?" Pan asked.

"Our fine waiter Donovan here has recommended the Lakkalikööri cocktail," Rikky told me cheerily.

"Uh, yeah. That sounds great," I said, mostly because I didn't want to make poor Donovan wait around when it was obviously so busy.

He offered a brief smile and in a gravelly voice he promised to have our drinks right out to us, then left.

"So." Rikky drummed her hands on the table and gave me a toothy grin. "What do you wanna do? How do you wanna go about this?"

"I don't know," I admitted. "This place is quite a bit

bigger than I expected. I thought we could glance around, and you'd let me know if you spotted Indu. But that seems kinda naïve now that I'm here."

"Oh, yeah. The Vulture's something else." She leaned back in her chair. "This is called the Red Room. There's also the Mudhole, the Tree Top, the Dungeon, the Dark Corner, and the Bridge. I figured we'd make the rounds and have a drink in each one."

"That sounds like a great plan," I said.

"You know what else is an excellent plan?" Rikky said, just as our drinks arrived.

"What?" Pan asked, but we were left waiting in suspense until after she took a long swig of her Lakkalikööri cocktail.

"Playing a game of *økkspill*," Rikky announced, and rather abruptly she sauntered across the room.

On the wall hung a big chunk of raw-edged wood with three separate bull's-eyes on it—a large white one at the top left, a medium-sized black one at the bottom right, and a small gold one positioned roughly in the center.

The players stood back from the board, maybe fifteen feet, each of them wielding five kasterens. The kasterens were like medium-sized hatchets, but odder looking. They had long, slender handles, and stubby, curved blades with visible hammer marks.

"What's that?" Pan asked me, and his eyes followed Rikky as she collected a set of kasterens.

"*Økkspill?*" I asked. "You haven't played before?"

He shook his head. "No, I don't think I've heard of it."

"I guess it is kind of a country troll game, and you probably haven't played many of those, living with the humans and then in a city like Mimirin," I realized. "It's a pretty fun bar game. You stand behind the line, and you throw the kasteren axes, trying to hit certain rings for points."

"So, like lumberjack darts?" Pan asked.

I laughed. "Basically, yeah."

His dark eyes held mine. "You know, I didn't get a chance to tell you earlier, but you look really pretty tonight."

I tried to hold his gaze, but I only managed to for a moment before I had to lower my eyes, because I could feel the heat rising in my cheeks. "Well, thank you."

"Hey!" Rikky snapped her fingers and stalked back toward us. "Who wants to play with me?" She was theoretically asking both of us, but her eyes were locked on Pan as she grabbed her drink off the table.

Pan shrugged. "I don't really know how to play."

"The guys back there wanna play doubles, so I gotta find a partner." She downed her drink, then slammed the mug down on the table. "I can teach you as we play. You've always been a quick learner."

He laughed. "I can't say no now." As he stood up, he looked back at me with a sheepish smile. "Are you gonna be okay here? Or do you wanna join us as the cheering squad?"

"Nah, I'll be fine here." I waved him off. "I'll keep the table warm."

"You wanna order another round of drinks while we're gone?" Rikky asked with a hopeful twitch of her eyebrow.

"Yeah, sure, no problem."

I watched them walk away—feeling a slight pang of jealousy when Pan put his hand on the small of her back as they weaved through the crowd—then reminded myself that my time here would be better served taking in my surroundings and checking out the other patrons.

Beyond the vulture décor, there were a few pieces of rustic Nordic art. A sign behind the bar was made of planks of wood and held together with twine. It'd been painted with runic symbols that, when translated, loosely meant, "To drink. To fight. To fuck. To live."

On the wall across from me, a candelabra sconce hung on the wall. It appeared to be made of vulture bones and painted bronze. Just beneath it, perfectly backlit by candles, was a glass display box showcasing a broken bottle. Admittedly an oversized bottle, made of semi-opaque jade-green glass about an inch thick. The neck ended in jagged edges.

Donovan the waiter came back to clear away the empty glasses—Rikky had already finished hers—and I took the opportunity to order more drinks and slip him a hefty tip.

He smiled when he pocketed the money, and I was once again struck by how much different the Omte looked compared to my imagined version. Donovan was obviously an ogre—his hands were so huge, the big mug looked like a child's toy cup in his thick mitts; his nose was wide and a bit bulbous; his brow extended slightly; his voice was deep and guttural.

But he wasn't angry or dumb or slovenly. He wasn't even unattractive, not really. His buttoned flannel shirt had to be tailor-made to fit his unique shape, and it did a good job of showing off a physique that landed somewhere between André the Giant and Superman.

Donovan returned quickly with the drinks and set them

down with a smile, and hopefully still carrying a bit of the goodwill that my tip had bought.

"Is there anything I can do for you?" Donovan asked, and he definitely had a unique way of speaking. His voice was like a bass drum, but he put more emphasis on the first syllable of the words, making it sound a little rhythmic.

"Do you know what that's about?" I pointed to the candelabra and the broken bottle display.

"You know not of the King's death?" he asked.

I smiled meekly. "I'm not from around here."

"Thor was the very good King, loved by many," he explained. "The King of the common troll."

"He sounds like a very cool guy," I said.

"Very," Donovan agreed solemnly. "He lived among us, and he drank in this bar many nights. Trolls argued over stories of the old heroes slaying monsters, and the King was pulled in. He never backed down from a fight. But the bottle got his throat. Before healers touched him, he died."

"That sounds like . . . a sad day," I replied hesitantly.

Donovan spoke of the late King with great reverence, but he also spoke of his death with pride. He seemed happy to display the instrument of the King's death, so it was mixed signals for me.

"Very sad," he agreed. "But we honor him here."

"Were you working here that night?"

"No, that was before my time. I have worked here only seven summers."

"Wow. That's still a long time," I commended him. "I bet you know all the regulars."

"I know many," he conceded.

"What about Indu Mattison?" I asked. "Have you seen him around lately?"

He shrugged and shook his head sadly. "I'm not so good with names."

"If only I had a picture," I muttered to myself.

The only thing I had to go on was Rikky's basic description—tall, sorta good-looking, salt-and-pepper hair, maybe forty, and eyes that were either brown or green. Bekk claimed she had no pics of him, and her description varied slightly—tall, black-and-silver hair, hazel eyes, and fit for his age, which she put somewhere between forty and sixty.

Donovan moved on to taking care of his other tables, and I turned my attention back to Rikky and Pan. They were waiting for their turn, with the other team chucking their kasteren axes at the target, and Rikky was leaning against Pan, resting her head on his shoulder.

I grabbed my drink and went about exploring the rest of the bar. I planned on sipping the drink—it was stronger than I was used to—but as I weaved out of the Red Room into the Dark Corner, I felt increasingly intimidated. I'd never considered myself small—I was average height and more than a little overweight, so "petite" had never really been the proper descriptor for me.

But now all the Omte seemed to tower over me—and not just the broad, bumpy ogres, but young women and lanky teens.

As I made my way out of that dim, dank section of the bar, my straw was coming up empty, and I realized that I'd accidentally finished my drink much faster than I'd meant to. I left the glass on a table as I made it into the Mudhole, where Loretta Lynn blasted out of the speakers.

I don't know how long I wandered through the Ugly Vulture, passing through each crowded room, before I started having the most surreal feeling. I didn't know if it was the liquor or the thumping bass of the rapcore version of an old troll war song. Or maybe I was overwhelmed and claustrophobic because of all the large bodies surrounding me. But I was suddenly completely untethered. I wasn't moving at all, but it was like I was floating away from myself, away from everyone.

Like I wasn't really an Omte. Like I wasn't really a troll.

Like I wasn't even real.

"Ulla." Pan's voice behind me pulled me back, and then his hand, gentle on my arm, grounded me. I turned to face him. He stared down at me, his dark eyes somehow darker, feeling endless but warm and safe and—

"Are you okay?" he asked, and I didn't know how long I'd been staring up at him.

"Yeah, yeah, I'm fine." I managed a smile, and then I was grateful for his hand, still on my arm, tethering me there with him.

"Rikky had one too many cocktails and she isn't feeling so hot, so I'm thinking we should get out of here." He leaned in closer to me, his voice rough in my ear. "If that's cool with you."

"I'm ready. Let's go."

Pan started to walk away, and I grabbed his hand, afraid of losing him in the crowd. He glanced back over his shoulder at me, long enough for me to see his smile, and he squeezed my hand as he led me through the crowd.

14

summer

I collapsed back on the daybed, watching the fireflies dance above the water beyond the screen of the guest room. Rikky had put on Donna Summer when we got back and insisted on dancing with Pan around the living room. She invited me to join them, and I did for a bit—twirling around with her to "Dim All the Lights"—but the weight of the day wore me down, and I excused myself to my room.

I slipped out of my dress and into an oversized T-shirt, and I clicked on an old copper fan, even though the air had a chill to it. Then I sprawled out on the bed to watch the fireflies and wait for sleep to take over.

It didn't, even though the music was turned down—so Donna sang Summer more quietly of how love never came easy. A moment later there was a soft rapping at the storm door, and I sat up to see Pan.

"Are you still up?" he whispered.

"Yeah." I sat up, pulling my legs to me and my shirt down

to hide my bare thighs. "You can come in and sit down if you want."

"Thanks. Rikky passed out on the couch," he explained apologetically as he sat down beside me. "I thought I should let her sleep."

"That's probably a good idea."

The sleeves of his shirt were pushed up to his elbows, and the top few buttons were undone, making him seem more relaxed than he had been earlier. More relaxed and more handsome, to be honest.

Pan lifted an arm, ruffling his black curls, and his shirt rose up, revealing the smooth olive skin over his taut abdomen and hips as he stretched. He put his arm behind his head, and I had to pull my gaze away from his exposed flesh.

"It really is beautiful out here," he said.

"Yeah," I replied, like I'd been busy admiring the view outside instead of checking him out. "Yeah. It really is."

"Sorry about tonight," he said at length.

"What do you mean?"

"I kinda ditched you at the bar. And we didn't really spend much time looking for that Indu guy. The whole night kinda seems like a bust for you."

I laughed. "It wasn't a bust. I learned some things. Kinda. I think."

"Very convincing," he said, which only made me laugh harder. "I was hoping to spend more time with you."

"Oh, yeah?"

"Yeah. I thought there'd be dinner and dancing, and that it would be a good time."

"You know, we are together now. We can still have a good time."

His eyebrow arched sharply. "Oh, yeah?"

"Yep." I stood up and extended a hand to him. "There's still music, so there can still be dancing."

"Truer words were never spoken." Pan grinned as he took my hand, and he got to his feet before slipping an arm around my waist. "I'm still not the best dancer."

"To be fair, I haven't taken any dance lessons since the last time we danced."

"Well, I can never be too sure with you. You're always up to one adventure or another."

"Yeah, that does sound like me," I agreed with a laugh.

It occurred to me, with his hand warming my back, that it wasn't the chilly night air causing goose bumps to form on my skin.

"You're cold," he said in a low, husky voice.

"I'm okay," I said, but when he wrapped his other arm around me, I didn't protest. I pressed myself gently against him, letting his body warm me, and I looped my arms around his neck and rested my head on his shoulder.

"Since tonight didn't go the way I planned, I'll have to make up for it by taking you out when we get back to Merellä."

"That sounds great," I said. "But I don't think tonight turned out all that badly."

"That is true."

I waited a moment, giving myself a chance to quell the butterflies in my stomach and build up my courage before saying, "You know . . . the night's not over yet."

"No, it's not," he murmured.

He pulled away from me, enough that he could look into my eyes. By then we'd given up any pretense of dancing. We were standing together, arms around one another, as the cool twilight air firefly-flashed around us.

The air felt thicker, and time seemed to slow—it felt like minutes between the desperate thumps of my heart.

And then—as I held my breath and he leaned in toward me—Rikky suddenly made a loud retching sound from the living room.

"Oh, shit." Pan grimaced. "That doesn't sound good. I should go make sure she's okay."

"Yeah." I stepped away from him.

He started toward the door but stopped and looked back at me. "Once she's settled and okay, should I . . . do I come back here?"

"Yeah." I smiled at him. "I'll be up."

"Pan!" Rikky shouted. "Panny, I need your help!"

15

social

I woke up in the daybed, cold and alone. The house was silent, other than the chatter and songs of the animals and insects that surrounded us. Last night, I'd stayed up for a while (or maybe just a bit?), listening to Rikky bemoan all of her life choices—particularly the ones that led to her throwing up on the floor and requiring Pan's help to clean it up—all while he reassured her in soft comforting words.

Now the sun was coming up, chasing away the chill of the previous night, but the thick fog lingered on.

I didn't want to leave my room yet—I told myself it was because I didn't want to disturb Pan and Rikky, and not because I was afraid of what I might walk into—but I couldn't sleep, so I went about gathering the things I'd left strewn around.

Eventually nature called, and I crept out of my room. On the way to the bathroom I walked past the couch, where I spotted Pan sleeping alone. He lay on his back, one arm behind his head, and his shirt was unbuttoned and open, exposing his tanned stomach and smooth chest. I was dimly aware that I was staring, but in my defense, he looked far hotter sleeping than anyone had a right to.

After I went to the bathroom, I braved the outdoor shower—spider and all. By the time I was done, exiting the bathroom wrapped in a pair of threadbare towels, both Pan and Rikky were awake. Rikky was in the living area, straightening up, while Pan made breakfast.

"Good morning!" Rikky chirped, seemingly oblivious to the fact that I was awkwardly clinging to the towels wrapped around me. "Sorry about last night. I feel like I put a huge damper on your investigation. That wasn't what I planned to happen, but the night got away from me, you know?"

"Yeah, yeah, don't worry about it," I replied amiably.

"Do you want some gator-egg hash, Ulla?" Pan looked back over his shoulder at me.

I shook my head. "No, I'm good."

"What are your plans for the day?" Rikky stopped folding blankets long enough to brush her dark auburn bangs from her eyes. "I don't have work today, so I can help you with whatever you need."

"Thank you, but I don't know for sure yet. I'm trying to meet up with someone today, but nothing's set," I explained.

"Well, let me know. I'll be doing stuff around here. Washing windows, cleaning cages." She waved toward the skylights, acknowledging the splatters of bird droppings on the windows. "Maybe work on some projects."

"I'll make sure to get my stuff out so it's not in your way," I said, since the porch I was sleeping in doubled as her workroom.

"No, no, I didn't mean it like that. You've got stuff to do, you should focus on that," she insisted.

"Rikky," Pan said in an admonishing tone. "Will you stop talking and let Ulla get dressed?" He gave me a side-long glance over his shoulder—it was brief and chaste, but my skin flushed anyway, a wave of heat with a prickle of goose bumps.

I lowered my eyes when he looked back at the food he was cooking, and I only nodded as Rikky offered apologies and I hurried to my room.

Honestly, I don't think I really breathed again until I was leaning back against the door, my palms flat against the cold metal. My crush on Pan was definitely intensifying, but I was determined not to let that get in the way of what I needed to do.

So I got dressed and got to work figuring out how to get in contact with Eyrun Gundt, formerly Holt. Her daughter Tindra had died five years ago, with Indu Mattison listed as the father on the census records. Right now Eyrun was the only living connection I had to Indu.

Other than Bekk Vallin, who I suspected had been about as forthcoming as she was going to be. She had given me more information than other Omte would have, and I hoped it was enough to lead me closer to the truth.

The first step was pulling out my Moleskine notebook. I had copied down all the information when I had been at the Postkontor, and I grabbed my cell phone to do a little sleuthing. Thankfully, Fulaträsk had much better reception and appreciation for Wi-Fi than Merellä.

When I flipped through pages, I paused when I saw the message that Jem-Kruk had left for me before he'd gone.

If you ever want to say hello—to me or to Eliana—
come find us.
X Jem-Kruk

My fingers grazed the jagged lines of his name, and an image of him the last time I saw him swam in my head. At the Midsommar ball he'd looked especially handsome, with his lush hair in braids and his mesmerizing eyes on me.

He took my hand in his. "And if we don't meet again, I want you to know that I truly enjoyed knowing you while I did, Ulla." He bent down and kissed my hand, and I swear I nearly swooned.

I shook my head, clearing away the memory, and I turned the page in the notebook. Jem-Kruk might be my friend, but he might very well be my enemy, and either way, daydreaming wouldn't help me find him or Eliana or anyone.

With my phone in hand, I got ready to do a little sleuthing. Bekk's files had given me Eyrun's address, but I didn't want to show up at her house unannounced and start asking questions about her dead daughter's absentee father. So I went searching through social media to find her.

Kingdom rules varied on social media use, but all of them frowned on it. Some tribes—like the Vittra—actually made it illegal. That didn't stop trolls from posting, but usually they did their best to mask their real identities and hide their more supernatural attributes and locales.

And then there were the occasional troll social-media stars, who seemed to enjoy hiding in plain sight. One of the most popular "beauty influencers" was a Trylle who owed her looks more to supernatural genetics than to blending techniques. Then there was the Skojare who dabbled in the cosplay community, where her gills passed for convincing makeup and prosthetics.

Eyrun turned out to be neither, but after a half hour of searching various terms, locales, and media forums, I finally stumbled onto pictures geotagged near the address Bekk had given me.

That's when I discovered *MommyBogger*—the name being a play on words for Mommy Blogger, since she was recording her life as "a stay-at-home mom living a country life in the bayou."

Her aesthetic seemed to be one part educating others on her "natural" life, hunting-and-gathering and raising "barefoot boys," as she put it. The other part consisted of carefully shot rustic pics—twine ribbons, mason jars, sunsets, and oversaturated puddles.

The pictures showed the nice life of a pretty young mother. One picture featured twenty-five candles for her birthday. Her two boys—Sylver, the older one, a toddler but very big for his age, and Glade, a baby with fat rolls on his thighs and mud in his dark curls—were her life.

There were a few photos that referenced Tindra. A stark picture of a rainbow, another of a wilting flower. Both had very short captions, unlike her usual wordy ramblings about the scent of rain on leaves. *Miss you today and every day, Tindra Rosemallow.*

This had to be the right Eyrun, so I opened the direct message and typed up a vague request.

Hello Eyrun,

I'm looking for my birth parents. I've been working with the Inhemsk Project, and I'm in Fulaträsk now. I was hoping to be able to meet with you while I'm here to ask you a few questions. I promise I won't take up too much of your time.

Thank you,
Ulla

I hit send. And then I waited.

16

Health

The house was nearly hidden in the fog. Eyrun Gundt's stylish little cottage—"a supersized tiny house," according to her profile—sat on dry land, unlike most of the homes in Fulaträsk. It was right on the edge of the city limits, where the swamp bled into the skeletons of long-abandoned farms. A dirt road connected the house to the outside world, so we'd considered driving the Jeep, but it was much faster taking the airboat.

Eyrun and I had messaged back and forth a few times, and despite some initial hesitation, I finally convinced her it would be better if we talked in person, and we agreed to meet. Rikky was busy tending to her animals, having discovered an injured possum just that morning, so Pan and I headed out together.

When we pulled up to her house, Eyrun was standing on the porch at the edge of the water, her arms folded over her chest and a nervous smile on her face. The first thing I noticed was that she partook in some deceptive photography. Nothing was an outright lie, exactly, but she'd employed flattering angles and strategic lighting to hide her long nose and her wide frame, as well as mask the chipping paint and more dilapidated aspects of her homestead.

"You find the place okay?" she asked us as we tied up the boat.

"Yeah, it was exactly where you said," I assured her.

Once we'd finished with the boat, we walked up the short trail to the porch. Eyrun hadn't moved yet, standing at the top of the steps as she looked down at us. "You are the girl I was talking to online, right?"

"Sorry, yes, I'm Ulla Tulin."

"And I'm Panuk Soriano with the Inhemsk Project." Pan stepped forward, extending his hand as he did, and Eyrun shook it tentatively.

It was his credentials that had finally gotten her to agree— head researcher at the Inhemsk sounded a lot more impressive than my title as "random intern."

"Eyrun," she replied tightly. "Should we go inside?"

I nodded. "Sure."

"My husband took the boys to the park," she explained as she led us into her house.

Inside, it was small, bordering on cramped. The front door opened into a kitchen overflowing with spices, home-canned vegetables, window herb gardens, and multitudes of specialized and antique utensils, overflowing from shelves and hooks and cupboard doors held shut with industrial-sized rubber bands.

The kitchen spilled into the living room, with a small round table straddling the two rooms. Beyond that was a love seat, a wood-burning stove, and an unreasonable amount of family photos, toys, knickknacks, and crafts stuffed into every corner.

We sat at the table while Eyrun poured us a glass of homemade strawberry-rhubarb juice. I took in our surroundings, and Pan made small talk about her son's art, slowly putting her at ease.

I'd begun to realize that Pan had this way about him. With his soothing baritone, somehow strong and light all at once, he was a calming presence. It was hard not to feel like everything was going to be okay when you were around him . . . even if it wasn't.

"So, what is it you think I can help you with?" Eyrun asked as she sat down across from me. "I can tell you right off the bat that I never gave a child up for adoption, and you look like you're eighteen? Seventeen? I would've been eight or nine when you were born."

"I'm nineteen," I told her. "I didn't suspect that you were my mother, but I thought you might know someone who may be connected to my parents."

"And who might that be?" she asked with pointed skepticism.

"Indu Mattison," I said.

Eyrun looked away and let out a "Huh." She didn't say anything more, just stared off in thought.

"We saw the name listed on the birth certificate of your child," Pan said, calmly trying to salvage the conversation, which seemed poised to go off the rails before it even really started.

She closed her eyes, almost wincing. "I suppose that is

an unfortunate matter of public record." Slowly she exhaled and opened her eyes again. "I didn't want his name listed. But they take birth record and population info very seriously around here. They won't let anyone slip by."

"We're sorry to upset you," Pan said quickly. "We never meant to bring up unpleasant memories."

Eyrun ignored him, resting her brown eyes on me. "You believe Indu to be your father?"

I didn't answer right away, because I didn't know what the answer was. I hadn't *let* myself consider that Indu Mattison might be my father. The idea of this Älvolk fanatic, impregnating Omte women for some reason . . . that wasn't exactly the ideal father I'd conjured when I was growing up.

But I also couldn't deny the possibility—he'd had babies between 1994 and 2006, putting my birth in 1999 almost right smack in the middle. The woman I suspected to be my mother had last been seen in the First City—where Indu was alleged to be from.

If he was not my father—as I hoped was the case—then it was still likely that he had crossed paths with my mother.

If he never met her, he still knew where Áibmoráigi was.

If he didn't, he could still tell me something more about the Älvolk and maybe put me on the right track to finding the First City and the Lost Bridge of Dimma.

No matter what, Indu was my biggest lead, and I needed to find him.

"I think he knew my mother," I clarified finally.

Her lips pressed into a tight, painful smile. "He knows many women. I'm sure he knew her too."

"Is there anything you feel comfortable telling us about him?" Pan asked. "Or is there a way we can contact him?"

"Your mother." She twisted her wedding band, anxiously spinning the punch-pink gemstone around her finger. "What was her name?"

"Orra Fågel."

"Orra Fågel," she repeated as she considered it. "Wasn't the Queen called Fågel before she married the King?"

"They're cousins," I said.

"I don't think I knew an Orra, or any of the Fågels," she decided at last. "That doesn't mean much. Fulaträsk is bigger than it looks."

"We didn't expect you to know much about Orra," I admitted.

"Right. You want to talk about Indu." She leaned back in her chair, folding her arms, and looked out the window. "I don't know how much I can tell you. I haven't seen him in years, since before our daughter drowned." She paused. "He didn't even come for the funeral."

"I'm sorry," I said quietly.

"Don't be. Just don't expect him to come to yours either," she said flatly. "It sounds mean, but it's not meant to be. It's only facts. For as many kids as Indu had, he knows fuck-all about being a father."

"Why'd he do it?" Pan asked, and we both looked over at him. "Do you have any idea why he kept having children if didn't want anything to do with them?"

"Because he believed it was his duty as an Älvolk," she explained bitterly. "His children are supposed to add to the numbers of his 'thrimavolk,' and he never did explain to me what exactly what that meant, just vaguely referenced needing to guard the Lost Bridge or protect the realm or whatever ogreshit it was he claimed to believe.

"Honestly, I'm not even sure that he knows what for," she said with a rough sigh. "He took an oath to spread his seed far and wide, and he was promised divinity and his heart's every desire."

"And what were you promised?" I asked gently.

Tears instantly formed in her eyes, but she smiled. "A daughter. A strong, healthy baby when so many struggled to conceive. He said his blood and mine would make a child of unrefuted strength, verging on an immortal."

She shook her head, but neither Pan nor I said anything, instead waiting for her to speak when she was ready. "I can't tell you how much of what he said was a truth or a lie or merely a delusion. All I can say is that . . ." Her breath caught in her throat, but she pushed on. "All I can say is that Tindra did not live forever."

"I'm so sorry for your loss," Pan said, and she held her hand up to silence him.

"Do you know how to contact him?" I asked, hoping to change the subject. "I know you haven't seen him in some time, but do you have a number or something else?"

"Not anymore." Eyrun shook her head. "I had a number once, but it went to some antiquated phone service where I left my number, and he'd call back when he had a chance. Or whenever he felt like it.

"The last time we spoke, it was a bad connection on the

phone," she went on. "It was so staticky, and I'd told him that Tindra had passed, and all he cared about was getting her body to be buried in Áibmoráigi."

"That's rather morbid," Pan said.

"That's exactly what I thought," she agreed. "Morbid and clinical and uncaring. I tried to discuss anything else with him, any other part of Tindra's life, but he was fixated on getting her where he wanted, focused entirely on the logistics of how to transport from an off-the-grid swamp community to a hidden village in the Arctic."

"Do you remember where?" I asked. "Anything at all about the name or the location?"

"I don't remember exactly what he said." She frowned. "But he mentioned the Kiruna Airport. He was ranting about it when I hung up on him."

We talked for a little while after that, but the conversation wound to a close relatively fast. She didn't really want to talk about any of this at all, especially not with strangers.

Just before we left, she said, "I'd wish you luck on your journey, but for your sake, I hope you don't find Indu. Your life is better without him."

17

Navigations

I sat on the couch, legs folded underneath me, with my notebook open. Pan had gone with Rikky into the narrow attic space above her bedroom to dig through her storage.

After a bit of shrieking and several loud thuds, Pan rushed down the ladder. By then I was on my feet, standing in the doorway to Rikky's bedroom.

"Are you okay?" I asked Pan as he wiped the cobwebs and dust bunnies from his face.

"Yeah, Rikky's got raccoons living up there, and she says it's fine." He rolled his eyes at that. "But I noped right out of there."

A little bit of something—a tiny downy feather—clung to his long, dark eyelashes. He stood before me, a little out of breath, his hair mussed from the encounter. His hands were on his hips, and the sleeves of his white T-shirt were rolled up, taut around his biceps.

I stepped closer to him, tentatively, and I reached out and plucked the feather from his eyelashes. He didn't move or flinch—he kept his gaze on me, then slowly closed his eyes and opened them again when I pulled my hand away.

He laughed quietly. "For a second I thought . . ."

"Found it!" Rikky yelled through the ceiling, followed by a scurry of little feet.

Pan stepped back from me, shouting back over his shoulder, "That's great, Rikky! I knew you'd get it."

I went back to the living room, waiting on the couch for Rikky to close up the folding attic ladder and hatch. She came in, laughing about the raccoons, and nudged aside Pan's laptop, was still open with his recent searches for Kiruna, and then she sat beside me and plopped a big old atlas onto my lap.

"Here it is," she said as she brushed the dust off the cover. "*Snorrik's Troll Guide to the World*. It has all the various maps from our history, but I can't be sure they're all that accurate. I looked through these before, and if I recall, there's one where they put Greece and the Dead Sea in Canada, so there are definitely some errors."

"I'll keep that in mind," I said and leafed through the book, carefully so as not to damage the brittle pages.

Pan leaned on the back of the couch and reached over—his arm brushing mine—to click his keyboard and wake the laptop back up. "So, this says Kiruna is about a hundred kilometers north of the Arctic Circle."

"I'm not seeing a lot of longitude or latitude lines on these maps," I muttered as I looked through them.

"Trolls, unlike Vikings, are not so great with cartography," Rikky agreed. "I always assumed it was because they mostly made maps to trick the humans about our locations, but then they never made accurate ones for themselves."

There weren't a lot of landmarks for me to go on in general, and when there were, they tended to be misconstrued—like one where Scandinavia took up the entire page and the rest of Europe (labeled *the Sutherlands*) was the size of my thumb in the bottom right corner.

I stared down at the disproportionate map, and the splattering of trees for forests and triangles for mountains and blue puddles for lakes, with labels like *Lake Mälaren* and *Giebmegáisi* and *Krystalsløret* and an island in a giant blue puddle marked *Isarna*. There were a dozen marked "cities," if they could be called that. One was simply titled *Sigrad Haus*. But there were others, like Birka and Oslo, that were real human cities that still existed.

"So, I'm guessing that Kiruna would be somewhere up in this . . . north region." I used my finger to draw a circle on the uppermost part of the malformed Scandinavian peninsula. "Indu mentioned the Kiruna Airport, so he probably thought that was the nearest one. So, there can't be that large of an area that it services."

"Let's see." Pan moved the laptop so it perched on the arm of the couch, allowing him to type more easily. But still his arm pressed against me.

I wasn't sure if I should move, and anyway, there wasn't anywhere else to go with Rikky sandwiched up on the other side of me. Besides, I didn't really want to move—it wasn't an exciting or particularly meaningful touch, but I liked it all the same. And I liked how he smelled—a wonderfully clean boy smell, that soap and rain and crispy musk that seemed to be the undertone of all soaps for men.

"So, you'll be surprised to learn that the Arctic regions of Sweden are very sparsely populated," Pan said when he'd finished reading the entry on Kiruna. "Which means it can't support a lot of airports, so the Kiruna Airport is the only one in a fairly large radius."

"Dammit." I sighed. "It's summer. Maybe it wouldn't be so bad if I kinda hiked around the countryside."

"It says here that area around there is incredibly mountainous," Pan continued reading. "Kebnekaise is the tallest mountain in Sweden." He glanced down at the atlas. "I think that's the same as the Giebmegáisi."

"I didn't say it would be an *easy* hike," I argued weakly.

"I don't know, Ulla. I think we're gonna have to come up with a better plan than us wandering around the wilds of Sweden," Pan said gently.

His phone rang in his back pocket, and he straightened up to grab it. "It's Sylvi. I'm gonna take this outside," he said, and he took long strides toward the door as he answered the call.

"I hope everything's okay," Rikky said, her eyes following him.

"I'm sure she's just checking in."

"What exactly are you looking for on the maps?" Rikky turned her attention back to me. "You know the Lost Bridge won't be listed, hence the name."

"Yeah, but I was hoping there'd be some kind of landmark on there that correlates to the location near Kiruna, and then . . . I don't know. It would magically all make sense to me."

She laughed—the kind where she threw her head back and let out a loud staccato sound. "Nothing in life ever works that way. Trust me."

"The woman who raised me, she always said, 'Put hopes in one hand and shit in the other, and see which one fills up first,' " I said.

"That was one that my mama was fond of saying too!"

Rikky and I looked through the maps for a few more minutes, until Pan came back into the house. His brow was knotted, but his expression was more blank than grim.

"What'd she say?" Rikky asked, and I added, "Are you okay?"

"Yeah, I'm okay. But I have to go back to Merellä," he said.

18

claims

Rikky was already on her feet, while I was still registering what Pan had said.

"Why? What's wrong?" She rushed to his side, but he stepped away from her.

"Nothing's wrong." That was what Pan said, but he had a dazed look on his face and he toyed with his phone. "It might be . . ." The furrow on his brow deepened, but a faint smile played on the corners of his lips. "I think it might be good news."

"What do you mean?" Rikky asked.

"The Kanin monarchy is reopening my case." His jaw tensed, and his eyes were moist. "You know how my mother told me that my father was the former Kanin King Elliot. He died when I was still a baby, but the kingdom has always refused to acknowledge my existence."

He paused, swallowing hard. "But now they're reopening my paternity case. I'm going to get confirmation one way or another." He looked down at his feet, but he couldn't hide the relieved smile. "I'll know who my dad is, and so will everyone else."

Rikky squealed and clapped her hands together, shattering the gravity of the moment, and Pan only grinned at her excitement.

"We *must* celebrate!" she insisted.

"Nothing's set in stone yet," he said, but his words fell on deaf ears.

Rikky was a woman on a mission. She was already pulling on a pair of muck boots and talking about how she had to go out to her "aboveground cellar" to get her really good strawberry wine.

Pan managed to stop her before she made it out the front door, but he had to actually step in front of her to do it. "I do have to leave in the morning. I have to get back to make my case. And with two long days of driving ahead of me, I don't want to start it with a hangover."

She waited a beat before asking. "So tonight is your last night here?"

"Yeah, it is."

"Okay, well, your farewell celebration definitely calls for the good wine." Rikky went on undeterred. "You can drink as much as you feel comfortable with, and not a drop more."

"That's a fair deal," he relented with a laugh.

"I'm a fair woman," she said as she slipped around him, and then she was out the door, presumably venturing into some sort of aboveground cellar.

Once she was gone, taking her high-strung energy with her, Pan looked at me with an embarrassed smile. "Sorry about all this." He rubbed the back of his neck. "I'm sure that Rikky will let you stay with her longer and help you figure out things here."

"I'm sure she would," I agreed as I walked over to him. "But I don't want to take advantage of her kindness. She's already extended herself so much. And, if I'm being honest, I don't know how much more there is for me to find here."

He frowned. "Are you sure?"

"Probably they know more than they're telling, but the Queen isn't talking, and I don't want to hang around here imposing on Rikky for some undetermined amount of time," I said.

And that was true. We'd already been at Rikky's place for four days, and that seemed like long enough to be taking up her space and time. Pan and I had pooled together before we got here—both of us had dug into our savings for this trip—but we both agreed that Rikky's hospitality deserved compensation.

He'd given her the money when he arrived, without either of us setting up an exact time frame, but it felt like enough to cover maybe a week. We were close enough to that expiration date.

"Besides," I said, smiling up at him, "we started this journey together; we finish it together."

"Good." His voice was low.

And then gently, deliberately—his eyes on mine—he took my hand and pulled me toward him. He wrapped his arms around me and held me to him. As I closed my eyes, I realized that nobody had ever hugged me like this before. I don't know that I'd ever felt quite so . . . *held* before. The hug completely enveloped me somehow, so all I could feel was the warm strength of him, his heart beating quick and loud in my ear.

"We'll find your family," he promised, and in his arms, with my head to his chest, I felt his voice rumbling through me, and I felt an intense heat in my lower belly.

"I know." I stepped away from him—acutely aware that Rikky would burst through the door at any moment—and walked away, pretending to focus on the caged squirrel while I slowed the racing of my heart and hoped the fan would cool the flush on my cheeks.

As if she had been summoned by my thoughts, Rikky returned a moment later carrying a cask of wine. She was in surprisingly good spirits about the whole thing—or at least it came as a surprise to me. I assumed she'd be upset about Pan's departure, but maybe I had misread things and she was just happy to have her space back.

Back at the inn in Iskyla, Mrs. Tulin often muttered, "Fish and guests start to smell after three days." That was probably true everywhere.

Since it was a celebration for Pan, she let him choose the music. He spent quite a bit of time flipping through the milk crate of records before deciding on Harry Nilsson. Pan made us supper and Rikky poured us wine. We talked and laughed as we ate, until I decided to take a break.

I went back to my room to pack up my things. Since we were leaving early in the morning, I wanted to have it all together to be sure I didn't forget anything.

Once that was done, I messaged Dagny to let her know I'd be back home soon, and then I messaged Sylvi to let her know that I'd be coming back. I'd paid up my rent until the end of July—well, Finn had, as a sort of going-away present/ college fund—so I knew my living situation in Merellä was covered until then.

My boss Sylvi hadn't exactly been my biggest fan before I left, but she let me go without too much complaint, so I hoped she understood. I didn't want to seem ungrateful or careless, but it was more important to try to find Eliana.

Although, in our days of researching, we had barely inched closer to Áibmoráigi or how to find Eliana. I vacillated between convincing myself that she was safe with family or that she was in terrible peril.

Before we left Merellä, I'd explained to the authorities everything that had happened with Eliana being kidnapped by her twin sister, Illaria. I had told Dagny and Elof, and I'd filed a report with Mimirin security—not that that had really done much good. There was very little proof of Eliana's existence *before* she went missing—there was even less now that she had gone on the wind with Illaria, Sumi, and Jem-Kruk.

Not that I really knew who they were.

Then again, I didn't really know who Eliana was either.

With my messages to Sylvi and Dagny taken care of, I decided to send one to Hanna. I didn't have much to update her on, but I knew she would worry if she didn't hear from me soon. I wrote a few lines assuring her that everything was okay, and I attached a couple pics I'd taken of Drake the snapping turtle for good measure.

By the time I had finished, it was still early. The fireflies hadn't even come out yet, but maybe it was the light mist holding them at bay. The music was still playing—it had recently changed tracks from the cheery "Gotta Get Up" to the very melancholy "Without You," so I guessed that Pan and Rikky were still up.

It was empty out in the main part of the house, but the front door was slightly ajar, and I heard the splashing of Drake. Sometimes Rikky liked to feed the turtle after dusk. She said it more closely mimicked snapping turtles' natural hunting instincts.

I went to join them, but I stopped at the door. They were standing on the dock with their backs to me. An outside light was on, creating a halo of yellow above them, and the mist sparkled like glitter. It was heavy enough that their clothes were damp, clinging to their bodies. Rikky had her arm hooked through his, and both of them watched the animals swimming around.

Then she said something—it was too quiet to hear over Nilsson's mournful singing, and anyway they were too far away for me to hear. Pan looked over at her, then she leaned over and she kissed him, fully, deeply, on the mouth. She kissed him.

And at least for a moment—a few beats of my heart—Pan kissed her back.

вreak

I shouldn't have watched. I knew that then. I don't even know why I did in the first place. Pan and Rikky were outside— I knew they were—and I was going over to join them, but instead I stood there like a creeper.

And I saw her kiss him.

And I saw him kiss her back.

And I saw him stop. He put his hand on her shoulder and pulled away.

And I heard him say, loudly, "This isn't a good idea, Rikky."

She didn't say anything, but she moved forward, like she meant to try again, so this time he took a full step back.

That's when I decided I'd watched enough (too much, really), and I knew it shouldn't hurt, but it did. Pan wasn't really my *anything*. I had no claim to him, and even if I did, she had kissed him. He had stopped it. Almost right away.

Pan had done nothing wrong.

Neither had Rikky.

But I wish I hadn't seen him kiss her.

Or at least I wish I had kissed him first. Before I had seen him kissing her in the mist.

I went back to my room and I pulled the blanket over my head and I wished I didn't feel this way. I wished I didn't feel sick to my stomach. But mostly I wished I would fall asleep and feel better tomorrow.

It ended up being a little of both. I fell asleep relatively quickly, after a brief obligatory bout of tossing and turning, and I woke up feeling a little better but not great.

I didn't really know how to act around Pan. Or Rikky, for that matter. Which made for a very awkward farewell. It didn't help that the conversation between Pan and Rikky was very stilted, full of lots of "ums" and "uhs" and very little eye contact.

Things finally started to feel more relaxed when Pan and I were miles down the road. Until then, we'd been traveling in silence, but then he switched radio stations, flipping over to Elton John. He turned it up and sang along to "Rocket Man," and eventually I joined in.

"I'm really surprised you knew that one," he commented once the song had finished, and he turned the radio down. "I didn't think you guys listened to a lot of pop music in those really isolated villages where you grew up."

"We do, sorta." I shrugged. "The changelings bring a lot of pop culture back with them, and everyone everywhere knows about the Beatles and *Star Wars*. But I would say generally speaking our tastes tend to be a little dated. In Iskyla, I heard a lot of Cher, Diana Ross, and Elton John."

"That doesn't sound all that dissimilar to music in my house growing up," he said with a laugh.

We lapsed into a silence, but it didn't last long before Pan broke it with, "Are you done talking to me until another classic rock song?"

I narrowed my eyes at him. "What do you mean?"

"I don't know." He shook his head. "You haven't been talking much this morning, and it seems like something is wrong."

I slouched down in the seat, staring out the window as desert landscape rolled by. "No, everything's fine. I'm just nervous about getting back."

"Have you heard back from Sylvi yet?" he asked.

"No, but I've decided to take that as a good sign."

"I'll try to put in a good word for you, for whatever my word is worth to her."

"Thanks. I'll take whatever I can get, and Sylvi definitely likes you more than she likes me," I said, which only made him laugh.

"She'll warm to you. It just takes time," he assured me.

"If you say so."

"Hey, I warmed to you eventually."

"What?" I looked sharply at him. "You didn't like me at first?"

He nodded. "Oh, yeah. For the first thirty seconds or so, I was *really* on the fence about you. And then you said, 'Hello.'"

I smiled. "That's what did it for you?"

"Yep." He barely suppressed his own laughter. "That's what won me over. I've always been partial to folks that know their greetings."

"I'm glad I *finally* won you over."

"Yeah, me too," he agreed.

Phoenix, Arizona, was roughly the halfway point in our nearly thirty-four-hour drive back to Oregon, so we stopped at a little motel on the side of the highway. Neither of us were exactly flush with cash, so we chose the cheapest option. It was a little rundown and still had physical metal keys for the doors, but it looked clean enough, and we got two queen beds in our room.

"You want the bed by the window?" Pan pointed to the poppy-patterned bedspread. "I'll take the one by the door?"

"Sure. Whatever you want." I tossed my duffel bag on the bed. "Is it cool if I use the bathroom first? I ate way too much sugar on the road, and I really gotta brush my teeth."

"Yeah, go ahead. I was gonna call Dagny anyway."

I'd begun gathering up my toiletries, but I stopped. "Dagny?"

"Yeah, since she's been dog-sitting Brueger for me, I wanted to call and check in," he reminded me as he pulled his phone out of the pocket of his snug jeans.

When he'd asked Dagny to take care of his dog, I'd been there. Technically, Brueger the Belgian Malinois was the property of the city of Merellä, used to herd the giant woolly elk. But Brueger had been sleeping at Pan's apartment since he was a puppy, and he didn't think it was fair to ask him to sleep out in the barn.

"Tell her hi for me," I said before ducking into the bathroom.

I freshened up, and when I turned the tap off, I could hear him through the door, talking on the phone first to

Dagny—in his normal voice, thanking her again—then to Brueger, in a slightly higher-pitched, excitable tone, asking him if he's a good boy.

I put a hand over my mouth to silence my giggle, but I won't lie that it made me feel like taffy left in the sun all day—so warm and gooey and strangely pleasant.

When I came out a few minutes later—having changed into light shorts and a tank top—Pan had gotten off the phone and changed into his own pajamas. Well, *changed* might have been too strong a word. He'd really just stripped down to his boxers, so he stood shirtless beside the bed.

"Is this okay?" He motioned toward himself. (And, for the record, he had that wonderful naturally lean, muscular physique that happened with taking care of yourself and a bit of good genetics, and not that insanely jacked superhero look, so he would still be soft when he held you, but I already knew that from when he'd hugged me, and from when we'd danced.)

"Sorry." He apologized and reached for his shirt, and I realized I'd been staring at him, frozen, like a maniac. "You're obviously not—"

I held my hand up to stop him. "No, it's fine."

"You sure?" He held his shirt like he meant to pull it over his head. "I did it because it's hot in here."

The air conditioner sputtered in the window, doing its best to slowly cool the room, but he wasn't wrong. It was stuffy and warm in here.

I laughed, trying to break the tension of the moment. "It's not that big a deal." Then with a smirk I added, "I can sleep topless, if that'll make you feel more comfortable."

"I never realized that was an option, but yeah, yes. That would make me feel much more comfortable," he said, so I threw a pillow at him, and he laughed.

"I should've known you'd answer that way," I said as I climbed into the bed.

"I think you *did* know," he countered before hopping into his bed.

"Good night, Panuk," I said, before clicking off the lights.

"Good night, Ullaakuut."

I heard the springs creaking and groaning as Pan got settled in. I double-checked my phone to make sure my alarms were set for the morning, and then I listened to the pathetic hum of the AC. He sighed, then rolled over. And then rolled over again.

"Are you okay?" I asked.

"Yeah. I just . . ." He muttered something to himself that I couldn't understand. "Was it because Rikky kissed me?"

"*What?*"

"You've been aloof with me today," he said. "And . . . and last night, Rikky kissed me. I was wondering if there was a correlation."

"Yeah, but not the one you think," I admitted.

The thin motel curtains let in enough of the streetlight that I could see his silhouette as Pan propped himself up on an elbow. "What are you talking about?"

"She's still so hung up on you."

"She's not—" he argued, but I cut him off.

"She really is, Pan. And you broke up with her because she wanted to go home and you wanted to stay in Merellä."

"That's not the only reason," he interjected quietly.

"By the time we get back, I'll have missed a week of my internship, and it ends three weeks from now," I said. "Maybe even less, the way things are going."

He waited a little bit before saying, "You could stay."

"I might," I admitted. "But I might not. I don't know what I'm going to do yet."

"Nobody knows what they're going to do, not really," he argued gently. "There's no way I could've known that I'd ever be here, with you."

"I know." I stared up at the ceiling and the blinking red light of the smoke detector, and I thought carefully how to word what I felt. "It's not that . . ." I sighed. "I want to figure out what I want to do first. My internship ends soon. And then I will make a decision about where I'll be living, and then . . . then I'll be open to dating."

I grimaced in the darkness, hating how awkward and presumptuous it all sounded, but I didn't see any way around the conversation. And I wasn't sure I was saying the right things.

If Finn were here for me to ask, I know that he'd praise me for being responsible and making smart choices, which was definitely a recurring theme in the Holmes household. All the kids—including myself—were encouraged by both Finn and Mia to make smart choices, to use critical thinking and logic.

Of course, Hanna—who spent nearly the entirety of twelve years under the guidance of Finn and her mother— would be *livid* if she knew I was sort of turning Pan down.

That fact really did reaffirm that I was probably making the right decision by waiting to get involved with someone until I knew for sure what kind of commitment I could make.

But I was still thinking about how he looked shirtless, and that crooked smile that he had when we were dancing together, and the way his arms felt around me . . . and then I was wondering why I even made the decision to say no—

"So," Pan said, interrupting my train of thought, "if I understand correctly, what you're basically saying is the real-life equivalent of the Magic 8 Ball saying, 'Reply hazy, try back later.' "

"What are you talking about?"

"You don't know Magic 8 Balls?"

I shook my head. "I have no idea what you're talking about."

"It was a clunky joke anyway," he said with a self-deprecating laugh. "I was really saying that you meant, 'Not never, just not right now.' "

"Yeah, that is exactly it."

Pan lay back down, his silhouette disappearing into the dark shadow of his bed. "That all sounds reasonable and mature."

"Why do you sound so disappointed?" I asked.

"Because I can't really argue it. You're right."

"Thank you," I said, feeling rather disappointed with myself.

20

correspondence

After eighteen straight hours in the Jeep, the ancient city by the sea came into view. From working in the archives, I'd learned of the claims that it was one of the oldest establishments in North America, dating back to the 1500s, and the stone walls and looming towers showed their age enough that it was believable.

It was dark when we got back to Merellä, so I didn't get to see the citadel in its full glory—although the smell of the metropolis was definitely out in full force. The heady aroma of salty sea air, elk dung, fresh hay, rotting fruit, and flowers in bloom.

Security guards at the gates stopped us, doing a quick scan of our IDs and our papers, and then it was the winding dirt roads through the quaint village, all stone and tiny Tudor houses, practically built on top of each other. And finally we rounded the corner and I could see the carriage house and the staircase to the apartment above it.

The light at the top of the stairs had been left on for me, and I felt rather touched that Dagny had thought to do that.

Even before we got there, I could hear Brueger barking. As soon as we parked, Dagny opened the door, and the dog bolted down the stairs and practically leapt into Pan's arms.

Pan laughed as Brueger slobbered and jumped all over him. "I wasn't gone that long, buddy. But I missed you too."

"If you're expecting me to run down the stairs and greet you like that, you're going to be sorely disappointed," Dagny said dryly, and she leaned on the railing of the landing at the top of the stairs.

"Aw, shucks," I joked, and I unloaded my bags.

"How was your drive?" she asked.

"Long," I said, and Pan immediately added, "Very long."

"Are you coming up, Pan?" Dagny asked. "Or are you heading home?"

"I'm just so excited to get home and sleep in my own bed," he said.

"Suit yourself. I made some lemon tea for Ulla and me to relax," she said.

"Dang, Dags, you really are the best roommate."

She rolled her eyes. "Hurry up. The neighbors are probably trying to sleep."

Pan said his goodbyes—my arms were full with my bags, so I didn't have to worry about navigating any possible hugs goodbye—and then he headed home, and I jogged up the stairs to my apartment.

Dagny poured me the aforementioned tea, and I sank

into the lumpy couch. To help set a relaxing mood, she lit a few candles and a stick of incense. Her silver archery arrow hanging on the wall glinted in the candlelight.

She asked me about my trip, and I filled her in on the highlights—what we found out, Indu Mattison, the Kiruna Airport, meeting Queen Bodil, a little about Rikky, more about Bekk, and I even mentioned Drake.

The only thing I avoided telling her was anything within the realm of my flirtation with Pan. I didn't even tell her that Rikky was his ex-girlfriend. I figured that if Dagny cared to know about it, she would ask.

"I never understood how their king died in a bar fight," Dagny said after I finished telling her about my visit to the Ugly Vulture.

"He really did!" I insisted. "They're even proud of it."

She arched an eyebrow. "Really?"

I nodded emphatically. "They even had the 'weapon' that killed him on display. It was a big broken wine bottle."

"Did he die saving a life or defending the kingdom's honor or some such thing?" Dagny asked.

"No, they were fighting over dragons."

She'd been taking a drink, and she nearly choked on it, stifling her laughter. "Dragons? Were they children too young to know that dragons aren't real?"

"No, they were fully grown adults—I think—who probably drank way too much *eldvatten*," I said, and she nodded in understanding at that.

"Well, I'm glad you made it back safe and sound." Dagny smiled and held up her cup of tea, almost like she was toasting me. "With you *and* Hanna *and* Eliana gone, it's been way too quiet around here. Even the dog was much cleaner and more civilized than you three."

"How have things been here?" I propped my elbow on the back of the couch, leaning on it as I looked at her.

"Not that exciting, honestly. Elof has been focused on analyzing Eliana's sample, but the whole thing has him baffled."

"Has Elof ever seen any Älvolk blood samples?" I asked. "In real life or case studies?"

She shook her head. "No, he's never found any concrete evidence of the Älvolk. The blood he's taken from those who claim to be Älvolk only comes back regular troll mixtures— mostly Trylle and Omte, for some reason. But that could be because they were lying or because Älvolk blood is no different than troll blood or because the Älvolk don't really exist."

"I think they exist . . . I mean, right?" I asked. "But there isn't real evidence . . ."

"That doesn't mean anything either," Dagny said. "Humans have been studying blood and DNA for decades. Trolls have only recently decided to really delve into troglecology and all that that entails. We've been able to piggyback on the humans' research in a lot of areas, but since they don't even believe we exist, they haven't exactly been studying us or recording pertinent data.

"So," she continued, "the reason we don't know more about the Älvolk or their biology is because they're good at hiding and we haven't been looking for very long."

"Basically, we don't know anything because we don't know anything?" I said.

She snapped her fingers. "Exactly." She attempted an

optimistic smile, but it looked strange and unnatural. "But thanks to folks like you, we will know more soon."

"Glad to be of service." I gave her a faux-salute. "Anyway, have you talked to Hanna lately?"

"She emails me approximately twelve times a day, even though I have repeatedly told her that I will only reply to one email per day, maximum." Dagny sounded so offended and bewildered by it that I couldn't help but laugh a little. "The most confounding thing is that she keeps sending me passages from these books she's reading for me to analyze, as if I'm some type of literary scholar."

"Really?" I asked in surprise. "She mostly talks to me about Eliana, and it's a set of demands, with a few complaints about her horrible summer."

"She does ask me about Eliana, and she frequently complains that her younger siblings are making her life more difficult," Dagny said. "But then it quickly devolves into important quotes from the 'research' she's doing to find Eliana."

"What research?" I sat up straighter. "She hasn't told me anything about that at all."

"I don't know why she wouldn't. It sounds like she's reading old fables that used to belong to her dad."

"What?" I shook my head. "They had a lot of kids' books there, but I didn't see any 'old' fables there. And Finn definitely isn't the type to be overly sentimental or into fairy tales."

"I don't know." Dagny shrugged. "She said they were her dad's, and they were mostly about Adlrivellir."

And then it hit me—Hanna wasn't talking about Finn; she meant her birth father, Nikolas. It'd been in her grandfather's study, before Hanna had stowed away with me on my way to Merellä, that I had first learned of Jem-Kruk and Adlrivellir when I saw the book on the shelf.

That could explain why Hanna didn't say anything to me about it. She had spent so much time trying to convince me that she didn't care about Nikolas at all. And now she was digging through his belongings, trying to connect his past with the events of her present.

"Why does she think Adlrivellir is somehow connected to Eliana?" I asked.

"Something that Eliana told her once." Dagny furrowed her brow as she tried to remember. "She was looking at the sky one afternoon, and Eliana asked why we only had one star in the sky. Hanna figured out she was talking about the sun, and that Eliana thought there should be three.

"It wasn't until she got back home that she remembered reading about a land with three suns," she went on. "Adlrivellir is a place from the old children's fables, and now Hanna believes that that's where Eliana is from."

"Could she be right?" I asked.

Dagny shrugged. "Anything is possible. But I still don't know where Adlrivellir is or how to get there. If it has three suns in the sky, I imagine it has to be quite far away."

21

internal

The Inhemsk Project offices were empty, but that was to be expected for a Sunday morning. I sat outside Sylvi Hagen's door on an uncomfortable plastic chair. Between me getting here early and Sylvi running late, I'd been waiting for thirty-seven minutes, and my thighs were going all pins and needles.

Not that I had any room to complain. Sylvi was doing me a favor by meeting me like this. She'd held my internship open for me while I was gone, and she'd wanted to meet with me as soon as I got back so I could start working right away. Considering that I had a coveted paid internship (however low-paying it may be), Sylvi was being remarkably generous and gracious.

I didn't understand it, but I would accept help when it was offered.

Sylvi finally arrived, looking very cool and aloof in her jeans, leather jacket, and dark-tinted aviators. She didn't say anything to me at all—she just went straight to her door and unlocked it.

It wasn't until the door was completely open that she finally said a gruff, "Well, come on in, then," without looking at me.

I followed her into her office—going slow and unsteady like a newborn calf because of the pins and needles in my legs. If Sylvi noticed my wobbling steps, she didn't acknowledge it.

She pushed her sunglasses to the top of her head, then she flipped through her planner and sipped her black tea. I sat across from her, waiting in an excruciatingly awkward silence.

Finally, without looking up, she flatly asked, "Did you find her?"

"What?" I asked, more out of surprise that she had broken the silence.

"The girl that you and the docent and Mästare Amalie are all so fond of." She waved her hand dismissively. "You went to find her. Did you succeed?"

"No." I swallowed hard. "I would not say that we were successful."

Sylvi looked at me at last, her dark eyes a strange bleary type of scrutinizing, and then she leaned back in her chair, linking her fingers together across her lap.

"Do you regret it?" she asked.

"No, I don't."

Her eyebrows arched slightly, but she gave no indication as to whether that was out of disapproval or merely surprise.

"Calder is expecting you back at work at eight A.M. tomorrow."

"Great. I'm looking forward to it," I said with a forced smile.

"Panuk told me that you're looking into the Älvolk," she said impassively. "Is that for your parents or for Eliana?"

"Both," I admitted.

She smirked. "It seems the old saying, 'All roads lead to First City,' is true."

"It does seem that way."

"All right." She went back to sorting through the papers on her desk. "I'll get the paperwork filed saying you've returned from your leave of absence. You can go now."

"Thank you," I said and got up to go.

"You're getting a lot more leeway most others would than get. Don't squander it," Sylvi said without looking up at me.

I paused at the door and turned back to face her, summoning my courage to ask, "But why?"

"Pardon?" she scoffed.

"Why am I the one getting the special treatment?"

She lifted her eyes. "Didn't you ever hear, 'Don't look a Tralla horse in the mouth'?"

I shifted my weight from one foot to another. "I'm not trying to be ungrateful. I only want to know what I've done—or what I'm expected to do—in exchange for this treatment."

A subtle, impressed smile formed slowly on her lips. "It's not as sinister as you may think. You seem to have friends in high places. The Trylle Queen, Mästare Amalie, the docent Elof, and even my top researcher Panuk all have sung your praises, though, to be clear, Panuk is the most vocal." Heat flushed my cheeks, and I lowered my eyes. "That kind of thing makes me skeptical. But maybe you've done something to earn that admiration." She wagged her head. "Or maybe you haven't."

"It doesn't really matter to me either way, because my point remains the same," she finished. "Don't take opportunities for granted."

"I am trying not to," I said carefully. "I left because I wanted to make sure my friend is safe, but I knew I couldn't stay gone forever, so I came back when the trail went cold. But if I can pick it up again, I will leave again. I hope that Eliana is safe, and I hope that I am not called away before my internship ends. But I will never regret helping a friend in need."

"Noble," Sylvi commented. "Naïve and wrong, but noble."

"I've been called much worse before."

"I'm sure you have," she muttered, and her attention returned entirely to the work on her desk. "And if you stay much longer, you'll be in the way. Panuk should be here shortly for our meeting."

"Sorry. And thank you again for all your help," I said, but she was done with me.

Once I left her office, I walked slowly and kept looking around, hoping to spot Pan—him on his way to the office, me on my way home—but I had no such luck. I knew I'd told him that I wanted to cool things off for now—even if it hadn't really heated up yet—but that didn't mean I didn't still enjoy being around him.

For the past week, I'd gotten used to seeing Pan every morning when I woke up, making unnecessarily elaborate breakfasts. And then every night he'd been there to go over our days with or to dance with, as old vinyl records crackled out songs. And as nice it had been staying up late and talking with Dagny last night, I still found myself missing Pan.

Maybe I'd made a mistake slowing things down with him.

Or maybe it was better this way, because I'd have fewer distractions and, like Sylvi said, I needed to take my position seriously.

22

Returns

The archives were, in some ways, a labyrinth disguised as a library and box storage. It was a cold, dungeon-like space made of stone and dark wood without any windows. The ceilings were surprisingly high for a basement—over ten feet, at least—and the bookcases stretched all the way to the top, so ladders were needed to reach more than half the shelves. The design meant the shelves were really walls, with arches and tunnels cut through, and they led to more than the occasional dead end.

Calder Nogrenn—the records keeper, head of the archives, and my immediate supervisor—manned the circular desk in the center of the room, straight down the tunnel from the main doors. The main purpose of the archives—according to Calder—was to maintain and add to the complete history of trollkind.

It was not a place made for customer relations, which explained Calder's personality. The intricately carved, beautiful circular desk he sat at made less sense since nobody ever really saw it but him.

I wasn't sure how he'd react to my return. I'd never really been able to tell if he liked me or merely tolerated me for efficiency's sake. The last time I had seen him, Pan and I had stopped unannounced at his apartment, and he had grudgingly told us what little he knew about the Älvolk.

He didn't look up when the door closed behind me—he was hunched over his desk, his nose buried in a scroll, the sleeve of his caftan stained with ink. My footsteps echoed off the stone floor, and he remained head down, focused on his work.

But he did finally look at me when I cleared my throat and said, "Hello."

"So, the rumors are true." His gray eyes rested heavily on me, and his olive skin was a weathered map of wrinkles and time. "You've returned."

"Does that mean you're not holding a grudge?" I asked.

"A grudge?" He scoffed. "I hardly care what you do. My work continues on, whether you are here or not."

"What can I do to help you with your work today?" I asked.

"Ragnall Jerrick and the Information Styrelse decided to go through many of our tomes from the early twentieth century. They've returned a large portion of them, but they still need to be properly shelved." With his thumb, he pointed behind him to a cart overflowing with thick, dusty books, and beside it was another three crates of books. It had to weigh over fifty pounds.

But I was strong. I could handle it, even if it wasn't going to be fun or pleasant. So I smiled and nodded.

"I'll get right on it, sir." I went around to the back of the desk and dropped off my bag before going back to gather the books.

I could've used the cart—it would've been easier that way—but it wasn't hard for me to carry anything under a hundred pounds, and the book cart's wheels were all squeaky and squawky. It was the kind of thing that would drive Calder insane, even over his radio blasting out Bach.

So I carried the stack of books through the maze of shelves, with tiny plaques and Calder's vague directions to guide me through. The only thing the books had in common was that they were published in the same two decades, but the subject matters were so varied that they had me going to every corner of the archives.

I'd only been working there since the beginning of June— minus my week off—so I wasn't exactly an expert on how things worked, but I had never seen such a large haul of books needing to be reshelved. In fact, it was usually only one or two books, if any.

That's what made the archives different from the library. The books, records, and folders here weren't supposed to be checked out or removed, generally speaking. They were intended to remain here to serve as a resource, but a safe- guarded one.

So I had to wonder why the Information Styrelse had suddenly requested dozens of books, and how unusual an occurrence it was. Calder probably knew, but I doubted he would tell me.

I made note of the titles, but most of them were so generic— *Common Surnames of Trylle Kingdom 1901–1925*—or random—*Country Food Recipes of the Kanin*. And another specifically devoted to a nearly extinct yellow flower called *Sorgblomma trollius funus*. It didn't sound like there was anything of serious value to glean from them, so I really had no idea what the Information Styrelse wanted them for.

Sylvi's warning about not squandering my opportunities had struck a chord with me, and I couldn't waste a chance to learn something useful. When I came across any title that sounded even remotely related to Áibmoráigi, the Älvolk, or Jem-Kruk, I took a few minutes to skim it before putting it away.

Even with my supernatural strength, by lunch my forearms were sore, feeling the strain more from the repetitive motions than anything else. And I was definitely craving a break. After I put away another armload of books, I headed back toward the desk, winding my way through the bookcases and thinking about how I was going to ask Calder if I could head to lunch.

As I approached, I heard Pan talking—telling Calder a cheesy joke about a ghost always going through books. I rounded the bookcase, and I spotted him leaning on the desk.

"Hey," I said as I walked over to him. "What's going on?"

"Hey!" He grinned when he saw me. "I knew you'd be hard at work, but I thought maybe you could use a break." He lifted up a brown paper lunch sack. "I grabbed us a couple of strawberry *gräddtårta* from the bakery and fizzy pink lemonade, if you're hungry."

"Yeah, absolutely," I said, then looked to Calder. "If that's okay."

Calder waved me off. "Yes, yes, yes. The sooner you go, the sooner you can get back to work."

"Thanks," I muttered.

There wasn't a real break room for the archives, just a large supply closet where we stored all the stationery and cleaning supplies. In addition to the shelves stacked with pens and papers, there was also an old couch, a minifridge, and a tea maker.

It was dimly lit, with cold stone floors and exposed drywall, but it was nearby, and it was private. Using supplies we had on hand—a moving blanket and couch cushions tossed on the floor, a few of the tea lights we kept by the dozens for emergencies, and my cell phone in a paper cup for a speaker amplifier—we managed to set up a nice little picnic.

"So, how's it been for you since you've been back?" he asked.

I shrugged. "It's been nice sleeping in my own bed again."

"Tell me about it!" He groaned in agreement. "Rikky's couch was fine for a couch, but it was awful for a bed."

"I didn't know you were uncomfortable. You should've said something. I would've switched with you."

"No, it wasn't *that* bad, really." He played it down with a sheepish grin. "I'm just glad to be home."

"Me too," I said and sipped my fizzy lemonade.

"It is strange not seeing you every day." Pan lowered his eyes, staring down at his hands as he plucked a strawberry from the top of the creamy tart. "I'd gotten used to you being around all the time."

And then I remembered that he had his important meeting with Sylvi yesterday—that's what he'd been called back for—and I nearly choked on my drink because I couldn't believe I'd forgotten to ask about something so important.

I coughed, and when he asked if I was okay, I nodded quickly and cleared my throat. "I'm so sorry, I've been going on and on. How did your meeting with Sylvi go?"

"Good. Good." His thick eyebrows pinched together, and he frowned. "But . . . she didn't really tell me much."

"What do you mean?"

He leaned back and rubbed his hands on his jeans. "When Sylvi called, she made it sound like she had finally gotten the Kanin to agree to start looking into my parentage. But that's not what's happening. A Mästare sent an official letter that basically says that they'll keep asking the Kanin kingdom to open a paternity case regarding me, and the Kanin acknowledged that they'd received that letter and said we can keep on writing letters, if that's our wish."

"And?" I pressed.

"And that's it." He laughed bitterly. "Sylvi assured me they were going to keep looking into it."

"What did she say when she called?"

"The Kanin were reopening my claim, and I should talk to her before they changed their minds."

I shook my head. "So . . . did they change their minds, then?"

"As far as I can tell, the Kanin have the same position they've always had—ignore and deny," Pan said with a shrug. "Sylvi showed me the letter they sent, so it's not like they told her anything different than what I saw."

I took a bite of my food, chewing as I considered what

Pan had said. "But I don't understand. Why would she call you back here?"

"That's what I'm saying." He rubbed the back of his neck. "I don't know. I'm not complaining, exactly. Maybe when they talked to her it sounded more substantial. Or maybe she thought that I'd want to know any little thing, and I would've thought that I would too. So here we are."

"I'm sorry it wasn't something more helpful for you," I said.

"Thanks." He stared down at his lap and inhaled through his nose. "I keep reminding myself that I still know who I am. This doesn't change anything."

I put my hand on his knee. "Exactly."

23

catacombs

For maybe the second time since I'd been working there, Calder left work on time. I'd returned from putting away books, and he was straightening up his desk.

"Heading out already?" I asked, teasing him for all the times he'd said that to me for staying *only* an hour or two late.

He lifted his head quickly, his gray eyes surprised. "I have an important dinner engagement, so I can't maintain my usual schedule. Are you comfortable locking up, or would you like to leave with me so I can lock up?"

"I have a little bit left to do. I can finish it and lock up, no problem."

"If you're certain," he replied, and he was already taking long strides toward the door.

I waved after him, but he never looked back. "Have a fun night!"

As soon as he was gone, I did exactly what I said I would—I rushed around finishing up the work I had left. The very second I was done with that, I ran back to the supply room and grabbed the heavy brass keys hidden behind the emergency candles. I'd been left alone with the keys to the castle, and like Sylvi said—I had to make my time here count.

It was actually Hanna's words I was reminded of as I unlocked the cellar-style doors. She'd been so focused on the fairy tales and Adlrivellir. I had to find out why.

I had never been in the catacombs before. Calder said the access was limited to those who required it. Since I felt like I might require it, that meant it wasn't *exactly* off limits.

The Catacombs of Fables were located directly underneath the archives. From what I gathered from Calder's grumbled answers, they had been created as a dungeon of sorts, to house prisoners back when the Mimirin had been solely under Vittra rule and still held prisoners (mostly those who had committed treason, traitors, and enemies of the kingdom).

The catacombs were intended for a specific type of criminal, one that the Vittra architects found particularly odious, so they were designed with the explicit purpose of being an unusually cruel punishment.

"The catacombs," Calder had told me once in his uniquely raspy voice, "were meant to drive us mad."

They were several stone boxes, underground and windowless, connected by winding tunnels. The walls were made of thick stone to hold the dead. When they executed prisoners, they encased them in the walls.

The interior was a claustrophobic maze, with the paths narrowing as the walls expanded with the dead. Living prisoners were thrown down here, and the only contact they'd ever have with the outside world was when random pieces of food were dropped through holes in the ceiling (now long since closed up).

After their use as a prison, the catacombs were transformed into a book dungeon. All the books that the Styrelse found dangerous or confusing, because the stories blurred our reality with human fiction and even our own fairy tales.

Presumably that's why all the books about Adlrivellir were kept here. The powers that be didn't want anyone mistaking the fiction for fact. But I thought I could handle it.

I went through the cellar door and down, down, down the many narrow steps into the catacombs. The steps had been worn from centuries of use, leaving smooth divots and sloping the stone downward. Other stairs in the Mimirin had been updated and replaced, but these had been left dangerously slippery.

The thing that hit me most was the smell—a damp earthiness that instantly brought me back to the crypts. That's where we'd gone after Finn's father died last fall; he'd been buried in the crypts high in the bluffs of Förening. It was a wet, rainy autumn day, so the younger kids stayed at home, out of the rain and mud. But I had been there, with Hanna and Liam, as Finn led us through the family tombs. Finn came from a long line of elite trackers, and that earned them plots in the Trylle royal crypts.

"Why are you showing us all of this?" Liam had been doing his best not to sound as uninterested as he obviously was, but it was hard for him, at only six years old, to hide it well. He'd dug his toes into the mud and pulled at a loose thread on his shirt.

"Liam, stop!" Hanna had hissed and elbowed him in the

ribs. "You shouldn't disrespect the dead." She'd been standing beside him, hanging on Finn's every word.

"It's not disrespectful to ask questions," Finn had admonished gently. "I'm showing you this because these are your ancestors, this is your history. It's important to know where you come from to help find where you should go."

The memory was instantly shattered when a big, fat spider dropped down in front of me, dangling from a gossamer tendril of web. I jumped, slamming hard into a bookcase, and my back collided painfully with the splintering wood.

It was another unfortunate case of my strength getting the best of me when I was startled. In my fear, I'd jumped forcefully enough into ancient bookshelves that they snapped. An avalanche of books rained down on me, and I fell to my knees and covered my head with my arms until it finally stopped.

I pushed the books off me and slowly sat up. My body already ached from my earlier work, but now I could add stinging cuts and splinters poking into my skin, and a book had struck me right in the temple, causing a big gash along my eyebrow.

"Ah, crap," I muttered, surveying the dusty carnage around me.

And then I spotted a familiar cover. My cell phone—which I'd dropped during the commotion—lay at an angle, and the light from it hit a shimmering emblem on the front of the book. The triskelion symbol with the vines.

As I reached for the book, the spider dropped down on the pile. I watched it from the corner of my eye.

I realized this wasn't just another book with the Älvolk

symbol. This book—bound in soft fabric with lightweight vellum pages—was the same book I'd seen in Hanna's grandfather Johan's study. Not the exact same copy, of course, but it was the same edition as *Jem-Kruk and the Adlrivellir*, although the title page was missing.

I flipped through the book to read more, but I noticed movement. The spider was scurrying around, and now I realized it wasn't the same spider. This one was larger—a lot larger, actually. Long, spindly legs stretched out from a bulbous body marked with a jagged strip of dark emerald green down its back.

There were multiple huge spiders crawling around, my head was bleeding, and I felt dazed and sore all over. I knew I had to clean up the mess, but just then I needed to get out of there.

Clutching the book under one arm, I wielded my phone like it was a holy cross warding off a vampire. Unfortunately, the spiders did not react like vampires.

In fact, an even larger one crawled out of a gaping crack in the wall. A massive spider with an abdomen as large as an apple, and a dozen opalescent eyes reflecting the cell phone's flashlight.

Before I could scream, I was running, racing frantically away from the spider. The faster I ran, the more horrifyingly apparent it became that it was futile—the halls were endlessly winding, I couldn't remember the way I had come, and more spiders were lurking around every corner—some of them as large as house cats.

"Why isn't anybody talking about all the damn spiders?" I asked—shrieked, really—into the claustrophobic tunnels as

I slowed, catching my breath and pressing my hand against the stitch in my side.

Maybe it wasn't something they put in brochures, but it really seemed like the kinda thing that leads to gossip and rumors.

But that wasn't really my most pressing concern. I was trapped, stumbling through the catacombs with no cell reception and giant spiders crawling everywhere. They weren't chasing me, but it still felt like they were closing in.

"How am I going to get out of here?" I whispered into the darkness.

I heard footsteps slapping gently on the stone floor, and in the dim light I saw a shadow dancing along the wall.

"Hello?" I asked, and the shakiness of my voice surprised me, but it probably shouldn't have. My skin crawled, like a thousand tiny legs were dancing all over it, and I didn't know how to get away. It took all my restraint not to devolve into hysterical screaming.

And then the shadow was taking form—a sliver of a troll, tall enough that the figure had to stoop beneath the ceiling. It barely even looked trollian—it was more like someone had been stretched out until they became a semi-opaque waif. But their dark eyes looked like they belonged to the baby Holmes twins Lissa and Luna. A look far too innocent, wide, and . . . *trollian* to belong to something so unearthly.

They were an Ögonen, and they were extending their long slender fingers toward me.

24

***

unsettled

I started to scream, but the attempt stopped in my throat. Or really, it had been stopped. I could almost feel the scream— ice-cold and frozen in place, a hard rock in my trachea, even though air passed through it as I breathed.

The Ögonen stood before me, holding their hand out with their fingers curled, making a clutching gesture in the air before my face.

I put my hand to my throat and let out a shaky breath, but I still couldn't make a sound. The Ögonen stared impassively at me, blinking once slowly.

They were entirely androgynous, with no mouth and two slits in the center of their oblong face for a nose. The light from my phone hit their chest, shining through their semitransparent ocher skin so I could see the subtle beating of their heart.

Let me go! I screamed, but the words never made it out.

My main focus was on the Ögonen stealing my voice, but in my peripheral vision I saw the spiders, crawling over the walls and ceiling, covering the books and floor as they swarmed around us.

The Ögonen moved their hand, pointing down the hall behind me.

And then I was running. I don't know if I had a choice or if my body was just moving, racing under the command of something else. When I came to a *T* intersection, I turned left without thinking or knowing why. My feet were following a path I couldn't see, and as long as they took me away from the spiders and the voice-stealing Ögonen, I was happy to let them.

One more sharp left, and there it was—a set of rickety wooden stairs. They were steep—almost like a ladder—and I ran up them without hesitation.

At the top was another set of cellar doors, and I charged into them, but they didn't give. I slammed my palm against the door and shouted for help—and finally, mercifully, my voice was free.

The door finally opened, and I ran out, practically tripping over the top steps, and I collapsed onto the stone floor.

"Ulla Tulin?" Elof Dómari asked. He stood over me, squinting at me as I brushed my hands all over my body, making sure that no spiders had hitched a ride. "Are you okay?

"Yeah, yeah." I stood up and ran my hands through my hair one more time. "I'm fine."

"You're bleeding, and you were screaming for help down in the catacombs. Forgive me if I don't entirely believe that you're fine."

"Sorry. I went down to get a book." I held it up to show him. "And there were all these spiders. Why didn't anyone tell me about the giant spider infestation in the catacombs?"

Elof pressed his lips into a thin smile, and he went over and locked the cellar doors. "That's because there weren't any spiders."

"No, there were, I swear." I pointed at the door. "I just saw them everywhere."

"No, you saw what the Ögonen wanted you to see." He started to walk away. "Come back to my office with me. I'll get you cleaned up and explain it all to you there."

He led me back to the old brass elevator at the end of the hall, and as Elof controlled the lever and sent us up to the third floor, I briefly explained to him my experience in the catacombs, and he didn't seem surprised by any of it.

We made it to his lab, and he unlocked the door—using a key from a ring of large brass keys. He instructed me to sit down on the squat stool next to one of the dwarf-height islands nearby. He flicked on the lights—not all of them, but enough so the classroom wasn't completely submerged in darkness anymore.

Elof gathered up a first-aid kit, then he sat on the stool across from me. "You know the Ögonen are the guardians of Merellä, using their intense psychokinesis to mask its appearance?"

"Yeah, I think I understand, basically." I understood the concept, but most sources were vague about anything pertaining specifically to the Ögonen.

Elof motioned for me to lower my head, so he could more

easily reach my wound and clean it. I leaned forward, and he gently dabbed the cut above my eyebrow and a scratch on my cheek with an alcohol swab.

"Sorry, this stings a bit," he said when I winced.

"It's okay."

"To do what the Ögonen do—essentially hiding an entire city with a bustling population in plain sight from humans—that takes a great deal of power. A cloaking spell of that size has them working at max capacity—so to speak—which is one of the reasons the citadel must be strict about admittance to the Mimirin and Merellä as a whole. Population control is a must.

"As powerful as the Ögonen are, they have their limits," he went on as he gently applied a butterfly bandage to my eyebrow gash. "Which is why you're able to see the city. Even half-TOMBs like Pan are able to see through the cloaking spell to the stone and flesh underneath.

"So." Elof had taken care of my largest scrapes, and he sat back on his stool. "To guard the areas from the likes of you, they have to use different tactics. And it so happens that it's far easier for the Ögonen to create visions than it is to hide something that is really there."

"You're saying that the Ögonen made me hallucinate spiders?" I asked. "To scare me away, like guard dogs?"

"Yes, exactly." He tilted his head. "Which means that you didn't have permission to be down in the catacombs."

I sighed. "No, I didn't. And I broke a bookcase, accidentally." I groaned. "I should go back down there to clean it."

"I'll send someone down," Elof said. "Unless you're granted permission from the Styrelse, it's best if you do not go back down again."

"I'm sorry. I didn't mean to make such a mess." I set the book down on the island and tapped the cover. "I thought this would help me figure some things out."

"The archives are not under my domain, so I will leave it to you to discuss with Calder how to proceed with that book," Elof said, and his gaze turned more severe. "And I do trust that you will tell him about what transpired today."

I nodded. "Yeah. Of course."

"Good." He relaxed again. "But there is something I discovered recently that I thought you might find interesting. It's about the Ögonen, actually."

"What do you mean?" I asked.

"How much do you know about chromosomes?"

I shook my head. "Not much."

"Humans have forty-six chromosomes, and like many other animals, ours come in pairs," he began. "In fact, most species work in similar ways with chromosomes in pairs or sets of three, from seedless watermelons all the way up to decaploids like certain types of strawberries, which have sets of ten.

"But they're usually consistent, with minor variations. Down syndrome in humans has a single triple bond, resulting in forty-seven chromosomes. And then there's the Ögonen. Every one I've tested has thirty-five chromosomes, compromised of seven pairs and seven trios."

"Why? What does that mean?" I asked.

"There is still much that we don't understand," Elof

admitted. "But we've recently been able to ascertain Eliana shares several sets of chromosomes with the Ögonen, and like them, she has a mixture of pairs and trios.

"But unlike them, she also has a few that match ours," he finished. "She seems to be connected to us both."

"What are the Ögonen? No one's ever given me a straight answer," I said.

"They're a type of troll, but beyond that, it's hard to categorize them," Elof explained as best as he could. "I suspect that we must have common ancestors from long ago, but the Ögonen lived in complete isolation. For eons, perhaps. At some point, around a thousand years ago, the Ögonen were no longer able to survive on their own. The Vittra eventually came to their aid, housing the Ögonen in exchange for their protection."

He paused, drumming his fingers on the island. "Or so the Vittra records say. It's hard to ever know how accurate our history books are. We've all lived so much in secret, deliberately hiding as many of our tracks as we can."

"And Eliana is related to them?" I asked. "What does that mean?"

"I don't know." He shook his head once. "I've tried talking to the Ögonen, but it's hard to communicate directly with them. They only speak in telekinetic images, which can be very tricky to decipher. I even had Mästare Amalie helping me to translate, and I don't know that I was ever properly able to convey the idea of Eliana or the questions I had about her." He sighed. "I suppose that's a really long way of saying that I don't know.

"But this is still good news," Elof reassured me. "This is

a connection we didn't have before, and everything we learn bringsus one step closer to understanding her and finding her."

"Good. Good." I stared down at the floor. "I'm glad one of us is making progress. I've been doing everything I can to find the First City."

He pointed to my book. "Is that why you took this?"

"Yeah. I was hoping this might give me something to go on."

"Have you tried talking to Calder about it?" Elof asked gently.

"I have," I admitted. "But I think he's getting annoyed with me."

Elof clucked his tongue in understanding. "There are other avenues outside of Calder. I would like it if you could come back when you're feeling better—and Dagny is around to do the procedure—so we can run another blood test."

"Oh, yeah, absolutely, I'd like that too," I said. Then, more hesitantly, I added, "I did have a . . . question. Could you compare my blood sample with a baby's to see if we're siblings?"

"You think you may have found a sibling?" Elof asked, surprised.

"No. I don't know." I frowned, thinking of Indu and all his dead children, and Bekk Vallin's rotund belly. Her baby's father was Indu Mattison, and I had begun to fear that Indu might be my father too. "There's this guy who claims he's Älvolk, but he's definitely some kind of . . . romantic, we'll say. I would feel better if I could rule him out."

"Understandable. I can compare samples to see if there's a familial match. Just send him my way, and I will do the draw."

"Thanks. I'll have to get back to you on that one."

He smiled. "I'll be here."

25

Adlrivellir

"Sweet Freya, mother of all," Dagny said once she saw me—a rushed prayer under her breath.

I'd been back at the apartment for about five minutes, but she hadn't looked up from her book. She was sprawled out on the lumpy couch, with a dog-eared copy of a Lois Duncan book in her hands and Jewel playing through her laptop speakers.

"What happened?" Dagny sat up and set her book aside. "Are you okay?"

"Yeah, Elof patched me up." I collapsed on the couch beside her, and then I ran through the events of the evening.

When I finished, she asked, "Do you want some lemon tea?"

"No. I seriously just want a hot bath and to go to bed."

"Coming face-to-face with an Ögonen can be unnerving," she said. "I've interacted with them a few times for work, and I don't know if I'll ever get comfortable with them just . . . pushing their thoughts in my head like that."

"Yeah, I can't say that I enjoyed it either." I shivered involuntarily at the thought of the spiders and the words frozen in my throat.

"So, do you think the book was worth it?"

"I don't know yet." I leaned over, moving slowly in a vain attempt not to exacerbate the aching pain all down my back, and I winced as I pulled the book out from where I had stowed it in my bag. "I haven't had a chance to read it yet."

Dagny took it from me and flipped through it. "Is this a fairy tale?" She rolled her eyes. "You've been listening to Hanna too much."

"No, it's not Hanna," I said, and she gave me a dubious look. "Okay, it's *mostly* not because of Hanna." I tapped the gilded sigil on the cover. "That's the Älvolk symbol. Finding more about them is a high priority right now."

"So that's why you picked this book? Because of the cover?" Dagny asked.

"I've seen it before," I said as she handed it back to me. "Have you heard of Jem-Kruk?"

She nodded. "Yeah, I remember reading stories about him when I was a kid. He was something like a Viking Robin Hood. A swashbuckler who saved damsels and slayed dragons."

"I don't remember there being dragons in Robin Hood," I said wryly.

"That's true. Maybe I used the wrong example, but you get the idea," she said. "It's been a long time since I read any of the stories, but I don't recall anything that relates to the Älvolk."

"I guess I'll find out." I got slowly to my feet. "I'm doing some reading in the tub."

While the tub filled up, Dagny insisted on lighting incense on a tray on the back of the toilet. "It sounds silly, I know, but you'll never have a more relaxing soak."

Fifteen minutes later, the bathroom was filled with hot steam and lavender smoke. I slid under the water—it was almost too hot, stinging my scrapes, and I knew when I got out my skin would look like a boiled tomato—somehow it was completely perfect and wonderful.

And then I dove into the tale of Jem-Kruk and his adventures in a far-off land. It was a single novel, but it was really a series of short stories detailing various escapades of Jem-Kruk and his friends.

It would be fair to say that the sun always felt the warmest after a storm. So it was after the Great Blue Thunder—which had unequivocally been the worst storm that either Jem-Kruk or Jo-Huk had ever witnessed, with thunder shaking all across Adlrivellir. Rain came down for three days and four nights, until the water filled the Valley, but it had finally come to an end.

On the very first morning that Jem-Kruk awoke to a silent world and a cloudless sky the color of fresh grapefruit, he knew what he had to do. First, he woke his brother, pulling him half asleep from their tree house. Jo-Huk was still quite sleepy, squinting his eyes against the bright light of the three suns Kyr, Nuk, and Veli. He was about to grouse about it, like a cranky bear disturbed too early in spring, and then he finally saw that it wasn't too early.

"The storm has passed," said Jo-Huk, in awe now

that he finally beheld the Valley. "But I worry it will come again."

"You worry too much, my brother." Jem-Kruk slapped him merrily on the back.

"It is as the *häxdoktor* said," Jo-Huk said, reminding him of the warning they had heard. "The suns set in the green sky when the good morning becomes the violent night. Before the storm, the sky was green, this morning it is good."

"If it is a violent night, then we must greet the day with open arms." Jem-Kruk spread his arms wide. "But now we must dry out!"

"Everything in our sight is soaked through. How shall we dry?"

"There." Jem-Kruk pointed to the mountain across the flooded Valley, before the caves where the *etanadrak* slumbered.

"It's too far, and the path is much too dangerous!" exclaimed Jo-Huk.

Jem-Kruk laughed, for he knew that was what Jo-Huk would say. Many called Jo-Huk the wiser of the two, but Jem-Kruk knew that wasn't true. He'd come to learn that what most called "wisdom" was nothing more than "fear" in fancy dress.

"The rains have gone, the air is sweet, today is the day we go to meet the suns!" Jem-Kruk threw his head back so that he was yelling at the sky in a gleeful threat.

Jem-Kruk ran on ahead, knowing that Jo-Huk would give chase, and he did. But Jem-Kruk knew that if Jo-Huk caught him, he would have to go back. Those were the rules they agreed to, but all that ever truly meant was that Jem-Kruk would never let himself be caught.

As they raced through the woods, of course, they did not yet know of the trouble that lay ahead of them. Before they reached the mountaintops, they'd first have to pass the fairy lagoon.

"What?" I whispered incredulously in the silent, steamy bathroom. "Are there gonna be fairies and mermaids too?"

It was one thing that information about Áibmoráigi was hidden away in old books, but it was an entirely different thing to take advice and directions from a silly children's book full of make-believe.

Or maybe I was too tired and my head hurt too much. But either way, I wasn't in the mood for this anymore, and I headed to bed.

routine

After twenty minutes of fighting with the internet, I finally enlisted Dagny's help. She was getting ready for work, standing in front of the bathroom mirror straightening her long black hair, and when she'd finished, she pulled it back into a slick high ponytail.

"Why are you so technologically illiterate?" Dagny asked. She'd been letting me use her laptop because she claimed it was easier to connect to the internet, and she took it from me to hook it up to the landline.

I shrugged. "I didn't grow up around a lot of electronics."

"That doesn't stop Hanna from being savvy." Dagny tapped a few keys, then pushed the computer across the bistro table to me. "She's great at troubleshooting, and you two grew up together."

"Her family has been nothing but awesome to me, but I didn't come into their house until I was fourteen. And then a lot of my time was spent helping take care of Hanna and her siblings. Finn insisted I get an education, but he didn't exactly value technology, so it didn't really make it into my curriculum."

"I don't know why trolls have to be so averse to electronics." Dagny sighed as she got her stuff together—packing up leftovers for lunch and getting her tumbler of gingered lemon tea. "So many elders and royals lose their damn minds over every shiny bauble or sparkly rock, but their eyes gloss over with disinterest if you hand them a tablet or even a decent digital camera."

"You can't fight the future," I said under my breath and opened my email to reply to Hanna's dozens of emails.

I'd read some of them before, and I'd even replied to the oldest ones, but it had been impossible for me to keep up, especially given the spotty service I had here in Merellä.

Dagny had been correct that Hanna's emails were in many ways a list of demands, or, more accurately, complaints and wants. Like a diary entry, but with my name at the heading.

That was until the most recent message that came in last night, which had a much different tone.

I haven't heard from you, but Dagny told me you're safe. She also told me that you're researching the same things I am. I didn't tell you at first because I thought you'd think it was silly, but now I know you're thinking the same way I am.

Eliana told me that she came from a land of three suns, and these stories are from there. These two brothers and their friend Senka do lots of things that you'd roll your eyes at. One time they rescue Senka from monstrous *etanadrak* and another time Jem-Kruk and Senka fight these man-eating mermaids that kidnapped Jo-Huk.

Okay, they seriously do have all these fun and crazy misadventures, and I could go on forever, but that's not what this is about.

The point is that they eventually travel to the "land of blue sky." It's different than their world with their pink sky, and it only has one sun. They say the Blárheim has no *etanadraks,* and that it is a world of ice, covered in white.

So, to me, this all sounds like the Arctic in Scandinavia. I don't know how they got here or where they came from, but it sounds like they somehow ended up here.

And get this—there's a whole chapter where Jo-Huk argues with his brother about going to Blárheim. Jem-Kruk's been before but Jo-Huk is worried because there are stories that say Blárheim is so far away that you can't remember who you were when you got there.

Does that sound like anyone we know???

"In five minutes I'm heading to work, and that laptop is coming with me," Dagny said, interrupting my reading. "You should probably get going as well."

"Shit, I gotta get ready," I said as I checked the clock.

Last night, after my long soak in the tub, I hadn't slept so well. I'd had all sorts of vivid, intense nightmares about spiders crawling across a frozen ocean, under a sky of dark melon-pink. So I'd gotten up early and read more of the book before deciding that I ought to check in with Hanna.

That was how the morning had gotten away from me, and I was scrambling to get dressed and throwing on makeup so I wouldn't be late for work in the archives. I had a Band-Aid over my eye, but I did my best to mask my injuries as much as I could.

I had to talk to Calder about what had happened in the catacombs, and I doubted that he would respond well, so I didn't want to add fuel to the fire by showing up late for work.

I ran all the way down to the archives and arrived with enough time that I could pause and catch my breath outside the door. Calder had his radio on, playing his angry classical orchestras.

He was immersed in his work, his head bowed over the documents he translated at the curved desk. I walked slowly toward him, preparing to launch into my explanation, but he silenced me before I had started.

"Elof told me that he sent you into the catacombs to retrieve something for him." Calder hadn't looked up at me yet. I didn't know how to answer or what to say, and he finally lifted his weary eyes to make sure I'd heard him. "It is an understandable mistake. But you are not to get any book or go anywhere in the archives unless I—and I alone—tell you to."

I gulped. "Sorry. I won't let it happen again."

"No, you won't." He looked back down at his work. "This time you were injured. Next time it would be worse."

"Right. Of course. Sorry." I grimaced at my rambling.

"The Styrelse returned another cart of books that need to be put away," he replied without further acknowledging my apologies.

"I'll get right on it." I scurried around the desk to drop off my bag, then went to work straight away.

Calder spoke very little the rest of the morning, but that was normal for him, so it was impossible to use that as an accurate gauge of his emotions. I figured it was better that way anyhow, so I kept my head down and did what I needed to do.

By lunch I was excited for a reprieve. As soon as Calder said I could go, I dashed upstairs and to the Inhemsk Project main office. I went in to ask if Pan was around, and Sylvi replied with a quick, curt, "He's not here at the moment."

I'd been hoping to have lunch with him, but since I wanted to be back promptly from lunch, I headed out to the street market on Wapiti Way. The summer sun felt wonderful on my skin after the chill of the archives.

At night, Wapiti Way was a normal wide street that ran through the center of the city. During the day it was a colorful bazaar. It had basic farmers' market fare of fresh fruits, vegetables, and prepared foods, but it also had flea-market goods, like homemade wind chimes, organic diapers, and even some black-market human goods, like copied DVDs and knock-off Rolexes.

Mostly, though, it was a loud cluster of troll life. Trolls haggled over goods, street performers played instruments and danced with floral scarfs, and a pair of wandering ducks quacked at a bleating goat that was tied up and for sale.

I pulled my hair up into a loose bun as I perused my lunch options. I picked up a peach to see if it was ripe.

"I see you've moved on to using the cloudberry method with other fruits," said a familiar voice from behind me, and I whirled around to see Mr. Tall and Handsome himself, smiling at me.

27

fairy tales

It had been less than two weeks since I had last seen him, at the Midsommar celebration when he'd given me a cryptic goodbye before absconding with Eliana into the night.

He looked just as good as I remembered, not that I should be surprised, and not that it even mattered. He was tall and slender, so he cut a slight profile, but his dark bedroom eyes made him captivating. That and the ease with which he carried himself, so that each movement felt casually impressive, like watching a prima ballerina doing mundane tasks.

His wavy hair hung loose above his shoulders, thick and untamed. His cavalier smile faltered, and that's when I realized how long I had been standing there, holding a peach and staring at him.

"Who are you?" I asked, wanting to hear him say his name himself.

"Jem-Kruk."

I shook my head, confused, disbelieving. "From the fairy tales?"

"What?" His face twisted up in confusion.

"What are you doing here?" I asked, then I looked around, scanning the market for anyone else. "Is Eliana here?"

"No, she's with her sister." He paused a moment before adding, "She's safe."

"Can I see her?" I turned to him. "Where is she? What's wrong with her? Why are you here?"

"You have a lot of questions, and that is entirely understandable in your position," Jem-Kruk said. "Why don't we go somewhere and talk?"

"Why?" I stepped back from him. "How do I know it's safe to go with you?"

He held up his hands, his palms out toward me. Several brassy, jeweled rings adorned his fingers, and a thick scar ran across the beige skin of his right palm.

"We'll go someplace out in the open," Jem said. "I know of a quiet place nearby, and I'll answer as many questions as I can."

"Okay," I relented.

I tightly gripped the strap of my hobo bag and I followed him down Wapiti Way, and we headed southeast. When we passed the woolly elk barn, I realized he was leading me on the same path the elk took when they were herded through the city to and from their various pastures.

That was where Jem-Kruk was taking me, beyond the cramped, provincial city center to the outskirts. We were still within the walls, but there was more room to breathe. A small orchard grew alongside the wooden fence that surrounded the pasture, and the Forsa River cut through the lush grass. The trees were all Sommar plums, and their big pink blossoms were in full bloom.

The giant woollies were lazily grazing, some of them lying in the shade of a tall oak tree, younger calves frolicking around them. Jem leaned against the fence, and I made sure there was distance between us when I leaned on the fence.

"You really don't trust me?" he asked, looking at the space I had created.

"I don't know you," I said evenly. "And I don't know if you're good to my friend or not. All I know is that you're here and she isn't."

He exhaled and nodded. "Fair enough."

"I want to talk to Eliana. I want to hear from her that she's okay."

"Where she's at right now . . ." He frowned and stared at the elk. "It's not possible right now."

"Why not?"

"She's too sick," he insisted. "Not now."

"Why are you here?" I asked.

"I heard that you were worried."

"How could you possibly know that? And why would you even care?"

"Two questions with one answer—we have a friend in common."

"You mean someone other than Eliana?" I asked. "Who?"

"I'll tell you, but I fear you won't like my answer," he said with a weary laugh.

"But these aren't hard questions," I argued. "The name of our mutual friend? Where Eliana is? What you're doing here and who you are?"

As I'd been talking, my voice had gotten louder, and the elk stopped grazing to look at us. A breeze came up, causing a few Sommar plum blossoms to fall around us, scenting the air sweetly.

"Illaria told me that you were concerned, but who told her that, I honestly have no idea," Jem-Kruk said.

"You're right. I don't like the answer," I grumbled.

"I told you my name, and why I'm here." He squinted into the bright afternoon sunlight, his long lashes hiding his eyes. "It's hard to tell a story backwards, is all."

"Then tell it from the beginning," I said simply.

"Eliana and Illaria's parents are old family friends, and I've known the twins since they were born," he began. "Both girls were high-strung, as you may have discerned, but they were fine and happy. Or at least it seemed that way. Until their mother fell ill and passed away.

"Eliana took it the hardest," he went on. "We live far away in a very isolated kingdom. Some have called us extraordinarily private, and that kind of environment led to Eliana and Illaria becoming quite sheltered.

"I can't tell you what's wrong with Eliana because I unfortunately don't know," he admitted with a heavy sigh. "There is an erratic paranoia about her, and she ran off. Illaria, our friend Sumi, and I went looking for her, and we eventually found her here."

"How did you know to look for her here?" I asked.

He seemed to hesitate before answering. "That's more complicated, but the simplest explanation I can give is that Sumi is very skilled at finding what she's looking for, and Eliana had said some things that led us to believe she'd head to this area."

"I met Sumi," I said, thinking back to the trio of brief interactions I'd had with her. The very first time, she'd helped me find Eliana, but she'd deliberately chosen to stay back. "She had a chance to grab Eliana, but she let her go with me. Why?"

"It's as you said—Sumi would've needed to grab her." He gestured in the air. "We didn't want to kidnap her or make it any more traumatic. Sumi was trying to give her space and only check on her, but Eliana got scared and called her a dragon before taking off. Sumi thought it'd be best to let her go with friends she felt safe with, and we could come up with a better plan.

"The cloaking that happens here messes with Sumi's abilities, and she struggled to find Eliana again, despite the close proximity," he elaborated. "We figured that Eliana wouldn't want to miss the Midsommar, and we were hoping for a more . . . happy reunion."

"Why can't I see her?" I asked again.

"She's with her family, and visitors aren't allowed," he explained. "It's not up to me, so there isn't a point in you begging or bartering."

I chewed the inside of my cheek and considered his explanation. The pieces seemed to fit, but the whole thing would be a lot easier to swallow if there were someone else to back up his story, especially someone like Eliana.

The split-rail fence was dry and rough under my skin, and I twisted my hand around it.

"I think I would feel more at ease if I understood what you're doing here now," I said finally.

"You were Eliana's friend, and you cared for her when she needed it," he said. "Truth be told, she doesn't remember you now. She hopefully will again someday, but not today. But I know that she wouldn't want you to worry."

"That's really why you came back?" I asked, and he nodded. "Where do you come from?"

He gave me a sly smile, his dark eyes sparkling in the warm sun. "All I can tell you is that it is far, far away."

"Why did you tell me to come find you?" I asked, remembering the note I had found in my things after Eliana had gone.

If you ever want to say hello—to me or to Eliana—
come find us.
X Jem-Kruk

"That was you who left the note?" I asked. I'd believed that he had, but I wanted confirmation, and I got it when he winced and ran his hand through his tangles of hair. "Why would you leave that note if you knew I'd never be allowed into your kingdom?"

His eyes were downcast, so his thick lashes hovered above his rosy, high cheekbones. "I made a dumb choice on the fly, but Illaria immediately told me how ridiculous I was being. I'm sorry about that."

"What is your kingdom called?" I asked.

"I grew up in a place called Adlrivellir. Lots of mountains, cool summers, and long winters. It's different from here, to be sure, but it's not as dissimilar as you may think."

"Are you a troll?" I asked. "Like me?"

"We call ourselves something else, but I believe we are the same."

"What are you called?"

"We are *álfar*," he said.

"But what about the books?" I narrowed my eyes at him. "How come you're the star of children's books?"

He shook his head. "I haven't the faintest idea what you're talking about."

"Is Jem-Kruk a popular name where you come from?" I asked.

He shrugged. "I don't know about popular, but I am certainly not the only Jem."

"Maybe whoever wrote the book is from your hometown," I realized.

"What?"

I shook my head. "Never mind."

"Are you finished with all your questions?"

"Hardly," I said, and I laughed. "But I suppose I can give it a rest for now. Are you going to stay in Merellä for a while?"

"A few days."

"Okay. But there is one more thing I want to know. When you first talked to me at the market, that was to find out if Eliana was safe?"

"No, I didn't realize you knew her then."

I looked at him more closely, my brow furrowed in confusion. "Why did you talk to me, then?"

He laughed. "Because I thought you looked like somebody I'd want to know better. So I got to know you better, and it turns out I was right."

28

Light-Headed

We were sitting under the Sommar plum tree, the grass softly tickling my calves, which were bare below my Bermuda shorts. Out in the pasture, a pair of woollies had some disagreement. They let out annoyed bellows before smashing their antlers together.

It was as if the *crack* of their antlers woke me from a trance, and I blinked into the waning afternoon sun. I had been talking with Jem—mostly abstract, nonpersonal things, about the weather, the elk, the fruit, and then eventually I was divulging everything, every thought in my head about my life and myself.

Before I knew it, I was telling him the story of my entire life. I left out anything embarrassing and details I didn't want to share. It wasn't a compulsion, exactly, but I couldn't seem to stop myself from telling Jem-Kruk about growing up a lonely child in a frozen town, and the overwhelming loving chaos of the Holmes household, and all the worry and wonder I had about my birth family, where I came from, and who I was.

"You seem like you're someone who knows precisely who you are," Jem-Kruk had been saying, just before the woolly elk had begun their fight.

"What time is it?" I asked, shaking my head to clear it.

"What?"

"How long have we been out here?" I rummaged through my bag, searching for my cell phone, which served mostly as a fancy watch within the Merellä city limits.

"Are you okay?" He reached out to put his hand on mine—soft, warm, heavy, like, almost strangely heavy, like he somehow carried extra mass in his bones.

And the way he was looking at me—it was lust or longing or . . . I don't know what it was, honestly, but he was handsome and dreamy, almost like he wasn't even here at all. Even though I could I feel the weight of his hand, so heavy on mine.

He was *real*, but the light hitting his sharp androgynous features gave him an ethereal perfection. The high cheekbones and razor-sharp jawline, and just the lightest dusting of freckles smattered across his tawny skin. He was like a painting, a video game character, something so very close to real life but somehow not quite.

I finally found my phone in my bag, and I pulled my gaze away to see the block numbers alarmingly declaring it after four in the afternoon.

"Oh, shit! I'm supposed to be at work!" I stood up. "I *am* working! I'm so . . . not even late anymore. I've straight-up missed work." I groaned and rubbed my forehead. "Oh, no. I've totally messed up. I don't know how I lost track of time like that."

"Are you okay?" Jem-Kruk had stood up, and he reached out to steady me, but I recoiled.

"I'm . . . it's fine," I said uncertainly. "I have to go."

And then I was walking away, not quite jogging, but traveling fast, and I didn't look back. My mind raced as I tried to figure out what to tell Calder, what could possibly excuse my absence.

I'd been gone for so long that the only acceptable excuse would be that I had abruptly fallen ill, so ill that I was initially too incapacitated to even phone the archives. That would be more convincing if he didn't see me, looking slightly frazzled and flushed but clearly not so sick I couldn't give Calder word about it.

I made a beeline for my apartment, keeping my head down so I wouldn't be spotted, and went over what I would say to Calder, getting it right inside my head.

"Ulla!" Pan shouted, and I looked up to see him sitting on the landing outside my apartment door. He stood and came down the steps toward me. "Are you okay? What happened?"

"I just . . ." I trailed off, because it all sounded too impossible to explain. "What are you doing here? Is everything okay?"

"I came back to the office this afternoon, and Sylvi told me you were looking for me, so I went to the archives, and Calder said you disappeared after lunch. I couldn't get ahold of you, and I was worried that something bad had happened."

His eyes narrowed, his gaze lingering on the butterfly bandage and the scratch on my cheek. "Did that just happen?"

"What?" I asked, and he reached out, his fingertips brushing across the tender skin around my wounds. "No, that was yesterday, from an incident with some bookshelves."

"What does that mean?" His jaw tensed. "Ulla, is somebody hurting you?"

I shook my head. "No, it's not that. It's not like that at all." I started toward the steps. "Come on up. I'll explain everything."

Up in the apartment, we stood in the kitchen, eating pears and drinking sun tea. Neither of us had gotten much to eat that day, and without Hanna living here the endless supply of tasty leftovers had ended, so the pears were a fast snack.

As we ate, I told him everything I knew about Jem-Kruk, and all that he had told me. I may have significantly downplayed how attractive Jem was and the effect that he sometimes had on me (as in—I didn't mention it at all), but otherwise I laid it out honestly.

Pan listened quietly, only occasionally asking questions, but when I finally came to the end of everything I had say, he was silent. He finished the last few bites of his fruit, then wiped his mouth with the back of his hand.

"I'll have to be honest with you, Ulla." He looked at me with pursed lips. "This all sounds incredibly sketchy."

"But it's in line with what we know about Eliana and the Älvolk," I pointed out.

He rested his hands on the counter beside him and leaned back. "Is it possible? With our world, we can't rule out much, that's true. But the difference between possible and probable

is *vast,* and the likelihood that he's being one hundred percent truthful with you is a lot lower than the likelihood that
he's dangerous."

"I get what you're saying," I admitted quietly.

"But you believe him anyway." His voice was low, un-
surprised.

"I'm not blindly trusting any of it," I argued. "But I know
he's got a connection to Eliana, and he's the only one I've got
so far. Everything else I'm going on, it's chasing rumors. But
he *knows* her."

"If you're going to keep talking to him—and I am assuming that you will—then you need to go about this the right
way." He rubbed the back of his neck. "So I'll talk to Sylvi,
and see if I can find out anything about him. Where is he
staying?"

"I don't know, actually. He said he'd be around for a
while."

"That'll give me another thing to talk about with Sylvi,"
he said, and I let out a dry laugh. "There's one thing that's
still bothering me." Pan tilted his head. "Why does he share
his name with a fairy-tale Viking? It's a strange name."

"As are Panuk and Ulla, so I don't think we're in a place
to talk about unusual names, at least not in this neighborhood," I said, and he laughed. "His is a different kingdom, so
the culture is going to have differences. But the other names
in the book—Jo-Huk, Senka, Iry-Ka—sound similar to me.
I don't think it really means anything."

"Yeah, maybe," he allowed, but he stared off like he
wasn't completely convinced.

29

korva

Dagny insisted on walking with me to the office in the morning. She said it was because she wanted to make sure I got there safely, as if Jem-Kruk or one of his friends would jump out of the shadows and kidnap me (as if he couldn't have done that already if that's what he wanted to do), a theory encouraged by Pan when he stayed for supper the previous evening. The two of them had debated and speculated about what Jem-Kruk's true motivations might be, while I made supper.

Some of their ideas were very outlandish—foreign spies or fictional characters come to life or alien overlords. But they had dismissed these notions almost as soon as they'd suggested them.

None of that really mattered, though, because that wasn't why Dagny was walking with me now, at least not the real deep-down reason. She felt responsible for delivering me, since she'd been the one to go to the trouble of setting up the meeting with a Mästare to discuss Jem-Kruk.

"I'll make the call," Dagny had said abruptly while she was talking with Pan, leaving Pan to shoot me a few confused looks. They'd been sitting at the bistro table, while I stood over the kitchen sink, cutting carrots.

"That'd be weird, wouldn't it? For you to call my boss when I could easily do it?" Pan had asked.

"No, not Sylvi. No offense, Pan, but this sounds out of the scope of Inhemsk," she had said.

He'd frowned. "It wouldn't have occurred to me to be offended before you mentioned it."

"Sorry." She had shrugged. "I just think it would be better for Ulla if this was brought to the attention of someone with more expertise in interacting with remote, private kingdoms."

Dagny then got up and went over to the phone, but she looked to me before dialing. "Should I call Elof and see what he can do?"

"Yeah, if you think it'll be the most helpful," I'd said.

And then she had been the one to play phone tag, and eventually resorted to using a courier to get the messages promptly back and forth to the Mästare.

While Dagny had been carefully writing a note in her delicate script, she told me, "So many of the faculty around here actively loath technology. I don't usually listen to gossip, but I've heard credible rumors that none of the members of the Styrelse will even *use* a cell phone."

Finally, she'd gotten confirmation that I'd be meeting with the Mästare on the fourth floor, and she wasn't invited.

So now she was ushering me to the meeting, to be sure we were early enough that we could leisurely walk down

the hall to Mästare Amalie's chambers. We passed the painting by Monet before the door to Eliana's room—or at least,
it would've been hers if she'd been around long enough to
sleep in it more than one night.

I'd been in Mästare Amalie's room once before, and we'd
been let in by her assistant. This time, a guard was standing
in front of her door, dressed in the same crimson uniform as
the security at the Mimirin entrance.

Dagny saw the guard and let out a resigned sigh. "Good
luck with your meeting, Ulla," she said and walked away
without even trying to get in.

"Ulla Tulin?" The guard put one finger on his temple
and narrowed his dark eyes at me, then he nodded once and
stepped to the side. "They're expecting you."

I thanked him, then opened the door and stepped into
the color explosion that was the Mästare's chambers. Everything about her space was bold, bright, and stylishly decadent. Walls of rich crimson with curtains of indigo, rugs of
gold and teal.

Amalie was sitting on her velvet sofa, drinking tea that
perfumed the air with the scent of blackberries. But she
wasn't alone.

A man stood at the window, staring out at the city. His
back was to me, and the way his hands were clasped behind
him only accentuated his broad shoulders. He was tall, over
six feet, and his head was shaved smooth.

"Ulla, how nice to see you!" Amalie said cheerfully, like
we were old friends instead of barely acquaintances.

She was a tiny woman, practically drowning in her rich
violet robe, and her silvering dark hair was cropped into a

pixie cut. With all her heavy copper jewelry and ruby rhine-stones, she looked like she was more accessory than woman.

"Mästare." I started to bow then managed to stop myself before going fully into it, but my cheeks flushed with embar-rassment, and I avoided eye contact with her.

The man turned around and immediately flashed a toothy grin. The crinkles around his dark eyes suggested age and wisdom, but the rest of his face was rather statuesque and eerily smooth. He seemed to be somewhere between twenty years old and eternal.

"Hello, Ulla, I'm Ragnall Jerrick, the Korva of the Mim-irin." He stepped forward—lunged almost, with a single long stride—and he extended his meaty hand toward me.

"Hello, it's, um, nice to meet you," I stammered and managed a nervous smile.

Korva was the top position in the Mimirin, maybe even in the entire city. It was sort of an amalgam of a dean, CEO, and mayor. Someone had once told me about the internal speculation about who really held the power—the Korva, the Information Styrelse, or the Mästares.

Regardless, Ragnall Jerrick was a powerful figure, and he looked it. His suit was an impeccably tailored long black satin with fitted tunic lined with a Saxon knot trim, and like the Mästare, he had a preference for rings.

"Shall we sit?" He gestured to the sitting area.

"Tea?" Amalie asked, and she began pouring a cup before I could respond.

I sat down, carefully smoothing my skirt.

"You look nervous," Amalie commented, then held the cup toward me. "Here, have some tea."

I took it from her, letting it warm my hands.

"I hope you don't mind that the Korva is joining us," she said.

"No, not at all." I smiled thinly.

"I don't usually intrude on matters like this, but Amalie mentioned your situation, and it sounded so interesting, I had to know more." He leaned back, crossing one leg over the other. "I'm always curious about the visitors to our shining city on the sea."

"You're curious about what I know?" I asked, surprised. "I don't really know much. That's why I'm here."

"Ragnall was speaking more about your friendship with the unwell girl Eliana," Amalie clarified. "We do have records of Jem-Kruk, but we are limited on what we can tell you."

"Records?" I asked. "What do you mean? Criminal records?"

"No, nothing like that." Amalie laughed and waved her hand. "Jem-Kruk is listed as a visiting docent, and he's staying at the staff housing in exchange for his input on projects in history and anthropology."

"You know him? You know where he's from?" I asked.

The Mästare looked subtly to Ragnall, then she replied carefully, "The information we have about his village is that it is a very isolated, relatively primitive community in the Arctic."

"So what he said is true," I said, more to myself than to them.

"We don't know what he's told you, obviously, and we are able to confirm very little of what he says," Ragnall elaborated cautiously.

I sipped my tea, buying myself time as I processed what they'd told me.

"You know where Eliana is from," I realized in dismay. "And you knew about her unusual blood?"

"We didn't realize she was connected with Jem-Kruk, not while she was here." Amalie looked to Ragnall again, and he nodded in response. "We have not performed any . . . biological examinations on any of the members of Jem-Kruk's community, not before Eliana, so we had nothing to compare her samples to."

"I can understand that . . ." I trailed off, and I willed myself to meet Amalie's intense, bright gaze. "When you were here with Eliana, why didn't you tell me you knew someone like her?"

"Because I didn't know that I had," she replied. "I hadn't spent much time with her, and she remembered so little about herself it was impossible to know who she really was."

"Knowing what you know now, who do you think Eliana really is?" I asked her directly.

She hesitated—her eyes flitting once more over to Ragnall, who kept his face locked in a gleaming toothpaste-ad smile.

"I suspect that she is an *álfar*," Amalie answered finally.

"How come I don't know more about the *álfar*?" I asked. "I hear about the five tribes all the time. Why don't we talk about them the same way?"

"That's a great question," Ragnall agreed jovially.

"Thanks," I muttered.

"The *álfar* didn't make contact with any of the tribes until around the beginning of the 1900s," Amalie explained.

"And in the early years, they were very, very private, even more than they are now."

"Over the years, everyone here at the Mimirin has worked hard to keep communication open between us," Ragnall said. "It has been a long, arduous journey at times, but we have made real progress in getting to know such a reclusive tribe."

Then, as I looked at them—Ragnall with his painfully wide, salesman smile, and Amalie with her more restrained, timid smile, though their eyes shared an eager intensity—it finally dawned on me what was going on here.

"You still didn't know much about them," I said and leaned back in my chair. "You didn't invite me here to tell me about the *álfar*—you were hoping *I* could tell *you* about them."

Amalie pursed her lips, but she didn't disagree. "They are secretive, but you seem to have earned their trust."

I laughed despite myself. "I wouldn't say Eliana and Jem have been forthcoming with me."

"You have to understand our situation." Amalie had been holding her cup of tea and saucer, but she leaned forward to set them back on the tray. "We have been trying for so long to unite the tribes, to work together so we can truly understand our shared histories and our place in the world.

"You could be an ambassador for us, helping to strengthen a friendship we've been trying to build for decades," she said emphatically.

"Not a real ambassador, of course," Ragnall added quickly. "Not a staffed position, but more of a symbolic role, helping all of trollkind."

"Leading an expedition for our heritage," Amalie added.

"What do you want me to do?" I asked.

"Nothing that you're not already doing," Amalie said. "Just talk to Jem, be friendly, get to know him. Later, we'll get together, the way we are now, and we'll have a chat about things. We may have a few questions, but nothing invasive, of course."

"Of course," I said, because what choice did I have? Amalie and Ragnall literally had the power to kick me out of Merellä, maybe even the entire kingdom, if they wanted to. And so they called me an ambassador, when what they really meant was spy.

30

BIOLOGY

"So, they gave you his address and sent you on your way?" Dagny asked, but I couldn't tell if her incredulity was directed at me or at the Mästare and the Korva.

"Basically." I leaned against the lab countertops beside her, idly toying with the folded note written on the Mästare's letterhead.

As soon as I left Amalie's chambers and the bizarrely intense meeting, I headed straight to the labs. Elof was finishing up a class, but as soon as it ended, I slid in the past the departing students.

Dagny cleaned up lab equipment in the sink, while Elof sat at his desk, dealing with his lesson planner. Since it was only the two of them, I felt comfortable telling them both all about the Mästare and the Korva's strange proposal.

"Right before I left, Amalie told me that Calder wasn't expecting me back until after lunch, and then she gave me his address," I said and held up the paper.

"Jem-Kruk's address?" She took the paper from me

without asking and hurriedly read it. "This is in the staff housing at the Mimirin. He lives here?"

"Is he my neighbor?" Elof got up from his desk and came over to us.

"Are you going to go see him?" Dagny asked, and she held the note out so that Elof could read it.

He scoffed. "That's one floor above me. He's practically been on top of me." Then he looked up at me. "How long has he been here? Why haven't I heard about this?"

"I don't think he's been here that much," I said. "A couple weeks near the beginning of June, and then he came back recently, according to Amalie. She also said he's been keeping a low profile."

"That makes sense, I suppose," Elof said, but he still sounded slightly offended about being kept out of the loop.

"Did you know about the *álfar*?" I asked.

"Not especially. They treat their biology like trade secrets, so they don't like talking to me."

"When I was growing up, there were all these stacks of old *National Geographic* magazines around the house," I said.

Mr. Tulin would've been a hoarder if his wife had let him, but magazines were something he refused to give up. It was mostly the ones with the best pictures—art, architecture, science, and nature. They were tucked away in nooks, stacked on end tables, left sitting in boxes under the window until they were sun-faded and warped.

"There was this one issue that had a big feature on 'lost tribes' and 'uncontacted peoples,'" I remembered. "All over the world, there are these little pockets of humans totally detached from the greater civilization. Some of the tribes have essentially never had contact outside of their villages, so they're even more cut off than we are.

"In Iskyla, that seemed impossible to imagine, so I was obsessed with these stories," I went on. "There are literally hundreds of these small communities. Tiny, intense clusters with specific traditions, beliefs, and languages.

"Much of their way of life seemed unusual or primitive, or at least very different than what I'd grown up around," I said. "And the more I think about the *álfar*, the more I notice the similarities to these lost tribes. Eliana was very odd, but she spoke our language, understood how to use electricity, and got along fine around the city, relatively speaking. Like she'd spent time with a lost world *and* in our human world."

I looked over to see Elof eyeing me up with an arched eyebrow. "Sorry. I didn't mean to launch into a monologue. I was just thinking aloud."

"All right, fine, I cave," Elof announced abruptly. "I'll tell you what I know."

Both Dagny and I looked at him, and she asked, "What are you talking about?"

"Dagny, I thought you knew me well enough by now." He *tsked* at her but he was smiling. "There's a super-secret hidden tribe of magical beings that defy cultural and bio-logical norms, and you think I didn't immediately want to know everything about them?"

She smiled. "How silly of me."

"What do you know?" I walked over to his desk.

"Not much more than you, unfortunately," he admitted wearily. "I've never had the pleasure of meeting your new *álfar* friends—other than Eliana—but I did meet a young man who claimed to be from Adlrivellir, and the Styrelse believed him.

"The main thing that got me *really* curious was his perfect English," Elof explained. "Trolls have adopted English as their primary language for centuries, but before that it was mostly old Norse and Germanic. Even now, many communities speak and incorporate the ancestral Scandinavian mixed with nearby human languages, like Inuit, French, Spanish, and German.

"It turns out that the *álfar* speak five languages." He held up his hand to demonstrate. "Two that we—both trolls and humans—have no record of at all; an old variation of Norse; English; and a psychic one that we apparently can't handle."

"What does that even mean?" I asked.

He shook his head. "I haven't the faintest, honestly. He became deliberately obtuse every time I pressed him on it. But no matter, because this particular story is about how come their English became so similar to ours."

"How did that come to be?" Dagny asked.

"When they met us, initially they were very excited," Elof explained. "This was a thousand years ago, and while the troll kingdom always lagged a bit behind humans, the *álfar* were trapped way back in the Dark Ages."

"I always thought our delays in technology and industry had to do with our reliance on our abilities," Dagny said. "Humans had to create advancements for themselves. Necessity is the mother of invention."

"Funny you should mention that, because that seems to track for the *álfar* as well," Elof said. "They have been reliant on their abilities, and it seems to be with good reason, though I have yet to see the full display of their particular talents.

"Regardless, the *álfar* were originally excited to join our worlds, or at least that's what was written in the scant records of the time," Elof said. "There were a few things—a couple letters, some drawings, a limerick—that establish that the trolls and *álfar* were mutually happy about the union, if slightly but justifiably trepidatious.

"And things fell apart very quickly," he went on. "The *álfar* living in the troll kingdom were almost entirely wiped out by the Grændöden."

"The Green Death?" I translated. "Didn't that wipe out a lot of trolls too?"

"It did, but that was hundreds of years later, in the thirteenth century," Elof clarified. "Are you familiar with it?"

"Some," I admitted. I'd heard of it because it had decimated the troll populations in Scandinavia, so there were hardly any of our kind still living in our homeland.

"*Candida viridi,*" Elof said. "It's a fungal infection that gets in the blood, causes candidiasis, and after a few painful days, their skin gets a greenish hue, and they pass away. We eventually figured out how to handle it, but the first time we encountered it, when we were breaking bread with the *álfar,* it was a massacre. There are few accounts from that time, but the first recorded mention of the Grændöden describes leaving man, woman, and child dead in their beds."

I snapped my fingers. "That's what happens with a lot of these lost tribes! They're not used to our germs or our environment, so they don't have the basic immunities that we take for granted."

"Not even we have an immunity for that, but it appears to have hit them worse," he said grimly. "Nearly going extinct had a sobering effect on the *álfar*, and they retreated into themselves. But they have never given up hope that we will reunite someday, or at least that's the conclusion Mästare Amalie has drawn, since they continue to speak our language."

"You disagree with that?" I asked.

Elof gave a disingenuous shrug. "Perhaps. It's possible. Maybe even likely."

"But?" I pressed.

He leaned forward and tented his fingers together. "When the *álfar* first met the trolls, they weren't just exploring their neighborhood. One of the reasons the disease was so devastating to the *álfar* was because there were so many of them living around Áibmoráigi." He paused, as if letting it sink in. "They were making an exodus."

"From what?" Dagny asked.

"I have no idea." He shook his head. "Maybe they were running from something or searching for something that they didn't have at home, like food or water."

"But after the Grændöden, they went back to where they came from, and they haven't really come back since," I said. "That means they must have made peace with whatever they were running from or found a new source of food or whatever."

"The Grændöden was near-certain death," Elof reasoned. "Whatever they went back to only needed to be a little bit better than that."

31

visiting

The door to the apartment groaned open after my agonizingly long wait in the hall, and when Jem-Kruk saw me standing there, he grinned slowly.

"You found me," he said simply.

"I can't really take credit for it. The Mästare gave me your address."

He stepped back and opened the door wider. "Come on in."

"I'm Dagny Kasten." She'd been standing beside me, and she introduced herself with a brusque handshake.

It had been her idea to come here, saying that was what the elders wanted—"Or why else would Mästare have given you his address?" she had reasoned insistently. "We might as well get it all done." Naturally, she was concerned about my safety (and her curiosity had no bearing, obviously), so she had to come with me.

At first glance, the suite looked better than Calder Nogrenn's apartment on a lower floor in the staff housing, even though it had the exact same tight two-room floor plan.

But as we went inside, I realized it had just been styled significantly better. The dark kitchen cabinets had been painted bright white, and the mushy-green-pea walls were a contemporary fog-gray.

The dusty clutter of Calder's place was entirely absent. Sleek seating, a stack of books, and several potted plants were the only furnishings.

While Dagny and Jem continued their cautiously polite introductions, I noticed the one thing that was definitely better here than Calder's place—the view. Beside the sofa was a large picture window with sheer curtains. I pushed them aside and peered out at the bustling citadel, and at the ocean beyond the walls.

"They tell me this is the best view in the staff housing." His voice was behind me, and when I glanced back, he was closer than I thought, with his dark eyes on me. My skin flushed, and I looked back out the window.

"I believe it." I scanned the roofs, looking for anything to distract me from the warm flutter in my belly. "I think I see our place over there."

He leaned in closer and asked, "Oh, yeah?"

"Don't be silly," Dagny chastized me, and she was suddenly at my elbow, pulling me away from the window. "We don't even live on that side of town."

"Uh, right, yeah." I cleared my throat, then sat down on the cranberry-colored sofa. "I'm so bad with directions. I'm always getting them mixed up."

"Uh-huh," Jem said as his eyes bounced between the two of us.

"How long have you been here?" Dagny asked.

She'd left me on the couch, returning to her slow walk around the tiny apartment, frequently pausing to inspect the few personal belongings that were visible. Books with the library stamp on the spines—*The History of Merellä, Troglecology in the 21st Century, The Traumatized Brain, The Girl on the Train, National Audubon Society Field Guide to Insects and Spiders,* and *The Winter Garden: A Horticulture Guidebook.*

Once she'd flipped through them, she moved on to the small pile of jewelry on the bookshelf—rings, leather cuffs, and bracelets—touching each piece.

"Not that long," Jem answered her.

His long, dark hair had been pulled back, woven in thick braids that were twisted into a knot at the back of his head. A few strands of hair had gotten free, and he absently tucked them behind his ear as his eyes tracked Dagny.

"Are you looking for something?" he asked, and she set his potted succulent back on the countertop.

"Can I use the bathroom?" she asked instead of dealing with his pointed inquiry.

"Yeah." He pointed to the door off the kitchen. "It's through the bedroom."

I waited until she'd gone into the other room to whisper, "Sorry about her."

"So, she is behaving strangely?" he asked, and a relieved smile spread across his face. "It seemed odd to me, but I don't know her."

"Yeah, she's coming on a little strong," I admitted. "She's just . . ." I trailed off, unsure of how to finish without offending him.

"Worried?" he supplied, and I reluctantly nodded. Jem sat down beside me on the couch, tilting his knees slightly toward me. "Are you worried?"

I chewed my lip. "Would you blame me if I was?"

"No, no, of course not," he said. "You don't have any reason to worry, not from me. But I can see how unusual and concerning this whole situation might seem to you."

"So, you're saying where you come from, it's *not* normal for a guy from a secret lost tribe to come back after kidnapping an amnesiac stranger?" I asked, and he laughed.

"You remind me of someone." His smile deepened, and he looked at me closely.

The light filtered through the curtains, hitting his deep-set eyes so that the flecks of bronze sparkled in the black walnut irises, and it complemented the copper constellation of freckles across his broad cheeks.

"Who?" I asked.

"Someone back home." He raised a shoulder in an indifferent shrug, and his gaze shifted, looking past me and out the window.

His exaggerated nonchalance piqued my curiosity, so I sat up straighter and asked, "A girlfriend?"

"A friend." He looked back at me with a knowing smile. "Not that *girlfriend* is really a term we use back home."

"What do you call it, then?"

"*Veloma,* or maybe *klampiveleska,*" he said, and that was the first time I really noticed his accent—a little more guttural and slowed down. With both words, on the final syllable, he added a strange elongated vibrato to the *a,* so it became a warbled *uhhh.*

"I suppose it depends on how you define girlfriend," he said. "*Veloma* means 'the one you choose to be with,' and *klampiveleska* is for more serious relationships—'the one you choose to be joined with.' "

Something about the way he said that made my stomach flip, and I looked away from him.

"I always thought the Nordic languages were lovely," I said, hating that it sounded a little breathless.

"That's the language of your tribe?" Dagny asked. I hadn't noticed her reappear in the kitchen.

"Uh, yeah." Jem leaned back on the stiff sofa, and he looked over at her. "Most everyone around town speaks it. Some of the outlanders will only talk in *irytakki*."

"Where is that town?" Dagny asked him directly. She walked over and sat down on the leather ottoman across from us and crossed her legs.

"Sverige," he answered coolly.

"Sweden," I translated for her.

"Sweden's a big country," she pressed.

He met her gaze evenly, and he let the silence hang over us for a tense moment. Finally, he replied, "Adlrivellir. It's in the far north, under the shadow of a mountain. In the winter the sun never rises, and the summer it never sets, but the sky is always endless."

"That sounds beautiful," I said. "I'd love to see it someday."

"It truly is," he agreed. "Have you ever returned to Sverige?"

I shook my head, but Dagny narrowed her eyes and asked, "Why did you say returned? We're not from Sweden."

"I've always been told that's where troll civilization was founded," he elaborated. "It's our homeland."

"It's interesting that you feel so connected to our heritage when your tribe chooses to live so separately," Dagny said.

"It's *because* I've lived so disconnected from your world that I find such an attachment with our past. That's our only shared history."

"Why?" Dagny asked. "Why do you care about us at all?"

"Where I come from, we have our way of doing things." He stared out the window, squinting into the sunlight. "But I've always known it wasn't the only way, and out here I get to see the other opportunities, the other ways it could have been."

"So then why do you go back?" I asked. "If it's better here?"

"I never said it was better here," he said with a wry smile, and my face burned with embarrassment. "But there are a multitude of things that I do truly enjoy here, and yes, some that I prefer." I'd looked away from him, but I could feel his eyes on me.

"Where I come from isn't perfect by any means, and it definitely has more than its fair share of dangers, but it's still my home," he finished.

"I've never really felt that," I said. "I've lived a few places, but I don't think I've ever been anywhere that I felt compelled to return to."

"You've never been to Sverige," he reminded me. the was looking at me and I couldn't tell if it was an invitation or not.

"What do you mean by *dangers*?" Dagny asked. "I feel

like you sort of glossed over your home being excessively dangerous."

"Dag, he didn't say that," I tried to correct her.

She directed her sharp gaze at him. "You said that where you come from has more than its fair share of danger, and that sounds like the very definition of *excessive*. So, what would you say, Jem? Is it excessively dangerous?" Her wide eyes blinked with faux-innocence.

Jem-Kruk leaned back, and there was a subtle shift in his demeanor. His legs moved away from me, now tilting more toward the door, and he folded his arms across his chest. He was still smiling, but his dark eyes had settled heavily on Dagny when he said, "I didn't realize that I'd invited in the inquisition when I welcomed you into my apartment today."

Dagny matched his gaze, unwavering. "Eliana is my friend too. She was obviously ill, and by your own words, you took her back to a very dangerous place."

"For what it's worth, I assure you that she's safe," he said.

She looked away from him, staring off into the kitchen. "Elof's next class starts soon, and I've missed enough work for today." She stood up. "I'll let you enjoy the rest of your afternoon."

"I should get going too." I gave him a sheepish smile, and he got to his feet at the same time I did.

"It's just as well, I have things I need to do today." Jem walked us to the door. Dagny went out first, and I trailed a step behind her. As I left, he leaned against the door frame, and he said, "Now that you know where I am, there's no need to be a stranger."

32

packed

I'd stayed late in the archives to compensate for missing so much work, but I didn't know that Calder even really noticed. Since I'd gotten back from Louisiana, he had managed to get more indifferent every day. I didn't know how it was possible for someone who couldn't care less to somehow defy logic and care even less than he was capable of not caring.

Regardless, by the time I got home, with ink stains on my fingers and dust in my hair, I was exhausted. It had been a very long, unusual day, and I was looking forward to taking a hot shower.

But my plans were thwarted the instant I stepped through the front door, and I found Dagny flitting about the living room, packing up her oversized vintage suitcase, and singing along to the Nina Simone playing on the stereo.

"What's going on?" I asked cautiously.

"Oh, good, you're finally home." She put her hands on her hips when she turned back to face me. "I thought you'd be home sooner, so you'd have more time. I've been packing my stuff up, and I would've done yours, but I honestly didn't know where to start."

"Pack?" I scratched my head. "For what? Did we get evicted?"

"What? No." She laughed. "For Sweden. Jem told us exactly where to go. So . . . I'm getting ready to go."

"Okay." I dropped my bag by the door and went into the kitchen to get myself a glass of water. "So, do you have any ideas about how we're going to get across the ocean to another country thousands of miles away?"

"Of course. I've got most of it figured out, other than what to pack of yours, obviously."

"Oh, good, if you've got it all figured out, then everything's good," I muttered to myself before gulping down cold water.

Dagny started rattling off a list of things she still needed to get together, but she was interrupted by a rapid knocking at the door. I stayed at the kitchen sink, letting her answer it.

"Hey, sorry, I hope I'm not bothering you," Pan said.

"Don't worry about it," Dagny said as she let him in. He came into our apartment, wearing his peurojen overalls with the antlered-heart patch on the chest.

"Is everything okay?" I asked, since he seemed a little out of breath, although the staircase up to our loft apartment had that effect sometimes.

"Yeah, yeah." He pointed to Dagny's suitcase where it lay open on the coffee table. "It's true. You're leaving."

"So I've been told," I said dryly.

"How did you hear about that?" Dagny asked. "I've only talked to Elof about it."

"And Elof talked to Sylvi about Ulla's extended absence, and she told me," Pan explained.

"Whoa, whoa!" I held my hands up and walked closer to them. "You actually already planned all of this?"

"Yeah," she said with a shrug. "I told you that I had most of it taken care of."

I gaped at her. "But . . . we can't just *go* to Sweden!"

"Why not?" Dagny asked. "You guys went to that Omte city in Louisiana. This is the path for finding Eliana, your parents, and maybe even rediscovering a lost tribe or the First City."

"That's actually why I rushed over here," Pan said. "I wanted to see if I could go along with you."

"You'll have to talk to Elof," Dagny said. "He's really the one taking care of most of the details. He's freed up some grant money from the Troglecology Department to pay for our airfare and some other travel expenses, but he's already had to allocate enough for the three of us."

"I've got some money saved up," Pan said quickly. "I can pay for myself. I'd like to go with you."

"Wait, back up. Elof is going with too?" I asked incredulously.

Dagny looked at me like I was speaking nonsense. "This is his life's work, and he's put an immense amount of effort and time into getting this all together on such short notice. Obviously he's going."

"Yeah, of course, obviously. How silly of me to *not* to assume that my flatmate's boss would be going with me on a transatlantic trip that I knew nothing about," I muttered. "Is there anybody else going with that I should know about? Calder? Pan's dog, Brueger? Is Hanna meeting us there?"

Dagny rolled her eyes and went back to folding an ivory turtleneck. "I don't know why you insist on being so ridiculous all the time."

"Wait, you didn't know?" Pan turned to me, his eyes wide with surprise. "Dagny didn't talk to you about this at all?"

I shook my head. "I've been working for the past nine hours, and I only found about this five minutes before you got here."

"What the heck, Dagny?" Pan demanded. His hands were on his hips, and he sounded so appalled on my behalf I couldn't help but smile.

"I was being pragmatic." She turned around to face us. "Ulla was working, and the reception is nonexistent."

"Dagny!" Pan scoffed. "You work in the same building. You could've just gone downstairs."

She stared down at the wood floor, twisting her bare feet sheepishly. "I know. I didn't mean for it all to happen this way, honestly. I was talking to Elof and things snowballed from there. Everything really did happen so fast, and I didn't realize that we'd accidentally left Ulla out of the loop until . . . well, until everything was done."

"That's not really an apology, but okay," I said grudgingly.

"I'm sorry, Ulla." She finally looked at me. "But I really think this is the right thing to do, and I thought this is what you'd want and you'd be excited about it."

I nodded. "You're right. But next time check with me before you sign me up for anything major."

"I'll do what I can," she agreed with a crooked smile.

"So, what exactly did you sign me up for?" I asked.

"We're flying out tomorrow night," Dagny said. "That's all I know for certain. Elof has been busy talking with the Markis Ansvarig in Sweden to arrange some transportation and sleeping arrangements." She snapped her fingers. "Which reminds me. I have to call him to get Pan added in. You are serious about that, right?"

"Yeah, I definitely want to do this," he said.

"I'll call Elof now, if that's okay," she said, and she was already heading toward the phone. "Should I go in the other room so I'm not bothering you? I'll go in the other room."

She didn't wait for a response, so we didn't bother, and she grabbed the phone and shut the door behind her, mindful of the cord.

"So . . ." Pan kept his voice low, even though Dagny was in her bedroom. "How are you doing with all of this?"

I laughed weakly and walked over to the couch, then collapsed on it. "Right now I'm mostly feeling tired and overwhelmed."

"I can imagine."

My hair was in a messy bun, and I undid it and then ran my fingers through the tangles. Pan pushed Dagny's suitcase to the side, and he sat on the coffee table across from me.

"Are you really okay with me tagging along?" he asked.

"Yeah, why wouldn't I be?" I smiled at him.

He shrugged. "I don't know. You didn't have much of a say in the planning of all this, so I thought I ought to make sure you had a say about me."

"Thanks. But Dagny's right. I want to do this." My stomach was doing anxious somersaults, and my heart hammered in my chest. As tired as I had been only a few minutes ago,

I now felt wired—in an admittedly bone-ass-tired way—and my mind was racing. "It's exciting. I should be excited."

"Should be?" he asked, his voice light and teasing.

"I am excited," I corrected myself, but the uncertainty in my voice was so blatant that we both laughed. "Are you excited?"

"Yeah. But I'm also nervous."

"Me too." I pulled my legs up under me. "But I think . . ."—I looked down at my hands, twirling my rings around my fingers—"if you weren't going with, I'd feel even more nervous."

"How does me being there make you feel less nervous?" he asked with a soft laugh.

"I don't know." I chewed my lip. "When you're around, things don't seem quite so bad. Like even if things get messy or difficult, you'll be there to offer advice or make me laugh . . ." I trailed off. "Sorry. I'm tired and rambling."

"I like it when you ramble." He leaned forward and placed his hand on my knee, tentatively, softly. I looked down at it, and he jerked his head back. "Sorry, I shouldn't have—"

"No, I didn't—"

"The timing is bad, I know." He rubbed the back of his neck with the hand that had just been on my leg.

"Yeah, it is," I agreed.

"I'm not trying to make you uncomfortable, Ulla," he said after a heavy pause.

"I know, I know, and you're not," I said. "We're in a weird space right now, but we can figure it out together . . . right?"

He met my gaze but didn't answer right away, and then Dagny came out of her room, rapidly listing all the things

Elof suggested we pack and do to get ready. As soon as she burst into the room, Pan stood up, and Dagny filled the space between us with her frenetic packing and loud proclamations.

And he never did answer my question.

33

Ambassadors

Mästare Amalie was talking with Elof when we arrived in the lab the next day. On the island beside me, all our official paperwork was laid out—passports, IDs, documentation, debit cards, everything that humans required to travel abroad and exist in their world.

"You've spoken with Patrik Boden, and you have his number?" Amalie asked Elof. As they confirmed their plans, I went over to see how they'd set me up.

With the passports, they went with very common American names to help us travel under the radar. That's why the name under my photo in the passport was "Emily Miller," and Dagny Kasten had become "Alexis Williams" and Panuk Soriano was now "Austin Williams."

"You two have the same surnames," I commented after I'd read them.

"I thought they'd more easily pass for siblings," Elof said.

They eyed each other suspiciously, but Elof wasn't wrong. Their skin had a slightly darker umber undertone than mine, their eyes and hair were the same color, and they both had rather full lips. Elof had apparently finished his conversation with Amalie, and he swiveled his stool toward us. "Do those look all right to you?"

"Yeah, they look great," I said.

"Wait, Pan, why do you even need a new passport?" Dagny asked. "Don't you have one? You were born in a Canadian human hospital, right?"

"We just call it Ottawa General Hospital," he said dryly. "But the Mimirin has super-intense safety protocols, and they really regulate the connections and trails left by passports and records. They prefer I don't use my legal name in the human world whenever it can be connected to Merellä or any troll business.

"But this way, I finally have a little sister I never wanted," he added, and he playfully punched Dagny in the arm.

She shot him a look. "I have two older sisters, and that's more than enough for me."

"So what's the plan?" I asked.

Mästare Amalie had been reading over the itinerary, handwritten in a sleek calligraphy under her elegant letterhead, but she slid it across the island toward us. As she ran through the list, she tapped each item with her long, midnight-blue fingernail.

We were flying out at eleven P.M. from Portland, and we'd be landing in Sweden thirty hours later. From the airport, we'd rent a car and drive to a port near Nikkala, where Patrik Boden would meet us and ferry us over to Isarna.

Isarna was a quiet island town in an archipelago in the Bay of Bothnia off the coast of Sweden. It was the largest troll settlement in Scandinavia, and it was unusual for a lot of reasons. One of the biggest was that it had dual fealty, meaning it belonged to both the kingdom of the Trylle and that of the Skojare. They jointly appointed a Markis or Marksinna to govern the city, called the Markis Ansvarig or Marksinna Ansvariga, the current Markis Ansvarig being Patrik Boden.

"Patrik has offered to be a city guide for you, and he's assured me that he'll help you get whatever you need to find Áibmoráigi," Amalic said. "We're all very excited for you to be going as ambassadors for the Mimirin like this."

"So, as ambassadors we get a free trip to Sweden, and you guys get what, exactly?" Pan asked her carefully. Amalie and Elof had really rushed through the explanation when they'd told him this morning.

"Information, as much as you possibly can gather," Amalie said. "When you return, we simply want you to tell us all about your trip. Nothing too invasive, I assure you."

"How come Patrik and the folks in Isarna haven't found Áibmoráigi yet?" I asked. "If they're so close, what's stopping them?"

Amalie smiled, but her jaw tensed visibly. "That is a good question, and that's why this is exciting for us all. Because I hope you'll be able to answer it very soon."

"Well, we'll have plenty of time to go over everything on the very, very long trip there. And since we have a long drive to Portland, we need to leave here by"—Elof paused to check his watch—"four o'clock. That gives you a little over two hours to pack up and get your things in order. We'll meet up outside the doors of the Mimirin then, and we'll be on our way."

"I should get going, then," Pan said. "I've gotta take Brueger to my coworker's for him to dog-sit while I'm gone."

"Dagny, can you spare a moment to help me get my schedule in order for my replacement?" Elof asked, and he was already walking back to the desk.

"Yeah, sure. I'm all packed up anyway," she said.

So was I, actually. Last night Dagny couldn't sleep until she had everything packed up, and with my bedroom being an open loft, I couldn't really sleep while she was running around making sure she had everything she needed, so I figured I might as well pack up too.

But since I was ready to go and everybody else was busy, I realized I had a window in my schedule. I waited until after Pan had left, and I snuck out of the lab before anybody else would notice. Neither Dagny nor Pan trusted Jem, and neither of them thought that I should visit him alone.

I understood their trepidation, but he'd never done anything to hurt me, and I had a feeling he'd be more truthful if I was alone. Dagny's abrasive questioning didn't exactly inspire an honest and open dialogue.

As I headed up to the fourth floor in the staff housing, I grew more and more anxious. By the time I got to Jem's door, my heart was racing and my mouth was dry. I knocked on the door, trying to be for gentle, but sometimes when I was nervy like this my strength got the best of me. Under my accidental hammer of a knock, the door popped open and swung inward.

"Oh, my gosh, I'm so sorry!" I said frantically, and I pushed the door the rest of the way open so I could apologize properly. "I didn't mean—"

My words died when I saw the apartment. All the big pieces of furniture were here, but all the smaller, personal possessions were gone. Some of the books were still on the shelf, but most of them had been cleaned out, and the piles of jewelry and even the succulent were no longer here.

"Jem?" I stepped farther into the apartment. "Jem-Kruk? Are you here?"

I peered in the bedroom. The bed was made, and no one was there. The top drawers on the dresser were open and empty.

Jem-Kruk was gone. Again.

34

Fate

"Okay, seriously, what's wrong?" Pan asked. We were waiting at the gate for our plane. Dagny and Elof had gone off to scrounge up something to eat, but the two of us had stayed behind.

"What do you mean?" I asked.

"You've been acting weird ever since we left the city. I thought you were nervous about making it past security, but you still seem . . . spacey. You keep staring off and looking anxious and biting your nails."

I'd been chewing on my thumbnail, and I self-consciously stopped and tucked my hands under my thighs. "I went to see Jem before we left."

"What? Why? What happened? Did he do something?" Pan asked.

"I wanted to tell him that we were going to Isarna to look for Áibmoráigi. I don't know if Áibmoráigi is the same thing as the Adlrivellir city he comes from, or if it's something else entirely. But I . . . wanted to see what he thought." I shrugged, unable to fully articulate why I wanted to see him one more time before we left. "But it didn't matter anyway. He wasn't there."

"You mean he wasn't at his apartment?" Pan asked. "Or that he was *gone*?"

"It looked like he was *gone* gone."

"Maybe he went home. That doesn't really mean anything," Pan said. "I mean, he said he came here to assure you that Eliana is safe. He did that, so why would he stay?"

"I don't know. Why did he want me to know that Eliana is safe?" I chewed my lip. "Why is Amalie so eager to help us? Something is going on, and every time I feel like I'm getting close to understanding what it is, something changes and I realize that I don't know anything."

"I don't know what's going on either. But if anybody can figure it out, it's the four of us." He looked past me to where Dagny and Elof were walking back toward us, bearing lemonade and apples. "And that's why we're going on this trip. So we can find out the truth."

I gave him a tired smile. "I hope you're right."

Since the flight had been booked last minute, none of our seats were together. I ended up in a tight window seat near the back of the plane, next to an elderly couple who fell asleep and started snoring before takeoff, but things could've been worse.

As tired as I was, I was still too anxious to sleep. I'd been on a plane before, but never one this large, never for this long. For a little while, I stared out the window, watching the country sleeping, thousands of feet below me.

Suddenly the darkness erupted in glittering flashes of

light. I gasped in surprise, and the flight attendant's voice came over the loudspeaker, telling everyone we could watch fireworks out the plane window. It was the American independence holiday, but I'd been so wrapped up in everything that I hadn't even noticed.

I watched outside long after the fireworks had ended, when most everyone else in the cabin had fallen asleep. It was a dark night, with clouds blotting out the moon, so there wasn't much to see, and I decided to make better use of my time by pulling out the book.

I ran my fingers across the gilded title *Jem-Kruk and the Adlrivellir*. I'd snuck it out with me in my carry-on bag, since I thought it might offer some insight about where we were going, especially now that I knew that Jem came from a place he called Adlrivellir.

The earth had finally dried from the Great Blue Thunder, making the passage across the Valley easy again. It was on the first clear day after the water had receded, when bright red flowers bloomed brightly on the green fields, that Jem-Kruk announced his intentions.

"I will go into the Valley to harvest the sweet Idunnian pear," declared Jem-Kruk.

"You can't," Jo-Huk argued. "The *etanadrak* guard the Idunnian grove."

"The waters drove them away, but if I hurry now, I can get the fruit before they return."

"But is the fruit worth the risk?" Jo-Huk questioned his younger brother.

"It is no risk." Senka dropped into the conversation—literally.

She had been climbing in the willows around them, nimbly hanging on to the slender branches, and when she wanted to be, she was lighter and quieter than the wind.

Senka crouched on the ground when she dropped, grinning mischievously up at them. Her long hair was a dull shade of lime, and it hung around her shoulders like a shawl.

"See, I told you!" Jem-Kruk shouted rather gleefully, but Jo-Huk had never been so easily swayed by Senka.

"How can you possibly promise such a thing?" Jo-Huk asked, rather dubious of her.

"Because. I will go with, and I can handle the *etanadrak*."

That was enough for Jem-Kruk, and no amount of protests from Jo-Huk would stop him once he was in action. Jem-Kruk and Senka were already racing out into the Valley, and he ran after them.

Many of the other animals had come back already. They ran alongside a pack of binna deer. The giant beasts nearly crushed them under their hooves, and Jem-Kruk and Senka whooped in glee as they darted through the shadows cast by the large antlers.

They kept running, long after Jo-Huk's legs ached and he couldn't keep up with them anymore. When he came to the field of flowers, he lost sight of them, as they weaved between the boulders.

On the other side was the Idunnian grove, but

Jo-Huk heard the bellows of the angry *etanadrak*. He finally made it through, and he saw them coming for Jem-Kruk and Senka.

They were giant slimy beasts, with rotund shells of emerald green, and a row of pointed teeth in their mouths. Senka and Jem-Kruk fought them valiantly. Jem-Kruk used his daggers, while Senka used her arrows tipped with the poison nectar of the mourning flowers.

One of the *etanadrak* managed to wound Jem-Kruk, a sharp fang catching the palm of his hand and spilling blood out all over. Jem-Kruk responded by immediately cutting off the beast's head.

Within short order, the three of them were sitting in the field eating fresh Idunnian pears, and though Jo-Huk hated to admit it, nothing had ever tasted so sweet. It had been worth the risk, after all.

35

midnight sun

By the time our final flight landed at our destination, I had discovered a kind of tired that I'd never known before. My body felt strange and gummy, and I lumbered through baggage claim and renting a car.

Pan drove, Dagny beside him helping with navigation. That left me and Elof to sprawl out in the back seat, and Elof had totally sacked out before we even hit the road. I planned to do the same, resting my forehead against the cool glass of the window, but then we got out on the open highway, away from the town and the mountains to the west, and I finally saw the full scope of the landscape.

I sat up straighter and rolled the window down, so there was nothing between me and the view. It was so utterly breathtaking. The vast, lush green flatlands, rushing up to meet the snowcapped mountains that arched across the land.

"Is everything okay back there?" Pan asked, trying to look at me in the rearview mirror.

Dagny craned her head around to look at me. "Are you getting carsick, Ulla?"

"No, no, I'm just . . ." I waved out the window. "It's beautiful here."

It did remind me a bit of the places where I'd grown up—the evergreen flatlands like what I saw during the summers in Iskyla, and the mountains a more epic scale of the bluffs of Förening. But despite the similarities, this was much grander. It was so *vast* and green, seemingly stretching on forever.

Elof shivered on the seat next to me, so I rolled up my window. I watched for as long as I could, admiring the majestic fields, until my eyelids grew too heavy. But even with my eyes closed, the lush scenery played on in my dreams.

I saw the fields, but I was soaring above them. A herd of giant woolly elk appeared from nowhere, their antlers reaching high into the sky. I dove down lower, so I was floating alongside, chasing them. They should've been running fast, their long legs bounding through a wildflower meadow, but they moved in slow motion, so their graceful strides appeared almost magical.

From the herd came the piercing call of one of the elk—a deep thunderous roar underneath a high-pitched whistling scream. It was a ghastly sound, as if two different demons were crying out in agony from the throat of one of the woollies.

This call was louder than I'd ever heard before, sounding more like it belonged to a fierce dragon than a monstrously oversized deer. Then I spotted the beast that made the sound. Unlike the others with their fur in dark shades of umber and mahogany, this one was pure white. Even the broad antlers were ivory colored.

The rest of the animals ran, but the white elk stayed behind. Its cinnamon-red eyes were locked on me when it let out another long, tortured bleat, and I put my hands over my ears, futilely attempting to block it out.

But the meaning got through loud and it clear: it was a warning.

"We're here," Pan was saying, and he gently shook me.

"Ulla, get up!" Dagny snapped. "We're here and the Markis Ansvarig is waiting."

I sat up, blinking back my grogginess, and tried to get my bearings. Elof and Dagny had already gotten out of the rental car, and they were unloading their bags from the trunk. We were parked in a lot next to a harbor, under a gray cloud of mist.

Pan lingered in the front seat, but as soon as he'd told me, "It's time to go, Ulla," he was out of the car.

When I got out after him, Elof was standing nearby, talking to a man in a trilby hat with a white feather in the brim.

"We're so happy to have ambassadors here," he was saying in a clipped accent. His hands moved the whole time he talked, gesturing in quick, fluid movements. "We don't get many visitors to the city."

"It is quite the journey," Elof commented with a smile. "But we're so grateful to have your hospitality."

"The gratitude goes both ways, it seems," he said, and his dark eyes landed on me. "We missed introductions. I'm Patrik Boden, the Markis Ansvarig."

"Ulla Tulin," I said and shook his hand. He smiled then, and it was sharp and clean, like a brand-new blade.

"Does everybody have their things?" he asked and checked his watch. "The next ferry leaves in ten minutes, so we should catch it while we have the chance."

"Here." Pan handed me my duffel bag, and Dagny checked the car one final time to make sure we hadn't left anything.

It was a five-minute walk to the ferry. The paint-chipped sign out front promised that the ferry made stops at all the islands in the nearby archipelago, including the uninhabitable national park Isarna. (That's what the sign *said*, to keep humans at bay.) The boat was rusty, and the wooden benches that served as seating had seen better days. But there was a canopy to keep out the drizzling rain, and a heater in the center to help ward off the chill.

I sat down as close to the heater as I could get, while Patrik told us about the amazing views of the bay that we could see even better from the bow. Dagny and Elof decided to take him up on his guided ferry ride, but I offered to stay back with the luggage and warm myself.

When the boat finally departed, it let out a loud blast of the horn, and I almost jumped out of my skin.

Pan sat down beside me. "Are you okay?"

"Yeah, yeah. I had a strange dream on the way here, and it's lingering." I rubbed my temple. "I think I'm just really tired, and this rain's got me shivering even though it's not even cold out."

He put his arm around me, in a casual way that managed to warm me in more ways than one. "We'll be there soon, and then we can all get some rest."

"I can hardly wait." I rested my head on his shoulder and softly added, "Thanks for coming here with me."

"Are you kidding me?" He nodded at the clear waters that stretched around us for miles, save for bright green patches of islands scattered about. "I wouldn't miss any of this for the world."

Once I had warmed up—and woken up some more—I was able to better appreciate the beauty around us. It was a tranquil, breathtaking boat ride. For most of the trip the visibility was very high, despite the light misting rain. But as we went along, it was like we were driving into a thick cloud, and that's when Patrik announced our stop was coming up.

The ferry ventured slowly forward until the thick coniferous forest came into view, materializing from the fog. We gathered our things and got off the boat, and as we walked down the long dock, the mist began to thin. By the time we stepped foot on the actual island, the mist had evaporated.

I looked back over my shoulder, watching the ferry disappear into the gray.

36

island

"I've arranged a special treat for you," Patrik announced, sounding rather excited, and I turned to see him walking toward a pair of Tralla horses hooked up to a carriage. "Since Isarna is free of motor vehicles, I arranged to have our two best Trallas take us to your hotel."

Back in Iskyla we'd had a few Tralla horses, but nothing as big or as stunning as these two. Trallas were a type of draft horse, bred exclusively by trolls, and almost entirely by the Kanin. Occasionally they were gifted to other tribes, often from the King to other royalty.

Trallas were renowned for their size, since they were larger than Clydesdales, and for their plush satiny coats and very high tolerance of the cold.

Patrik walked to one of the horses, this one a lovely lavender-silver color, and her shoulder was well over a foot above the top of his head. She lowered her head so he could stroke her nose. "This beautiful girl is Agda." He went to the other one, a charcoal dapple steed with big dark eyes. "And this is her nephew, Eldil. King Linus gave us these horses after he took the throne, as a coronation gift for the Trylle's help in securing the crown for him."

Eldil and Agda were a beloved King and a favorite Queen from the Kanin's recent Strinne Dynasty. They were related to Pan, actually, through his father, and I wondered if he realized that as the big horse gave him a nuzzle.

I tried to give the horse a friendly pat, but Eldil decided he'd rather sniff and slobber in my hair. I laughed and ducked away from him, and then I climbed up into the carriage. It was a large open cart and looked suited for a Victorian hayride, with padded benches and seating for at least a dozen, but it was only the five of us.

Once we were all settled in, Patrik took the reins, and the horses pulled us up the hill. We moved slowly at first, as the road wound through the trees, but our pace quickly increased on a straight open stretch. There was a little bit of open land, a few acres set aside for gardens, pastures for the sheep and horses, and even an archery range.

"This the Trylle side of the island," Patrik explained. "We don't have any real divisions, everyone is free to live where they want, but we tended to group up together anyway. But it's not that big an island. We're a community at heart, and we intermingle often."

The houses and buildings on this end of town were made with green shiplap and gray bricks. As we headed down the main street, we saw a few shops lining the road: a veterinarian's office, a bakery, a flower shop, an apothecary. There were many small houses and cottages, and even a small apartment complex with a garden courtyard.

Right in the center of town was an old stone building with a vaulted roof and a bell in a tower. Patrik pointed it out, telling us, "That's Öhaus, the town hall. I'm sure you'll see a lot of it on your visit."

"How come?" Dagny was sitting in the seat right behind him, a row closer than me, and I easily heard him, but she leaned forward anyway.

"That's where we keep our records," he answered.

She looked back over her shoulder, staring longingly at the building. "We could stop now. Since it's on our way to the hotel."

"Don't you want to get settled in?" he asked.

"I would like to, yes," I interjected before Dagny derailed my plans for a shower, getting something to eat, and then getting some sleep.

"We should rest up," Elof agreed. "We can head to Öhaus first thing in the morning."

Dagny scowled, but she relented and sat back on her seat.

Right after the town hall, the green houses gave way to blue; the floral vines proudly displayed on the shop signs turned to fish. The whole aesthetic had quickly shifted from country village to nautical seaside. Here there were no flower shops or vets, but they had a bait shop and a restaurant, and the Skojare had their own apothecary and market.

Patrik turned off the main road, taking us down a narrow dirt path that led to the shore. Boats and docks lined the rocky coast for half a mile, but that was soon replaced by seaside houses cloistered in trees.

It was there, when we rounded the final bend, that we finally arrived at the Grand Bottenviken Hotel. It was a fairy-tale lodge, with the shiplap painted cornflower-blue, and the pillars supporting the porch decorated with flowered vines twisting around them.

Inside, Patrik and Elof checked us in, while I paused to admire the fish swimming in the long tank in the small lobby. The hotel stay, like the rest of the trip, was covered by the Mimirin, and I felt a twinge of guilt about this until I remembered that I was actually working here. They expected me to spy.

Finally, Dagny handed me a big brass key to my room, and I headed upstairs. I glanced around my room, taking in the sparse, rustic space. The big bed with a down comforter was my main concern, but the blackout curtains were also appreciated and a definite necessity. In the summer this close to the Arctic Circle, it was the land of the midnight sun, as the signs at the airport had frequently reminded me.

I closed the curtains, blotting out the sun and the view of the blue waters lapping against the shore beyond the hotel walls. Then I stripped down to a T-shirt and underwear and climbed into bed. Before dozing off, I tapped out a quick message on my phone to Hanna. I'd told her what we were doing before we left for Sweden, and she'd been worried, so I wanted to put her mind at ease.

Hey Hanna—

We just got into the hotel, and we're all doing fine. It's really beautiful here, and Isarna seems like a really interesting place. I'll try to take pictures tomorrow to show you.

On the way here, I've been reading a book about Jem-Kruk, and it sounds a lot like the one you mentioned in your other messages. What's it called, and where did you find it?

I hope you're having a fun summer and helping your mom and dad around the house.

Talk to you soon,
Ulla

I hit send, and within seconds I was asleep.

37

Displayed

In the morning, I met Dagny, Elof, and Pan in the lobby for a breakfast of hard dark bread and bitter tea. When we finished, we headed down to Öhaus to meet Patrik. He'd offered to send another carriage, but it wasn't far, and after days cramped in flying tin cans, it was nice to get out and stretch our legs.

Or at least that's what Dagny said, and I went along with it. The morning air wasn't cold, exactly, but it was crisp and cool enough that my hooded sweatshirt barely kept it at bay. Isarna was a very quiet town, especially compared to Merellä. As we walked, the only sound was our feet on the ground and a few seabirds calling each other.

We made it to downtown only passing two other trolls— both of whom were distinctly Skojare, with bright blond hair and visible gills. There had been half a dozen cats, though. Lounging about or strolling casually. I'd stopped to pet a particularly large fluffy tabby that crossed our path, and it seemed friendly enough.

From the outside, Öhaus looked like a much, much smaller and older version of the Mimirin. Troll architects definitely had a style.

Pan held the big double doors open, and as we went inside, I found Öhaus was not at all what I was expecting. The hardwood floors were covered in antique Swedish rugs with geometric patterns in bold blues and stark whites. Framed art and documents hung on the walls, and there were glass display cases set up all around the room.

Instead of the usual government offices, this was a museum.

On the back wall was a massive tapestry, nearly floor-to-ceiling. It depicted five ships on a violent sea, and under the crashing waves a water serpent chased after them. Patrik stood in front of it, using a waist-high display case as a table. Papers and old books were piled up around him, and a stack of file boxes was on the floor beside him.

"It is so nice to see you all again." Patrik stepped out from behind the case to greet us. "I presume your stay at the hotel has been pleasant so far?"

"Yes, it's truly lovely here," Elof agreed warmly.

Dagny had already stepped away, peering into a glass case that contained what appeared to be an emerald-encrusted animal skull. "What is all this?"

"Ah, you've discovered Safri. She's a local favorite," he said as he went over to join her. "Safri was an artic fox that used to belong to a former Marksinna Ansvariga, and she was beloved all around the island. After she died, the Marksinna chose to honor her memory this way.

"Isarna has a rich and unusual history, and we want to

keep it alive by having it on display in the Öhaus show-room," Patrik explained. "That's why I thought this would be a perfect place for us to find what you're looking for."

"You seem to have prepared," Pan commented. He'd made his way over to the materials first, taking a cursory inventory of what was laid out for us.

"Yes, we went into our storage and our archives looking for anything we have that references Áibmoráigi, the Lost Bridge, or the Älvolk," Patrik said in his clipped, cheery tone.

"To be safe, we even included the records on the Vígríðabifröst."

"The Battle of the Bridge?" I translated.

He nodded once, a quick, efficient gesture. "That's the war in which the bridge became lost."

Dagny eyed the piles, and she sounded impressed when she said, "You're very thorough here."

"Thank you." The Markis's smiled widened. "We have a saying around here. If a job cannot be done correctly, it should not be done at all."

"Isarna really seems like your kinda place, Dag," I teased, but she nodded readily.

"Where should we start with all of this?" Elof asked.

"I compiled a list of the known Älvolk." He reached for a stapled set of papers, and when he held it out, I saw the letters indented the paper, like it had been written on a typewriter. "These are the ones that we know by name and see around town from time to time."

He handed it to Elof, and I read over his shoulder, scanning until I saw a familiar name—INDU MATTISON. It wasn't until I saw it, and a wave of nausea rolled over me, that I realized I'd been hoping he wouldn't come up. That my trail wouldn't keep leading me toward the weird creep hell-bent on impregnating trolls around the world.

But here we were.

I stopped reading the list and pretended to be very interested in a display of stony gray jewelry, which was made entirely from beach pebbles.

"Wait, you have records of the Älvolk?" Pan asked. "Like a list? How'd you manage that?"

"Like I said, they come and go," Patrik reiterated. "They're not here often, but I wouldn't classify it as infrequent either. We suspect that they live somewhere nearby."

"Don't they live in Áibmoráigi?" I asked.

"That is what they claim, yes," he replied.

Pan stepped away from the display case, moving closer to where the rest of us stood around Patrik. "Have you followed the Älvolk to see where they live?"

"We have," Patrik said, conintuing his trend of cagey answers.

"Is it Áibmoráigi?" Dagny asked bluntly.

"I can't say for sure, but I think perhaps it is, yes," he allowed.

She narrowed her eyes at him. "So where is it?"

"You mistake the truth of the First City," Patrik answered cryptically. "It is not that it cannot be found—it's that we can't remember when we do."

"What are you talking about?" I asked.

"The Älvolk that guard it have honed a very specific telekinetic power," he elaborated. "Yes, they cloak the city so it can't be seen by hiking humans or from overhead planes, but if it is spotted, well, then they remove the memory of it. You can't remember where it is, how to get back, or even anything about your time there. You blink, and it's gone."

"That is some real *Men in Black*–type shit," Pan said when Patrik finished.

I looked over at him. "What?"

"Come on, you guys had to have seen that movie," he insisted, and when we shook our heads, he rolled his eyes. "Whatever. It's just after somebody sees something they don't want them to see, they erase their memory."

"I didn't know that the Älvolk were that powerful," I said.

"It seems to be the only power they truly have," Patrik replied, sounding more subdued.

The Trylle had the strongest telekinetic abilities, and some of them could be quite dramatic. The former Queen created precognitive paintings, a Marksinna kept flowers in bloom in winter, and there were others who could move things with their mind. Most of them had some form of mild persuasion, but I'd never heard of anything like this.

Erasing memories? Playing with our thoughts? That was terrifying.

"Do you think we'll be able to find Áibmoráigi?" Pan asked.

"You very well may," Patrik responded indifferently.

"But you don't think we'll remember it," I said.

"That is how this usually goes, yes."

"Then why help?" I asked in dismay. "Why even do anything at all? If you know it's a futile pursuit."

Patrik smiled again, but this time it was dulled. "Because I don't know it's futile, and the Korva of the Mimirin told me to help you."

Elof clapped his hands together. "Let's get to it, then."

Patrik started by breaking down the information he'd gathered into categories—modern records, ancient records, and rumors/legends. Dagny jumped at the modern records, and I gravitated toward the legends.

We'd only been at it for a short time, maybe twenty minutes, when the doors opened and a man strode inside. He wore a long indigo jacket, like a trenchcoat caftan, with an embroidered Nordic pattern on the edges of the sleeves and collar. His coal-black hair was silver at the temples, and his face was lined like that of a man in his midforties, maybe older.

Patrik leaned over to whisper to Elof, "That's one of the names from the list," and I was close enough that I overheard.

The man looked over at us, and he walked right to Dagny. "Hello. This will sound strange, but I am your father."

38

Relations

"I know my father, and you aren't him," she replied without missing a beat.

"Ulla?" he asked her, sounding very confused.

"No, that's me." I raised my hand weakly, and I couldn't even force a smile. "That's me."

"Oh." He narrowed his eyes at me, then glanced back over at Dagny. "You're Ulla Tulin?" I nodded. "Sorry about that." He shook his head, then smiled and walked over to me. "She looked more like me. It doesn't matter."

He waved it off, but he wasn't wrong. Both he and Dagny had black hair, compared to my dirty blond; darker olive skin compared to my pale tan; and dark eyes where mine were amber.

"This isn't exactly how I pictured this would go." He sounded kind of rattled, but his mouth seemed fixed in a permanent smirk.

"I can't say it's picturesque for me either," I muttered.

"My name is Indu Mattison, and I believe that I am the father of . . . of *you*. Ulla."

"Um." My mouth felt dry, and I swallowed hard to see if that would help. "Okay."

"Should we go somewhere to talk?" he suggested. "I'm sure you have a lot of questions, that we have a lot to discuss. There's a nice tea shop down the road."

"I can go with you, if you want," Pan offered.

"Sure. Okay," I said, not because I wanted to go, but because I didn't know how to say no. And even if I didn't want it to be the truth, if it was I needed to face it head-on. And Pan's presence would help.

We walked a short way down the road, Pan and Indu amiably carrying on mundane chatter about *gädda* fish, which I was grateful for because it kept the silence from closing in. Thankfully, Tella's Te'Butik was only a few doors down from Öhaus on the Trylle side of the island, and it was a cozy little tea shop/café.

We sat at a little table by the door, me and Pan on one side and Indu across from us. Folk music with too much flute and twangy lyre was playing softly on the stereo, and the whole place smelled like stale potpourri.

Indu ordered us a small pot of white tea for the table, and a small tray of finger sandwiches he called "sweet jam breads." The way the waitress talked to him, I gathered that he was a regular, and I couldn't believe how enmeshed the Älvolk had become on Isarna, despite how little anyone really knew about them.

"Violetta Indudottir," he said, beaming down at me. "That was what your name was to have been."

"Violetta Indudottir," I repeated, and it felt strange on my tongue. Not like a sting, but not like a butterfly. Something sharp and sweet, something that made tears form in my eyes, but I blinked them back. "Why after you? Why not my mother?"

"They don't use surnames in her tribe."

"What tribe is she?" I asked.

"She's—" He started to reply, but the waitress returned with a ceramic teapot, delicately painted with blue vines, and a small platter of dark rye-bread triangles layered with a cloudberry jam.

Once the waitress had gone, he finished, "Well, she's *álfar.*"

"What? No." I shook my head, but he poured the tea into our cups, unfazed. "If you're Älvolk, my mother is Omte."

"Why? How are those two things connected?" he asked, incredulous.

"I did a blood test. Elof told me that I'm Omte." I motioned toward myself, my mismatched eyes. "And, I mean, look at me. I'm Omte."

"It's all understandable, and try the tea while it's still warm," he directed between bites of his jam sandwiches. Pan did as he was told, sipping the tea and making an audible *mmm* afterward.

"The Älvolk are powerful, and not many of the other tribes make for suitable mates," Indu explained. "I didn't know my mother, but it was likely she was Omte or had some Omte blood in her. I mean, she must have, since you do!"

"So I'm . . . I'm half-*álfar.*" I leaned back in my chair, digesting what he'd said. "That's the part that Elof couldn't figure out. What was my mom like?"

"She was a beautiful, amazing woman. Truly something special, and so loving. She adored you, even before you were born. She's the one who picked out your name." His smile was nearly wistful when he said, "*Violetta.*"

"Then why did you . . ." I furrowed my brow, trying to understand. "If she loved me, and you did, then why was I abandoned in Iskyla?"

"Iskyla? That's where you ended up?" He scowled and shook his head. "I never checked. I thought she wouldn't go that far with a newborn."

"My mother ran off with me? Is that what you're saying?" I asked.

"Your mother? No," he insisted emphatically. "No, she would never have given you up. It was that overzealous guard Orra. She kidnapped you when you were only days old."

"You're talking about Orra Fågel? She *kidnapped* me?"

Indu looked at me in confusion, then he waved his hand. "This will be easier if I go back to the beginning. I'm an Älvolk, the same as my father, Mattis Elrikson, and his father, Elrik Ulfson, before him.

"As an Älvolk, I was raised to guard and protect Áibmoráigi and all the secrets within," he summarized. "We were once solitary, but over the last century we have begun to interact with the modern tribes."

"The modern tribes?" I snorted, thinking of their reluctance to use technology or advance past our ancient traditions.

"That is what we call you. The arrangement has been mostly beneficial, but there have been some setbacks." He frowned, his eyes downcast as he spoke.

I wondered if he was thinking of some of the horror stories that Pan had read about back when we'd been in Fulaträsk. The ones with *blodseider magick* and sacrifice.

I wondered if they were just stories, or if they were true.

"One of the setbacks happened around twenty years
ago," Indu said. "The Omte had a young King, and, like
many unfortunate young men, he'd become obsessed with
childish tales of treasure. He'd originally pursued legends of
his namesake, the Nordic god Thor, but when those proved
to be untrue, he'd latched onto the Älvolk and the First City.

"Then he came here, trampling over the countryside,
causing trouble everywhere he went." The distaste was drip-
ping from his words. "This 'King,' if you could even call
him that, he was an elk in a flower garden. Such a destructive
force.

"Of course, he couldn't travel alone, royalty never does,"
Indu said with a derisive laugh. "Orra Fågel was a guard, or
relative of some kind? Cousin, perhaps? I can't say anymore.
But they grew enraged that your mother and I wouldn't help
them find Áibmoráigi or cross the Lost Bridge. As revenge
against us, Orra kidnapped you and hid you away."

"That doesn't explain how you met my mother," I pointed
out.

"No, I suppose that was the story of how I met your
kidnapper," he admitted, and this time his smirk seemed
like it was on purpose. "Your mother was an *álfar*, a hidden
tribe from across the Lost Bridge. She never allowed me
to cross, the way we can't allow just anyone to visit Áibmoráigi."

"But she came over?" I asked.

"Yes, the *álfar* are able to cross on occasion," Indu explained. "We never know ahead of time, and I doubt we know every time. But sometimes they will visit us. All of our mothers are from other tribes, and some Älvolk, their mothers are *álfar*, and they like to keep in touch with them."

"*All* mothers are from other tribes?" I asked. "Are there no female Älvolk?"

"All Älvolk are male, but the thrimavolk are our daughters," he said.

I sneered. "So there's males and daughters? That's it?"

He narrowed his eyes slightly, and when he answered, the words were slow and deliberate. "There may be other designations outside of us, but in Áibmoráigi, the sons are Älvolk and the daughters are thrimavolk."

"Right." I gave up on pressing, because I doubted I'd get anything from him. But I couldn't really be surprised that an ancient cult that maybe dabbled in *blodseider magick* also had really regressive ideas about gender.

"What are the thrimavolk?" Pan asked, getting the conversation back on track.

So far, he'd mostly been sitting there quietly, sipping tea, munching on food, and lending me moral support with his presence. He wasn't saying much, but I didn't need him to. Knowing that he was here with me and I didn't have to face Indu on my own made me feel a lot more capable and strong.

"They're a form of guard," he said, still speaking in that careful way, and then he looked at me. "My daughter, your half-sister Noomi, she is a thrimavolk. She can explain it to you better when we go to Áibmoráigi and you meet her."

My heart double-jumped, and I heard Pan choking on his tea beside me. "We're going to Áibmoráigi?"

"Yes," he said matter-of-factly. "You're my daughter. I want to show you who you are."

39

⟡

Bitter Tea

"Is my mother there?" I asked, focusing on other things that mattered instead of letting myself get carried away with the excitement of going to Áibmoráigi.

Indu took a deep breath before answering, "No, unfortunately, she passed away recently. She'd fallen ill, and she didn't recover."

My arms had been folded across my chest, but they fell to my lap as the strength suddenly left them.

"She's dead?" The words felt like lead, catching in my throat, and it took effort to keep my voice even. "My mom is dead?"

"Yes, I'm sorry to be the one to tell you," Indu said, and for his part, he did sound genuinely saddened. "We hadn't been close for some time. After you were kidnapped, she was so distraught she went back with the *álfar* and rarely visited."

"I'm sorry, Ulla," Pan said, and under the table he put his hand on my arm, gently rubbing it with his thumb.

"She rarely visited?" I asked. "Why didn't she try to find

me? Why didn't you? If this woman kidnapped me for revenge."

"We did try to find you," Indu insisted. "Both of us. But we were young. I had hardly ventured outside of Áibmoráigi then, and we didn't know the modern tribes or where to go for help. I did track down Orra within a few weeks. You weren't with her, and she refused to tell me what she'd done with you. Fearing the worst, I . . . took care of her myself."

"Took care of her?" I asked, unable to completely hide the tremor in my voice. "You killed her?

"We thought she'd murdered you, so I did what was right," he reasoned, letting anger harden his words. "Yes, I killed her."

I winced, and my chest ached over a loss that I didn't know how to explain.

This was the first confirmation I'd gotten that the woman who had left me as a child was Orra Fågel. The woman I'd been imagining from the stories that Mr. Tulin told me since I was a baby. The woman who, when Mr. Tulin offered to let her stay, thanked him with tears in her eyes.

"Your mother had a funeral for you," Indu went on. "You were our daughter, and she stole you from us. I did what was right, for you and for your mother."

I nodded and swallowed down the attachment I had for a woman I had never known, who abandoned me after a winter storm. I had no real memories of her, only an old man's stories and my imagination filling in the gaps.

"But if you thought I was dead, how did you find me now?" I asked, pressing on. "How did you know I was your daughter?"

"Your friend Bekk Vallin contacted me. She told me about you, and I realized that you were the daughter that Orra had taken from me all those years ago."

I narrowed my eyes. When we'd been in Fulaträsk, Bekk had told me that she had no idea how to contact Indu. But that had apparently been a lie.

"How did you know I was here, though? At Öhaus? Bekk doesn't know where I am."

"Isarna's an island, and it's not that big," he replied vaguely.

"I keep hearing that," I said with a sigh "So, Bekk. Is she your girlfriend?"

"No, I wouldn't say that."

"But you are the father of her baby?" I asked more directly.

He nodded. "I am, yes."

"Bekk's baby, Noomi, how many siblings do I have?" I asked.

Bekk had shown me evidence that he'd fathered at least four children, but only one of them had survived infancy, and none of them were still alive. I had to wonder if Noomi and I were the only survivors, or if there were others.

"Well, your mother had two before I met her, so there's Eliana and Illaria—" he was saying, and I immediately gasped and sat up straighter.

"Whoa. What?" I leaned forward, resting my palms flat on the table. "What'd you say?"

"Eliana and Illaria are your older sisters," Indu said, and when Pan cursed under his breath, he gave him a puzzled look. "I assumed you knew that, since you knew them."

I kept shaking my head, so much so that I got a little dizzy by the time I stopped. "No, I didn't. No, they didn't . . . I never . . . No one told me. I didn't know."

My mind raced through every interaction I'd had with Eliana, everything about her. She was a tiny, cheerful, color-changing, green-haired girl. She was nothing like me.

Neither was Indu, and he was certain he was my father.

Was that what Eliana was doing in Merellä? Was she look-ing for me? How would she have known that I was there?

But . . . she couldn't be my sister. I would've known, wouldn't I? I always thought that I would know if I ever met any members of my real family, I would just . . . *know.*

I hadn't known with her. I didn't know with Indu. Maybe I didn't know anything.

And yet, somewhere deep down, when he said it . . . it felt true. Or maybe I just wanted it to be true?

"Eliana and Illaria are my sisters," I said, trying it on for size, and just hearing it aloud, from my own mouth, made me feel light-headed. "Shit. Okay." I cleared my throat and tried to regroup. "So . . . how many siblings do I have?"

"You have two sisters from your mother, and four from me," he said.

"All girls?" I asked.

He smiled, or, more accurately, his smirk deepened. "All daughters."

"So, you have five kids altogether?" Pan asked him.

"I tried for more, but things are . . . complicated." He leaned back in his seat. "We can go over all that when you come to Áibmoráigi. When would you like to come to the city?"

"I don't know. I haven't had time to think about it."

"Tomorrow?" Indu pressed. "Would that work?"

I glanced over to Pan, who shrugged encouragingly, so I said, "Sure."

"We could meet outside Öhaus around ten A.M.?"

"Uh, sure," I said, sounding less and less confident the more he asked me questions.

"I've really enjoyed talking with you, but I should actually get back," Indu said, and it felt rather abrupt, but I don't know if it was. Everything he'd told me had left me in a bit of a daze. "Is there anything else you want to know before I go?"

"Yeah," I said. "Yeah, the names. Of my sisters. Who are they?"

"Here." He got up and got a pen from the waitress, and he came back and scrawled them down on a lacy paper napkin. "You're processing a lot, so I'll write them down for you." He folded the napkin in half, then handed it to me.

"Thanks," I mumbled.

"I look forward to seeing you tomorrow and getting to know you better."

"Yeah, me too," I said, but I wasn't sure if I meant it. He started for the door, but I called after him before he left. "Wait. You know Eliana. Where is she? Is she okay?"

"She's safe with her sister. Eliana is sick, but they're taking care of her," he assured me.

"Do you think I'd be able to see her while I'm here?" I asked.

"Possibly. I'll talk to Illaria and see what we can do," he said, and then he was out the door.

"How are you doing?" Pan asked me after Indu was gone.

"I don't know? I really don't know." I laughed tiredly, and then I opened the napkin, reading the names he'd given me.

Noomi Indudottir (her mother was Skojare)
Bryn Aven (her mother Runa Aven is Skojare)
Minoux Moen (with Asta Moen, also Skojare)
Juno Indudottir (due in August with Bekk)

"Oh, *jakla*. I know her."

"What?" Pan leaned over to see. "Which one?"

"Bryn, she's my friend." I rubbed my temple. "Is it okay if I head back to the hotel?"

"Yeah, absolutely. Of course it is."

"Can you walk with me? I don't feel like going by myself right now."

He nodded. "Yeah, I'll always be happy to walk you home."

40

Appetites

The Grand Bottenviken Hotel had a small bar/dining room set off on the main floor, and that's where I holed up with Pan and Dagny. After Pan had walked me back to the hotel, he decided to stay with me, and he texted Dagny to let her know what was up. Fifteen minutes later, she showed up at the bar demanding that I explain everything to her.

"Shouldn't you be helping Elof?" I asked when she sat down across from me.

A bench ran along the back wall, allegedly made with reclaimed wood from old Skojare Viking ships, and I sat in the corner, my back pressed against the wall and my legs stretched out on the seat. The place was deserted except for the three of a us and a lone employee serving as the bartender and waiter.

Pan was at the other end of the room, ordering at the bar, but he was still close enough that I could overhear him and the waiter. They were talking about the fish mounted on the wall behind the bar, something long and olive-green with a fierce expression, and the waiter was saying it was the largest *gädda* ever pulled from the bay.

Dagny sat on the other side of the table from me, and behind her were the large picture windows with views of the bay. The sun was high in the sky, making the dark water shimmer, and the blue stained-glass trim around the windows appeared especially vibrant.

"Elof can handle it," she said, dismissing my question immediately, and kept her intense gaze locked on me. "You just met your dad, and Pan told me you'd had some other major revelations."

"Yeah, you can say that," I said dryly.

"What does that mean?"

"My mom's dead, and Eliana's my sister." I decided to go for it right away, but I wasn't sure if I made the right choice, given how shell-shocked she looked.

Pan returned with a pitcher of sweet ale and a plate with six beet-salad sliders, and by the time I finished telling Dagny everything, we'd finished half the pitcher and the two of them had eaten half the sliders.

"Do you believe him?" Dagny asked directly.

"Yes. Sort of." I scowled, because that didn't feel right. "I don't know." I turned to her. "Would you?"

"As of right now, I can't rule out anything he's claiming, but that doesn't necessarily mean that I believe it," she said, choosing an answer that was aggressively neutral.

"Do you think he's really my dad?" I asked her.

Naturally, she countered with, "Do *you* think he is?"

"I don't know. I mean . . . yes." I considered it, and finally decided, "I don't think he's lying to me. He's taking us to Áibmoráigi tomorrow. Why would he do that if I wasn't his daughter?"

"I'm going with you tomorrow," Dagny said.

"I didn't exactly confirm who Indu was extending his invitation to, but it seemed like Pan was included," I replied carefully.

"Good." She folded her hands flat on the table. "But I wasn't asking. I'm telling you that I'm going with. Elof will certainly insist on going also, and good luck to you on fighting him on that."

I nodded, because there was no point in arguing with her. "Right. So all four of us will head out there with my dear old dad, and then maybe when I'm there he'll have a chance to explain this all to me in a way that makes sense. Because right now I feel like . . . I'm going crazy. Am I crazy?"

"No, no, of course not," Pan said quickly, his voice calm and warm. "You're reeling from a lot of info. You found out that you're half-*álfar,* and I don't even entirely know what means."

"The *álfar* are from Alfheim, and that is a place hidden across the Lost Bridge," I said, reminding him of what little we knew. "Whether it's a place nearby or some other realm or maybe even below the crust of the earth, we don't know."

"*Yet,*" Pan added.

"There," Dagny said. "That's something to ask Indu tomorrow. What is an *álfar*? Do you want me to write it down? I've already made a list of questions I plan to ask him as an ambassador."

"No, I'm pretty sure I'll remember that one." Along with

all the other horrible questions I'd have to ask him. Like, why are so many of his children dead?

I moved on the bench so my feet were back on the floor and I was facing Dagny and Pan more fully. "But I've already got a lot of info that I don't know what to do with. Should I talk to Bryn?"

"Who's Bryn?" Pan asked.

"I knew her for a while. She got me out of Iskyla, and she helped find me a place to stay and introduced me to what amounts to my foster family. None of this would've happened if I hadn't met her. And now Indu says she's my sister."

I groaned and rubbed my temple. "But she already has a dad. I met her parents at this memorial event five years ago. Shouldn't I tell her that her dad might not be her dad? Or would I be stirring up trouble, especially if turns out that Indu is full of shit?"

"Maybe. Probably," Dagny allowed. "But is that the most pressing concern you have?"

"No." I looked at her, and I still felt dazed and overwhelmed. "What is my most pressing concern?"

"Getting ready to go to Áibmoráigi tomorrow and thinking of questions that you want to ask your father," Dagny suggested.

"I would also say that eating something and decompressing should be fairly high on your list." Pan nudged the plate of food toward me.

My stomach was getting grumbly, but the sliders—their buns all soggy and purple from the beets—didn't look that appetizing. It must've been nearly lunchtime, because a few couples had come into the restaurant. They were all sitting away from us, near the windows, but I lowered my voice a bit after they came in anyway.

"How does one go about decompressing after receiving several bits of life-changing news?" I asked.

"I know of three ways." Dagny held up her hand to count down on her fingers. "Food, fresh air, and friendship. I'm already here for the friendship, so got that." She folded one finger down. "I'm going to talk to the waiter now and see if they can scrounge up something a bit more decadent. And then we can go for a walk around town, taking in the sights and clearing our heads." She folded down the next two fingers in rapid succession.

I took a deep breath and nodded. "That's a good idea. I promised Hanna I'd take some pictures while we're here anyway."

"Perfect." Dagny looked around for the waiter, but he was oddly focused on wiping down the bar. "I'll be right back."

When she went over to talk to him, Pan watched her for a moment, and then he got up and slid onto the bench next to me. Quietly, with his dark eyes resting heavily on me, he asked, "How are you doing?"

"Honestly?" I shook my head and gave him a sad smile. "I'm here, and you're here with me. So it can't be that bad, right?"

"That's sound like something I would say."

I laughed. "Yeah, it does."

"Glad to see I'm finally rubbing off on you."

Dagny returned a few minutes later with some type of fruit bars that were slightly too sweet and utterly delicious.

While we ate, she chatted with the couple at the table nearest to us to plan out our hiking route, and by the time we were done eating, she knew exactly where we were going.

That's how we went through town, Dagny on one side of me, Pan on the other. The fresh air did feel amazing, crisp and clean, and except for the times when it smelled like fish, it was really nice. We strolled around town for an hour, maybe a little longer, and I really was feeling a lot better. With their help, I had even made a clear plan of what I wanted to talk to Indu about tomorrow.

We split up outside Öhaus. Pan and Dagny went back to help Elof, and I said I would join them later. First I wanted to head up to my room to write down everything I wanted to talk to Indu about. There were big obvious questions I wouldn't forget, but there were a lot of smaller ones that still mattered, and I didn't want important things overlooked because I was feeling overwhelmed and frazzled.

At the hotel, I went in and headed toward the stairs to my room, but the girl working the front desk called after me.

"Miss?" She stepped out from behind the desk, tentatively holding something toward me. It was a white envelope, closed with an indigo wax seal. "A gentleman stopped by, and he left this for you."

My name was scrawled across the front, so I took it from her, and she gave me a timid smile. She looked about thirteen, with long brown hair and bright blue eyes (another Skojare-Trylle union on the island, I imagined), but there was something familiar about her sheepish boredom.

It wasn't that long ago that I was just like her, working at an inn, trapped in a tiny subarctic town and longing to get out.

"What's your name?" I asked her.

"Minnie."

"Thank you, Minnie. You're doing a really good job here."

She gave me a weird look, then muttered, "Thanks?"

I took my note and headed up to my room.

41

Directions

"This doesn't seem weird to you?" Dagny asked, predictably skeptical, but that didn't mean she was wrong. The four of us—Dagny, Pan, Elof, and myself—were crowded into my little hotel room, taking turns interpreting the note I'd been sent.

After I'd read the note, I'd done research online and written out my questions for Indu. Before I'd finished, I'd heard Dagny, Pan, and Elof talking in the hall on their way to their own rooms, and I'd called them into my room to help make sense of this.

"Of course it seems weird to me," I said. I stood in front of the window, the thick drapes open to let in the bright early-twilight sun. "But every part of this seems weird."

Pan was the one holding the note now, rereading the slip of paper over and over again before finally asking, "What if it's a trap?"

"It might be." Elof sat on the end of my bed, next to Dagny. His expression was almost eerily placid, while hers was scrunched up as she tried to solve a puzzle when she didn't have nearly enough pieces.

"That's not very comforting, Elof," Pan said with a disapproving look.

"It's not meant to be," Elof replied with a shrug. "I don't know this Indu Mattison. Ulla knows the most about him, and she doesn't seem to trust him that much." He paused long enough for me to scoff in agreement. "And the stories I've heard about the Älvolk don't instill a lot of confidence in me either."

"So, what should we do?" Dagny asked.

"I want to go," I answered when Elof didn't, then I corrected myself with more conviction. "I *have* to."

Without hesitation, Pan said, "If you go, I'll go. I won't let you do this alone."

"I can handle it," I told him, even if I couldn't be sure that was true.

"It doesn't matter if you can or you can't." He looked at me, his dark eyes solemn. "I started this journey with you. I want to finish it with you."

"And I want to see what the Älvolk are up to in the First City," Elof said, and I lowered my eyes, breaking the intense look with Pan.

"So we're all going," Dagny decided, then stood up and took the note from Pan. "Whether it's a trap or not."

I was summoned back home on an urgent matter, and the travel is so long, I will not be back to Isarna to meet you as we planned.

If you can begin the journey yourself, there is a

place we can meet on Lake Sodalen. It's northwest
of Kiruna, near the mountain station. The road ends,
and you'll have to travel by foot. Humans run a quiet,
discreet restaurant on the lake, Norra av Nord. I will
be there at 1700 h tomorrow. If you wish to go to
Áibmoráigi and find out more about yourself and our
destiny, meet me then.

I hope to see you. But if not, I want you to know
that I am glad to have met you, and that I am happy
to have a strong, beautiful daughter like you.

Yours,
Indu

"So we leave in the morning, very early if we hope to make it on time." Elof stood up. "We should all get some rest. Tomorrow will be a very long day."

Elof and Dagny left, Dagny already muttering to herself about figuring out the quickest way to go. Pan stayed behind, and when the door had shut behind them, he turned to me.

"You okay?"

I rolled my eyes and a bitter smile stung my lips. "You keep asking that."

He took a step closer to me but seemed to change his mind. He looked past me, squinting in the sunlight, and chewed the inside of his cheek. "You don't mind that I'm going tomorrow?"

"I don't want you getting hurt," I admitted.

He smiled crookedly. "I don't want you getting hurt either."

"So we're even, then."

"It seems that way." Slowly, almost hesitantly, he walked over and leaned against the wall beside me. "I don't trust him, Ulla."

"Indu?" I asked, and he nodded.

"He might be your father, but you need to be safe around him," he said emphatically. "There's something really off about him."

"I'm not letting my guard down," I promised him.

"Good." He smiled again, this time a soft, subtle one that barely played on his full lips. "I should let you go and get some sleep," he said, but it sounded more like a question.

"It's probably going to be a while before I fall asleep. You can stay if you want."

"How were you planning to pass the time?"

"Anxious pacing, obsessive worrying, scrounging up what passes for room service out here."

"That all sounds good," he said with a laugh. He paused before he went on, a light smile still on his lips but his smoldering gaze had locked onto mine. "But may I make a suggestion?"

"Go for it."

"How about . . ." He trailed off, his eyes flicking down to my mouth, and he leaned in closer to me, tentatively, giving me time to pull away if I wanted, but I didn't pull away, and my breath had gone shallow.

I closed my eyes when I felt his lips brush against mine, gentle at first, but then more fervently, his tongue parting my lips. Heat rushed through me, coming from deep in my belly, where the butterflies swirled warmly.

Then he stopped, his eyes searching mine, and the way the sunlight hit him then—his eager bedroom eyes glimmering hopefully, and the nervous smile that twitched on his mouth—he was so handsome.

His breath was heavy and his voice husky when he asked, "Or is that not okay?"

"No, that's . . ." I trailed off, overwhelmed by how badly I wanted to kiss him again. "I want to do more of that."

So I kissed him, and I felt his restraint crumble. His hand was on my side, pressing into the soft flesh beneath my shirt, and he pushed me against the window. I wrapped my arms around him, kissing him deeply.

I was so focused on him—on my fingers in his hair, his mouth on mine, and his hands roaming all over—that I didn't notice my feet slipping on the floor, not until it was too late, but Pan caught me with ease.

I laughed—giggled nervously. "Maybe we should try the bed."

"Beds are always better," he agreed.

With an arm around my waist, he stepped backward, and then we tumbled back onto the bed. He knelt on it and pulled off his flannel shirt, so he was down to a white tank top that wonderfully showed off his firm biceps. I decided to do the same—pulling off my shirt so I was left in my pink bralette.

Then we were kissing again, and I wrapped my arms around him. His hand went to the thin fabric covering my breasts, and it was slipping off them when I heard the door creak open.

"Hey, so I talked it over with Elof, and—" Dagny was saying as she sauntered into my room, while Pan sat up and I scrambled to pull on my shirt. "Oh!" Her eyes widened, then she turned slightly to the side and used one of her hands to partially shield her eyes. "Is this happening now? For real?"

"No, it's not—" Pan began, then he grimaced and shook his head.

"It wasn't . . ." I'd gotten my shirt on, which did little to help the burning in my cheeks. "What are you doing in here?"

Dagny peeked around her hand, and we must've been dressed enough—Pan was slowly buttoning his flannel shirt up again—because she turned back to face us. "You left the door unlocked."

"Well, *you* left the door unlocked, since you're the one who left," I countered. "So that's on you, really. All of this is."

"Was I interrupting?" She stepped back toward the door. "Do you want me to come back later?"

"Clearly, you were interrupting, but you're here, so . . . Why are you here?"

"Just letting you know that we booked transport for the last leg of the trip," she explained. "Elof wasn't sure if he could handle all that hiking, so we got a couple guys to drive us out on their Polaris UTVs to Norra av Nord. That cuts the time in our trip by a lot, so we can leave a couple hours later. So, good news, you two have more time to—"

"Dagny . . ." I protested.

She waved me off. "Oh, please. It's only weird if you make it weird. You're grown up, you're nice, have fun."

"Thank you for your awkward blessing," I told her, but I still didn't feel comfortable meeting her eyes.

"I'll leave you guys be." She headed toward the door, and

back over her shoulder she said, "If I need anything else, I'll be sure to knock."

"Thanks. That's generally a really great policy!" I called after her.

"Don't stay up too late," she said and closed the door behind her.

I looked back at Pan with a sheepish smile. "So . . ."

"So." He'd been standing beside the bed since Dagny burst in, but he climbed back on and leaned over me. He brushed back my hair from my face, letting his thumb trail across my cheek, and he kissed me gently. He stopped, but he caressed my face a moment longer before saying, "I should head back to my room."

"Yeah? Are you sure you don't want to stay?" I asked hopefully. "A bit longer."

"I do. I *really* do." He straightened up and let his hand fall to his side. "But the next few days are going to be long and stressful, and I don't want us to rush into anything and then have it all blow up because we're overwhelmed and far from home."

I swallowed the uncomfortable lump in my throat. "Those are perfectly reasonable reasons."

"I am taking a page from your playbook back in Fulaträsk."

"That's why your argument sounded so succinct and smart," I teased.

"Yeah. That's why."

I pulled at a loose thread on the hem of my shirt, which suddenly seemed very important. "But this is just a . . . pause, right?"

"Oh, yeah, this is definitely just a pause until we get back," he agreed immediately.

"Until we get back," I echoed.

"Ulla," he said, so I'd look back up at him again, and when I did, he kissed me—softer, sweeter than before. "I mean it. But I gotta go now." He stood up. "Good night, Ulla."

"'Night, Pan."

sodalen

Our time on the island of Isarna ended the way it began: a carriage ride from the hotel to the ferry, taking us back to mainland Sweden. From there, I drove the rental car, Dagny once again serving as the copilot, and we spent hours admiring the vast Arctic summer in full bloom.

Dagny had carefully mapped our route based on Indu's note, and it turned out to be very accurate. A little over five hours later, we found ourselves at the end of the road. The last hundred kilometers, the road took us through a narrow valley, winding alongside rivers and lakes, with the snow-capped Scandinavian mountains towering over us.

Even though we made it to the end of the road a little early, the guys with the UTVs were already there. Which was good, because it didn't allow much time for any awkward conversations with Pan. We'd hardly spoken all morning, at least not directly to one another, beyond clipped banalities, like, "It's a nice morning."

The UTVs were basically a hybrid of a four-wheeler and

a Jeep Wrangler, with big wheels, three seats, and roll-top bars with a roof. After the road ended, the terrain was too rough for any standard vehicles.

I rode with Dagny one the driver, the guys following behind us in their UTV. Dagny had offered to sit in the middle, since it was easier to ask the driver questions, and she wanted to make the most of her guided tour through the valley. That was fine by me. I hung on to the bar and leaned back, letting the chilly air blow through my hair as I took in the surreal splendor around me.

The path ended with the mountains forming a cul-de-sac around Lake Sodalen. It was the largest of the lakes we'd passed in the valley, and "over thirty meters deep," our driver told us, shouting over the engine in his cheery Swedish accent.

On the far northwestern side of the lake, Norra av Nord sat in the shadow of the highest peak. Sitting there, out of the bright evening sun, on the edge of mirrored lake, it looked like a restaurant at the end of the world.

It seemed to be the most improbable location to do business, but every step along the way there had been humans. Hiking, kayaking, taking photographs (mostly taking photographs, honestly). Not *a lot,* but more than I anticipated for someplace so far out. In Iskyla, we'd never had this much tourism, but then again, we hadn't been home to stunning vistas and such tall mountains.

The UTVs dropped us outside the restaurant. Everyone took turns going in to get something to eat and to admire their small souvenir section, while the others watched out front for any sign of Indu. I'd gone in first, settling on a bottle of water and a wooden Swedish Dala horse for Hanna. I walked a few feet away from the restaurant, where humans milled about, and I opened my duffel bag and traded the souvenir for my Moleskine notebook.

I had written down a few questions, the way Dagny had suggested, but that's not what I was looking at now. We were heading to Áibmoráigi and the home of Älvolk, and I wanted to refresh myself with everything I knew one last time.

It was chilly in the shadows, and I pulled the sleeves of my sweatshirt down over my hands. My notebook fell open to the page where I'd tucked the maps. When I'd been in the archives, Calder had let me look at a book about the Älvolk, and I'd traced the maps and diagrams of the Älvolk. On the back of the maps, I had written only one thing, a phrase I had copied from the same book: *The sun sets in the green sky when the good morning becomes the violent night.*

Behind me, I heard footsteps as Pan walked over to join me, and I put the notebook back in my bag.

"He's late," Pan said.

"I'm not that surprised, honestly," I admitted.

"How long will we wait?"

I shrugged. "Until they ask us to leave."

"I don't think they do that around here." He looked to the south side of the restaurant, where a few tents were set up in a camping area.

"Then I'll wait forever. If you want to head back—"

"I don't," he interrupted me, and I looked over at him. "You know that I don't. I'm wondering what we'll do if he doesn't show up."

"I don't even know what to expect if he does show up."

He laughed lightly. "Fair enough."

We stood out front long enough that my legs started to ache, and I stamped my feet to get the blood moving. Pan waited beside me, and behind us Dagny and Elof were sitting on the porch outside the restaurant, talking about the flowers, the food, the birds in the sky.

And then, when I was starting to think we really had to come up with another plan, I saw something off in the distance. Slowly rounding the summit of the tallest mountain and walking into the valley was an elk. It wasn't until it got closer and I saw the man beside it, leading it, that I could really appreciate its full size.

"That's a woolly," Pan gasped as he came to the same conclusion that I had.

"But I thought all the woollies were in Merellä," I said.

"So did I." He turned back. "Elof, are you seeing this?"

Elof got up and came over to stand with us. "Those are supposed to be extinct outside of Merellä."

"You didn't know about this?" Pan asked him.

"No. But I don't think I know as much about the giant woolly elk as you do."

"Should we go out to meet him?" Dagny asked. "If that's Indu strolling over here with his elk, why are we waiting here? We can just walk over and meet him."

Pan shrugged. "Yeah, let's do it."

We grabbed our bags and we walked across the field. The elk's bridle was made of bold cobalt and white rope and was a near-perfect color match for the tunic Indu wore. A saddle sat on the elk's back, on top of a blanket covered in blue and red runic designs.

Indu greeted us with his usual smirk and a cold apology. "I'm sorry for my late arrival. I had to be sure that we were ready for you in Áibmoráigi."

The hair stood up on the back of my neck, so I asked, "Ready for us?"

"Rooms for you to stay," he clarified with a broader grin. "The journey is too long for you to venture back tonight. And I had to get Ealga ready." He petted the giant cervid towering over him, his fingers raking through the thick brown fur. "I thought you might need extra help getting to the city."

Pan shook his head in disbelief. "Elk can't be ridden."

"I don't know about your elk, but this one can be," Indu countered.

Pan stepped forward, tentatively petting Ealga on his big snout. The elk huffed loudly, sniffing him, but he didn't seem to mind the touch.

"You're certain it's safe?" Elof asked as he eyed the woolly.

"Yes, it is the only animal that we ride through the mountains. They are surprisingly nimble for such large beasts, like overgrown mountain goats," Indu explained, and then he commanded, "Ealga, *knäböja*."

Ealga sniffed Pan's head once more, then he stepped back, bent forward, and knelt down on his front legs. He moved slowly, mindful of the massive broad antlers, and he kept his chin up throughout the maneuver.

"Hop on," Indu said with a hearty pat on the back of the elk.

Elof looked uncertain, but he stepped closer to it, and Indu helped him up onto the saddle. Ealga stood up, moving more quickly this time, and Elof gripped tighter to the reins with an uneasy smile. "He seems to tolerate me so far."

"Let us go, then," Indu said, and he started leading Ealga back the way he had come.

"How far is it?" I asked.

"Not too far," Indu replied, like that meant anything.

So we walked on, mostly in silence. Elof occasionally talked to the elk, offering reassuring compliments and promises of friendship, but Indu definitely preferred silence. I asked him a few questions, but he replied as vaguely and as quickly as possible.

Our path slowly steepened, rock outcroppings now breaking through the lush grass. Indu had been right about the woolly having a much easier time handling the mild ascent than the rest of us did. I was strong enough for it, but I wasn't used to the hiking boots I'd gotten for this trip—or any boots or shoes, really—and they made me second-guess my footing and slip from time to time.

We'd been traversing the mountain for a half hour, maybe longer. The mountain face had become sheer, and the only easily passable area—basically a three-foot-wide ledge that ran along the mountain—was blocked by a giant boulder.

"Where do we go from here?" Elof asked.

"This is where we go." Indu handed the bridle rope to Pan, and then he turned his attention fully to me. His perpetual smirk had deepened into something more genuine, and he put his hands on my shoulders. "Do you want to see where you were born?"

"What?" I asked.

"You were born in Áibmoráigi. Are you ready to see it?" he asked again. "Are you ready to go home?"

And the weight of the moment suddenly hit me, and I couldn't speak, so I only nodded. It was all so surreal, like I was floating above myself, watching as Indu smiled at me and put his hands on my temples. On either side, he pressed a forefinger and a middle finger against my skin, and then he put his thumbs over my eyes, and the world went dark when I closed my eyes.

This was all gentle first, so soft I could hardly feel it. But suddenly there was pressure, on my eyes, on my temples, inside my skull. And I wasn't floating above myself anymore, I was jerked back into my body, into the pain that jolted through me.

My body went limp, but I wasn't falling. Indu held me up by my skull, and I was dimly aware that Dagny and Pan were shouting my name. Then I did fall, landing in the dirt on my hands and knees. The pain was still there, like my head was going to explode.

"*Leat fámus,*" Indu whispered, and somehow his voice made it through the yelling, the elk's bellowing, even my own cries of pain.

And just like that—it stopped.

"What did you do to her?" Pan was yelling in anger.

"I'm okay!" I shouted weakly. "The pain stopped."

All of this had taken maybe thirty seconds, and now I

was on the ground, on my hands and knees, and with my eyes closed, gasping for breath.

"Are you okay?" Pan was beside me, and his hand was on my back. "Ulla?"

"I think I'm okay," I said, but my whole body still trembled. "What the hell was that?"

"Open your eyes, Ulla," Indu said. "And then you will see."

43

unseen

I sat back on my knees, and I opened my eyes, and there it was.

The boulder was gone, and the narrow ledge has become a broad plateau that spread out before us, and on that was the ruins of a civilization. Crumbling structures of stone and iron, many of them overgrown with vines and weeds. Once, certainly, it had been a sprawling beautiful city, if the remnants of towers and collapsing vault ceilings were any indication.

"What is this?" I asked.

"Ulla?" Pan was still with me, his arm around my waist, and I felt better knowing that he was here, he was real, this was really happening.

"Do you see all of this?" I asked him.

Pan shook his head in confusion. "I just see the boulder that was there before."

"The boulder's gone and . . ." I blinked at the lost city that had appeared on the mountainside, and I looked over at Indu. "What is this?"

He'd been crouching beside me, but he straightened up again. "It's Áibmoráigi. I'm sorry that process is distressing, but keeping our city hidden from all the tribes means we have to use very powerful magic. It's so effective because it worms itself deep within your brain, but the side effect is that it's very painful to remove."

"Is there another cloaking spell?" I looked back at the crumpled castles nearly falling off the edge of a cliff. "Nobody lives here."

"What do you see?" Pan asked.

"Ruins. It's all in ruins." I shook my head.

"These are the ruins of the *first* First City," Indu explained. "We rebuilt below it." He stepped toward us, holding his hands toward Pan. "Here, I will show you, as I showed Ulla."

"Is it safe?" he asked me.

I shrugged. "It was agony while it happened, but I feel fine now. Mostly fine."

"It is the only way you can get into the city," Indu told us.

I stood up and wiped my hands off on my jeans. "Show me the city before you hurt my friends."

"You shouldn't go in there alone," Pan said and got to his feet. "I'll do it."

I grabbed his hand, stopping him from walking toward Indu, and he looked back at me. "Pan, it does hurt, and we can't know the full effects yet."

"That's exactly why I'm going with you." He turned back to Indu. "Hit me."

Watching Indu do the whole routine with Pan wasn't

much better than experiencing it myself. This time, though, I saw how his face turned beet-red, and the way the veins stood on his face and neck during the agonizing moments before Indu finally released him with the words *leat fámus*.

He bent over, struggling to catch his breath, and I put my arm around him, steadying him.

"Shall I help you two?" Indu asked, turning to Dagny and Elof.

"We will wait," Dagny said, but I could see how torn she was about doing the safest thing rather than the thing she wanted most to do. She nodded as if to reassure herself, and added, "That seems the most prudent thing to do."

"We'll set up a campsite here," Elof said. He had gotten off the woolly elk, and he stood next to Dagny, his brows pinched together anxiously. "If you are safe, or if you are not, come back and let us know. We won't leave here without you."

Pan was standing, but he seemed weak still. While the *leat fámus* thing had left me weakened, weak for me was still much stronger than the average troll. I put my arm around his waist, and he put his arm around my shoulders, leaning on me slightly, as we followed Indu and Ealga into the city.

Dagny gasped when we went through where the boulder had been, even though she was probably expecting just that. But I don't know how much you can prepare for watching your friends disappearing into a big rock.

"This was once Áibmoráigi," Indu explained. He motioned to what was left of a large domed building, now little more than a curved stone wall, crumbling and mossy. "That was once our meeting hall."

"What happened here?" Pan asked. "Avalanche or something?"

"No, our magic keeps us safe from that," Indu said. "But we were unprepared for the Grændöden."

"The Green Death?" I asked.

He looked back, his eyebrows arched in surprise. "You know of it?"

"I heard that it wiped out most of the *álfar* living here."

As we followed the overgrown roads that wound through the rubble, I spotted a large building that didn't look quite as forgotten as the rest. The wooden exterior was weathered and faded, but it wasn't overgrown like the others, and the roof appeared intact.

"That is true." Indu nodded. "But that was only the beginning. The fallout led to an uprising between tribes, and it was Vígríðabifröst that decimated our city."

"You fought with the other tribes?" I asked, trying to decipher what he meant. "In a battle for the bridge?"

He stopped walking so he could face us fully as he answered. "We fought a war that we lost. They destroyed our city, they outlawed the Älvolk, and they tried to erase us from history. But we could not be stopped so easily. To survive, we went underground."

He made a clicking sound at Ealga, and he led the elk into the building. From the scent alone, I gathered before we stepped inside that it was a stable. Pan and I followed hesitantly behind him, since he left the door open.

Through the barn doors and to the right was a large space with large butcher blocks in the center. Meat hooks hung from the ceiling, and the far wall was covered in various knives and tools. A pletheroa of antlers were left piled in a corner, while a large elk hide had been pulled taut to dry.

They butchered the animals right next to where the others slept, and that made my stomach turn.

Indu and Ealga walked down the stone aisle, past other elk chuffing in their large stalls. A young woman, maybe a couple years younger than me, was waiting outside an open stall, and Indu handed her the rope.

"He needs a brushing," Indu told her curtly, then he looked back at me and Pan. "If you could follow me this way."

The aisle eventually ended with a locked door, and on the other side was a spiral stone staircase leading down into the earth. I walked in front of Pan, glancing back over my shoulder at him as we descended.

The stairs ended at a large stone room. Other than the rugs on the floor and a few wooden chairs against the wall, it was empty. The only notable details were the stone arches— one on the north wall, one on the south wall.

Each of their keystones were marked with different but familiar symbols. The northern one had triskelion with vines that I recognized as the Älvolk sigil, and the leaves were marked with amber gemstones.

The other was one I had only seen once before, and it had been a tattoo on Jem-Kruk's friend Sumi. A serpentine dragon biting its own tail to form a perfect circle. On the keystone carving, green emeralds had been added for eyes.

"This is our main hall," Indu announced loudly, his voice echoing off the walls. "The Älvolk live in the north wing, and the thrimavolk live in the south wing." He gestured to the arched doorways that led out of the hall.

"Does Eliana live here?" I asked.

"No. She has never lived here, and she has not visited in quite some time. Years, I believe."

"What about Jem-Kruk?" I asked. "Or Sumi?"

"I don't know who either of them are," he replied curtly. "There is so much here that you have to see. I'm surprised that you're so focused on what isn't here."

"You're right." I smiled thinly. "Where should we start?"

"If you want to see others, I would suggest that we start with the thrimavolk. You could meet your sister," Indu suggested.

"Yes, I would like that."

"That would be this way." He went toward the arch marked with the dragon.

44

sisters

Through the archway was a spacious living area. The stone walls and floors were softened with colorful rugs and tapestries. At one end there were sofas lined with elk fur and leather, poised around a fireplace. Instruments—a lyre, a guitar, various drums—were stacked in a corner next to a bookcase.

The other end was more of a game area. There was what looked like an *økkspill* board on the wall, with the kasteren axes in a basket on the floor. A small table had a chessboard on it, and there was something that looked sort of like foosball but with wooden figures on ropes.

"These are the main living areas for the thrimavolk." Indu stopped in the middle of the room, his hands folded behind his back, as we took in the bright and slightly cluttered space. "The girls spend most of their downtime here, when they're not training or going to services."

"So this is basically a female wing?" Pan asked.

"That would be a scientific way of referring to it, yes," Indu replied carefully.

"Does that mean the wives stay here? Or girlfriends?" Pan pressed.

Indu licked his lips and spoke slowly. "We have no wives."

"But the thrimavolk are your daughters? As in your biological children?" Pan clarified.

As he'd been talking, he'd been subtly moving forward, putting himself between me and Indu. Not blocking me, not entirely, but his shoulder was in front of mine now, and he hadn't taken his eyes off Indu since we'd gotten down here.

"Yes. I have five biological daughters," Indu answered, and his smirk seemed to fade for the first time. "All of the thrimavolk are children of Älvolk."

"All girls?" Pan asked.

"Yes, but I made sure of that," Indu said.

I narrowed my eyes at him. "You made sure of that? How?"

"I always ate a powerful herb before I lay with a woman." Indu lowered his eyes when he said that, his dark olive skin flushing subtly in embarrassment. "That's how to ensure that your child will be a girl."

"Why?" I asked, and Pan looked back at me, his eyes pained and flickering with something darker. "Why was it so important to you to have daughters?"

"For the thrimavolk, of course," Indu replied, like that would be obvious.

"And what are the thrimavolk?" I asked.

"We are the only warriors strong enough to protect the kingdoms, not just from our world but the next," a strong female voice announced.

I jumped in surprise—I'd been so focused on Indu, I hadn't seen two tall young women come striding down the hall toward us. They wore long tunics similar to Indu's, except theirs were dark red and cinched around the waist with a black fabric belt.

The features of the girls were dramatically different—the one on the left was blond, blue-eyed, stick-thin, and the other slightly shorter, with tawny skin and dark eyes—but their hair was styled exactly the same. Long hair pulled back, with multiple braids tight to the scalp and interwoven with dyed leather straps, until they came out in ponytails. And they each wore two solid lines of cobalt and white painted from eye to eye above bold red lips, an effect that looked more like war paint than makeup.

It was the blond one talking, her voice deep with an accent heavy on her vowels. "And when the time comes, we will be the only ones strong enough to cross the bridge and take back what is ours."

They walked right up to us and stopped in unison, like trained soldiers.

Pan moved back and put his arm around my shoulders. "Oh. Wow. That is quite the mission statement."

"You guys definitely have more exciting job descriptions than we do," I agreed with an uneasy smile.

"That was quite the introduction, better than I would've hoped for," Indu said, sounding strangely delighted by this whole uncomfortable situation. "Ulla, *this* is your sister Noomi. Noomi, meet your little sister Ulla."

"Hi, it's nice to meet you." I started to extend my hand toward her, but she was glowering at me, her arms clasped behind her back, so I quickly retracted and leaned back into Pan, grateful for his arm around me.

"How would you know?" Noomi countered. "You haven't met me yet."

"Yeah, no, that's true," I stammered.

"I'm Pan. I'm her—" Pan stopped himself, probably realizing that saying anymore would only make us uncomfortable, and Noomi definitely didn't care. "Hello."

"I am Tuva," the shorter one announced, her dark eyes quickly shifting between me and Pan. "I am the chieftain of the thrimavolk."

"Noomi is her second-in-command," Indu interjected with pride. "They run things down here."

"You're both very impressive women," I said, trying to compliment them, but they both stared blankly at me.

"We were planning a feast for you tonight," Indu said, as if he had suddenly remembered. "I will head upstairs to see to its completion, and while I am attending to that, Noomi and Tuva can show you around. By the time dinner is ready, you will have made a choice whether or not you want to stay on for a few nights, and if you do, you can tell your friends to come join us."

"And if not?" Pan asked.

"If not, then you'll leave," he said flatly. "You're not being held against your will."

"To make it perfectly clear: you are not a prisoner," Noomi told me. "You're not being pressured or coerced to stay. In fact, you're hardly even welcome here. If you want to go, Tuva and I will be the first ones to show you the door."

"That is very clear," I said.

"I will check on you shortly. I'm sure you will come to enjoy each other's company." Indu gave Noomi a knowing look before he departed.

"So." Pan folded his arms over his chest as he eyed them. "How many of there are you?"

"Sixty-eight," Noomi replied instantly.

Tuva added, "Sixty-nine with you."

"If she makes it," Noomi grumbled.

"Not all the daughters can make it," Tuva said, speaking more softly, almost like a secret.

"And no men can?" Pan asked pointedly.

Noomi smirked, her wide slender mouth looking like her father's. "No, this isn't the work for boys."

"Are you Vittra?" Tuva asked him.

He shook his head. "No."

She leaned toward him and sniffed the air. "You smell like there's Vittra in you."

"I don't . . ." He glanced down at me. "Is that a compliment?"

She nodded. "I like the Vittra. They're strong and put up a fight."

"I can't tell if you're threatening me or flirting with me," he said.

"I think it's a bit of both," I said.

"She's right," Noomi said.

Tuva smiled wide, revealing her teeth, and then she snapped them together hard enough to make a *clacking* sound. I flinched, and Noomi chortled in response.

"What do you do here?" I asked, trying to ease the growing tension.

"Here we relax," Tuva replied simply, then pointed to the narrow corridor that broke off from the main room. "Down the hall are our rooms and bathrooms. At the very end, we have our gym and our study, where we do our training and our services."

"Training and services? What's that?" I asked.

"We spend most of our time training and preparing for the War to Come," Noomi replied gruffly.

"What War to Come?" Pan asked.

Noomi shrugged. "Whichever one comes next."

"There will always be another war, and we will be prepared for it," Tuva clarified. "But that doesn't mean it's all doom and gloom down here. We have games. We climb the mountains and hike. We have a choir."

Pan laughed in surprise. "You have a choir?"

"Yes," Tuva said. "If you stay for supper, Indu wants them to put on a performance for you."

"We look forward to hearing it." I smiled at them, even though they had yet to reciprocate.

"Does that mean you feel safe here?" Noomi asked.

"Should I?" I countered evenly.

She hardly thought before answering. "I wouldn't if I were you, but I don't trust anyone."

"You are Indudottir," Tuva said confidently. "You will be safe here. Your friends are allowed here for a short time, but they cannot stay for long. Áibmoráigi is home to the Älvolk and the thrimavolk, and nothing else. If you are not one of those two, your stay can only be temporary."

"We tried that before with Illaria, and it is not something I wish to do again," Noomi said wearily.

"Illaria?" I pounced on the name. "You know Illaria?"

Noomi scowled and exchanged a look with Tuva before finally answering, "She lived here for a while, until her sister fell ill and she had to go back home to care for her."

"Why did she stay here?" I pressed. "Indu said he wasn't her father. Is she thrimavolk?"

"No, she wasn't," Noomi said. "He dated her mother—your mother—when Illaria and Eliana were young. Their father had died, and Illaria became way too attached to *our* father."

"Indu needed to set more boundaries for her," Tuva added. "She was an ardent follower of our beliefs, but there was no place here for her. It is good that she went home."

I swallowed my uneasiness and forced a smile. "I only want to stay here long enough to get to know you and our father and find out what life is like here for you."

"Our life here is good," Noomi assured me in her flat, stilted style. "We have food, we have shelter, we have purpose, we have family. There is nothing more that life has to offer that we do not have."

45

Hymnal

The dining room glowed under the candles in the iron chandeliers. It was a surprisingly warm, lovely setup, with flowers and food spread across the table, and this was a nice introduction for Dagny and Elof. Things had been going well, so Indu and I had gone to retrieve them, and they joined everyone for dinner.

The table took up the entire room, and there still wasn't enough room for all of us. That was understandable, given there were twenty-seven Älvolk, sixty-eight thrimavolk, and then the four of us guests. Still, the seating seemed to be overwhelmingly inadequate, since over half of the thrimavolk had to eat elsewhere in a smaller dining hall.

Indu seated us at the end of the table. He sat himself to my right and Noomi to Dagny's left with Pan and Elof in the center. Tuva sat next to Noomi, but the rest of the thrimavolk were peppered around the table among the men.

Before the meal was served, Indu stood and everyone fell silent. "Tonight we all have much to celebrate. It's not often that we have guests, but it is a fitting way to rejoice at the return of my daughter, my morning flower." He raised his glass and smiled down at me. "Join in my welcoming them into our home! *Skol!*"

Everyone around the table shouted *Skol,* but I felt more like an animal on display than an invited guest. Indu had attempted to introduce us to the many young women and older men who sat around the table, but there had been far too many for us to remember.

Once the meal was served—heavy in root vegetables and bread with sour cheeses made of elk milk—seven girls marched in from another room. They wore elaborate costumes of deep cranberry and dark indigo, with bold embroidery in yellow thread creating intricate patterns along their boat necklines and down the centers of their garments. Their garb was something like a dress, with the solid fabric ending midthigh but brightly colored tassels continuing all the way down to the floor.

Their hair and makeup were very similar to Noomi and Tuva's, but these girls were more embellished, with jewels pasted to their foreheads and lots of chunky necklaces and earrings.

After the girls came out in a processional, they lined up in a semicircle at the end of the table across from us so we'd have the best view. Everyone at the table fell silent, putting down their utensils and looking at the girls.

Then they began to sing. It was a mournful, almost bluesy song, or maybe that was because of the way they accentuated their throaty baritones. I couldn't really tell if that was their natural vocal range, or if they'd trained to sing in such an unusually low manner.

It was a beautiful song, and their unique style of singing made it hauntingly melodic. The lyrics were in a language I didn't completely understand, something that sounded vaguely Nordic.

As far as I could tell, the song was something about a summer bird looking for a morning flower, but the bird was never able to find what it was looking for before nightfall.

When they finished we all applauded, and the choir bowed before exiting in a single file.

"That is a uniquely talented choir you have there," Elof said, sounding genuinely impressed as he watched them leave. "You have a truly special group here."

Indu lifted his glass as if to toast him. "That we do. We are all truly blessed here." He smiled as he surveyed everyone around the table.

Other than Noomi, Tuva, and the ones in the choir, most of the girls weren't wearing makeup of any kind. That made their scarification more obvious—dots carved into their flesh across their cheek and foreheads, shaped into simple horizontal patterns.

Now that I'd spotted the scarification on the others, I could more clearly see it on Noomi. She had had three staggered lines—each one made of five dots—beginning at the corner of each of her eyes.

The men didn't have any scarification that I noticed, but many of them were older, their faces lined with wrinkles, so maybe it was harder to see. There were a handful of younger men, in their teens and twenties, but facial hair helped hide their faces.

No one had given their ages, but Noomi and Tuva did

appear to be the oldest of the thrimavolk, and they looked about midtwenties, maybe a little older. The youngest at the table with us were in their lower teens, but Noomi made a comment about the "youngens eating in another room with their unrefined table manners."

When we finished our meal, the choir came in for another song, but by then I could hardly keep my eyes open. The day had been exhaustingly long, including a hike partway up a mountain, and I had a dull ache behind my eyes that I suspected was a lingering effect from whatever Indu had done with the painful *leat fámus*.

"I'm sorry, but I really need to get some sleep," I told Indu, speaking quietly as the girls sang something about a snail, if I heard correctly.

"Of course. Your journey has been long," Indu said, then looked across the table to Noomi. "Your sister will show you and your friend Dagny to your room. I can escort the men to their room now also, if that is what you wish."

"I'm actually not tired yet." Elof leaned back in his chair and looked at Pan. "What do you say? Would you stay up and join me for dessert?"

Pan shrugged. "I could stay up a while longer."

"I don't know how you two can do it." Dagny yawned as she stood. "I can't wait to get some sleep."

As I walked past Pan on the way out, I put my hand on his shoulder. "Be safe."

"I always am." He put his hand over mine and smiled up at me. "Sleep well, and I'll see you in the morning."

Noomi led us down the narrow corridors of the thrimavolk dormitory. They had given us a brief tour earlier, but it hadn't been much to see because most of the doors were shut, their occupants inside quietly busying themselves.

The rooms we had seen had mostly looked the same— each one contained two sets of bunk beds, with two or three girls sharing each room. There were a few personal effects scattered around the rooms—books, hairbrushes, dolls, jewelry, that kind of thing—but for the most part the spaces had a clean, almost sterile feel to them. The linens on the beds were military-taut.

Noomi took us to the room at the very end of the hall, and she smiled when she remarked, "It's right next to the bathroom."

Normally that would probably be a plus for your sleeping arrangements, but not in a place that didn't have running water. The bathroom had composting toilets made out of stone and wood, and it didn't smell as bad as I would've feared, but there was something unpleasant seeping through the door. Water brought up from a well was warmed, and some of the younger girls refilled the basins in the bathroom.

Our room itself was fine, following the same medieval institutional vibe the rest of the place was giving me. I tossed my duffel bag onto one of the bottom bunks, and Dagny sat on the bed across from it.

"Someone will get you in the morning when it's time for breakfast," Noomi told us as she lit the kerosene lamps on the two nightstands. "If you have trouble, knock on the bedroom three doors down. That is your nearest neighbor."

"There are empty rooms down here?" Dagny asked.

"There are many empty rooms."

"Then why do so many of you bunk up?" she asked,

referring to the four beds. "Wouldn't you rather have your own space?"

"No." Noomi stood rigidly in the center of the room, eyeing Dagny. "Would you like your own room? We assumed you'd rather be together for comfort."

"Together is fine," Dagny said, without checking to see how I'd respond, but that was what I would've answered anyway.

"Good." She walked out of the room and said, "*Idjá,*" before shutting the door.

Once she was gone, Dagny said in a hushed voice, "This place is intense."

"It is." I had my back to her as I spoke, focusing on pulling my old T-shirt out of my trag, eager to change out of dirty jeans and sweatshirt. "I want to talk more to Indu and Noomi tomorrow and see if I can find out anything about my mother or Eliana. But regardless of how that conversation goes, even if they don't tell me anything, I think we should leave."

"Elof won't want to leave so soon," she said in a bleak, resigned way. "He'll want to find out everything he can. I'm sure he's down there now interrogating them over pie."

I kept my back to her as I changed, but I trusted her to avert her eyes anyway. "Well, he better get as many answers as he can before tomorrow night, because that's when I'm leaving. I'll camp outside the restaurant on the lake if I have to."

"You think it's dangerous to stay another night?"

"I don't know." I sighed, then climbed into bed, pulling the stiff comforter over me as I tried to settle onto the firm mattress. "Ask me in the morning. Right now I'm exhausted, and I don't feel safe or comfortable here."

I stared up at the bunk above me and breathed in deeply, letting the cool, moist air fill my lungs. Tears stung my eyes and I blinked them back. "None of this is how I expected it go when I finally met my family," I admitted.

"I'm sorry, Ulla. I'm sure you'll feel better in the morning." She stood up. "I'm going to go to the bathroom to freshen up, as much as I can, and get changed."

I closed my eyes, and I swear I was asleep before she'd even left the room. My sleep was dark and dreamless, and it was wonderful, but it didn't last long enough. Sometime after Dagny had gone to bed, someone burst into our room.

"Indudottir," she was saying, and then she was shaking me awake, her deep voice like a growl in my ear. "Indudottir, wake up!"

"What?" I sat up and squinted in the darkness. In my sleepy state I could only think to say, "I'm Ulla. I think you've got the wrong room."

"No, Ulla, I know it is you," she said, and I realized it was Noomi, yanking me out of bed. "Your friend wants you."

"Dagny?" I asked.

"No, I'm okay, I'm right here," Dagny answered from the other side of the room.

"Not her, the other one. Pan. He's in the *medica* with the *häxdoktor*. He's hurt, and he's asking for you."

46

safety

The *medica*—the medical ward—was on the floor below, down another narrow stairwell. At the bottom of the steps was a sparse room with two beds, and the back wall was covered with shelves stocked with metal utensils, gauzy bandages, and tiny bottles of medicines and potions.

But my eyes went right to Pan, sprawled out on one of the beds. Elof stood on a stepstool beside a tall man in a dark hood—the *häxdoktor,* presumably—so he was chest high to the bed, presumably so it would be easier to see and talk with Pan. A kerosene lamp hung above Pan, bathing him in a warm yellow glow, and his white T-shirt had been ripped open, the fabric now stained with blood.

There was blood everywhere, actually. On the floor, on his jeans, soaking the bandages on the floor.

I gasped and rushed over to him, half expecting to see a pale corpse, but Pan smiled at me with bleary eyes.

"Hey, Ulla," he said weakly. He reached out for me with his right hand, and I saw a fresh bandage wrapped tightly around his forearm.

I took his hand and put my other hand on his chest. "What happened?"

"It's okay, it's okay," he said, assuring me with his crooked grin. "I was playing *økkspill* with Noomi, and the axe slipped."

"It's not my fault," Noomi interjected flatly. She'd brought me down here, and now she waited a step behind me, her hands clasped behind her back.

"He is all right now," Elof said, and his clear, authoritative way of speaking instilled far more confidence in me than Pan's easy smile and glassy eyes. "We've given him a transfusion."

"Yeah, I feel weird, but good." His eyes widened empathically. "Like really good."

"That could be the *dadarud*—a pain-relieving root we gave him," Elof explained. "It also has some mild hallucinatory properties, but he is definitely not in any pain at the moment."

"See?" Pan squeezed my hand and stared up into me eyes. "I'm great."

"I'd like him to sleep down here in the *medica*, though, so I can keep a better eye on him," the *häxdoktor* said. "He does really need some rest, but he will be fine."

"Perhaps we should clear out to let him sleep," Elof suggested.

"Is it okay if I stay a few minutes longer?" I asked.

Elof nodded. "Of course. We'll be right outside if you need us."

When they were gone, I turned back to Pan. His dark curls lay flat across his forehead, and I gently brushed them back. "Are you sure you're okay?

"Yeah, I'm fine. Honest." He laughed lightly. "You're so pretty when you're worried."

"Thanks? I think?"

He laughed again, harder this time. "No, I'm just saying you're beautiful. I feel like everything I'm saying is coming out weird, but I mean what I say anyway."

"You sound drunk," I commented.

"No, I didn't drink anything, not really, but since they gave me that girl's blood I have been feeling pretty darn good."

"Pretty darn good?" I teased.

"Yeah, really." He put his hand over mine. "I also feel like I really wanna kiss you."

I chewed my lip. "I don't know if you should in your condition."

"No, I know that I should." He propped himself up a bit with his good arm. I leaned down and kissed him gently on the mouth, but I cut it short, pulling back.

"What's wrong?" Pan asked.

"I'm still freaked out from you getting hurt."

"But I'm okay," he insisted.

"I know. I don't think I could've forgiven myself if something really bad happened to you because you followed me here."

He relaxed back down on the bed, content with just hold-ing my hand. "I would follow you anywhere, and it's worth whatever risk there is."

"You're so cute when you're all high on Älvolk medicine."

"I'm always cute," he joked.

"That's true," I agreed with a laugh, and he yawned loudly. "You're tired. I should let you sleep."

"Stay with me until I fall asleep." He tugged at my hand. "Please."

I nodded, so he scooted to the side, as much as the nar-row bed would allow, and I squeezed onto the edge beside him. I rested my head on his chest, and he wrapped his good arm around me. It didn't take him long to fall asleep, but I stayed with him a little bit longer, listening to his heartbeat and savoring the way his arm felt around me.

Eventually I untangled myself from him. I went toward the door when something caught my eye. Under the apoth-ecary table I saw a pink gemstone glinting in the light, and I crouched down to pick it up.

It was a friendship bracelet, woven with neon thread, dried flowers, and a few glimmering plastic gemstones. There was one large bead in the center: a Linnea twinflower covered in clear resin. I had seen it before; I had actually been the one to buy it for Hanna, back in Merellä. She'd used it on a bracelet that she had made for Eliana.

This was Eliana's bracelet.

She'd been here since she'd left with Illaria, and Indu had told me that it had been years since she'd visited here. But she was here, in the *medica*.

Indu was lying about her. How much of anything he said could I really believe?

I palmed the bracelet and hid it in my fist, and I was shaking slightly when I left the *medica*. Elof and the *häxdoktor* were talking outside of the room, and Elof assured me he'd be checking on Pan throughout the night.

As tired as I felt, I was strangely wired, and I didn't feel like sleeping. The dungeon-like dormitory felt more than a little claustrophobic, so I decided the answer was fresh air. On my way back to the room, I noted some thrimavolk standing guard—down the hall at the bottom of the steps that led up to the main door through the stables.

Dagny was already asleep again when I got back to our room, and I quietly pulled on my jeans and got out my Moleskine notebook and my cell phone. I'd turned it off when we got here to conserve the battery, and I turned it on now. It was after two in the morning, so the sun had risen after a brief civil twilight, and I grabbed the solar charger from my bag in hopes that there would be enough sunlight now. I fastened the bracelet around my wrist so I wouldn't lose it.

I didn't take the notebook with me—I didn't want to risk losing or damaging it—but for a minute I studied one of the maps I'd traced. I didn't think the thrimavolk would physically stop me from going outside, but I wanted to see if there was a way to get out without them knowing.

It was something that Finn had always taught me to do. Make sure you know all the exits.

This is exactly why I had copied the maps of Áibmoráigi from the book back in the archives—so I would know how to get around if I ever found myself there. The map showed a well with a ladder in it next to the bathroom in the girls' dorm. The water it tapped was miles below the surface, so a doorway opened into the tunnel.

After the commotion because of Pan's injury, everyone had apparently gone to sleep, and the halls were dark and quiet. I used my phone flashlight to light my way, and the door to the well was fairly easy to find.

The door was heavy iron and didn't open easily, and it took my superior strength to open it, but I managed to do that with only one loud grunt from me and one tiny creak from the door. It opened to a big hole—one end running down to the water, and the other going up toward the sun.

I slid my phone in my back pocket and grabbed the mossy ladder that ran up the stone well wall. Then I leaned back and closed the door carefully behind me. I made it up the ladder only slipping and worrying about death three times.

Outside, I breathed in deeply, relishing the fresh air in my lungs even if it was stinging cold.

The ruins of the First City sat on a flat plateau jutting out from the mountain, and the edge of the city ended in a sharp drop-off. I walked over to the edge of the cliff, and I sat down and folded my legs under me, watching the sun rise over the mountains. I touched the bracelet on my wrist, toying with the flowered bead.

"Where are you, Eliana?" I whispered.

My phone dinged in my pocket.
It was a message from Hanna.

I tried calling but I couldn't get through. I'm assuming you're safe and just far out, because that's what you told me you'd be up to. But you better be taking lots of pictures. If you get enough signal, we should video chat. I hate that I'm here and missing out on all the action.

Sorry I've been silent for a few days. Mom grounded me from the internet because of some stupid fight I had with Liam, who was the one being a snot and not me. But that's a story for another day, as you would say.

Have you heard anything about Eliana yet? I keep asking Dad to help, and he says he's talked to the Queen and the Chancellor, but he doesn't think there's really anything we can do, since we didn't know that much about her.

I would just feel a lot better if I could talk to her, or even if I just knew that you'd talked to her or something. She's my friend, and it sucks that I don't have any way to talk to her.

The book I'm reading is called *Jem-Kruk and the Adlrivellir*. You probably haven't heard of it. It was in with my dad's stuff, not Finn but my bio dad. My grandfather Johan actually wrote the book. Mom says he was some kind of children's author and a historian, which is why I think some of the stuff he wrote is so accurate. He based it on real stuff he knew.

Anyway, I'm sure you're busy, and I gotta go. Call me when you get a chance.

-Hanna

Along with the message, she'd included a couple photos she'd snapped of the book info, a title page that had been missing from my own copy.

JEM-KRUK AND THE ADLRIVELLIR
An Adventure Story for Children

By Johan Nordin

UNDERVERK PRESS
Publishers   Förening
Published in conjuction with
the Trylle Kingdom overseen by
HRM King Mikel Dahl
MCMXC

Hanna's grandfather wrote the book. He knew so much about Jem-Kruk and the place he came from. How had he known all this? And why hadn't he told me he'd written the book when I was at his house? Why would he hide it?

Eliana's bracelet felt heavy on my wrist. She'd been here, and Indu and Noomi—my father and my half-sister—were hiding that from me.

Why? And what the hell was going on around here?

The bracelet tickled my wrist, and when I looked down, I saw it wasn't the bracelet but a inky black spider crawling up my arm. I flicked it away and scooted back from the edge of the cliff, right into waiting arms. Long fingers wrapped around my face, cold and strong, and blotted out the sunlight.

47
❦

visionary

I tried to scream, but I couldn't. It was trapped in my throat, like with the Ögonen when they'd caught me in the Catacombs of Fables back at the Mimirin. But this time I was paralyzed too, my limbs frozen in place as I gasped in the darkness.

But suddenly there was light in the darkness. A green fog that I was flying above, and then I zoomed in toward it. None of it was of my own accord. Rather, I was being dragged along by some unknown force, pulled into the emerald cloud, which smelled of sulfur and ash.

My vision cleared. I couldn't turn my head to look around, but behind me I heard something chasing after me. It made a thunderous roar, twisted with a painful shrieking.

Then I was plunging down, underneath the cloud and into cloud water. But that only lasted a moment, an icy few seconds where I couldn't breathe, and then I was surging out, gasping for air as I flew up over a waterfall.

I was spinning, spiraling really, and the waterfall was below me, disappearing back into the darkness it had sprung from.

Suddenly I was falling again, and a grassy field came into view hundreds of meters below. I fell through the sky, where rust-red vultures circled, and I was plummeting toward the meadow. It was empty, except for three yellow flowers, and I closed my eyes shut, bracing for impact.

But instead, I landed on my back gently on the soft grass, and I opened my eyes to the bright blue sky above me. I was lying on the cliff in the ruins of Áibmoráigi again, and I was gasping for breath.

I sat up and scrambled back from the edge, frantically looking over my shoulders until I saw the Ögonen standing to the south of me. They looked like the ones I had seen back at Merellä, with the light shining through their semitransparent ocher skin.

They had no mouth but wide dark eyes, and they stared down at me. Slowly, they raised their slender arm and pointed toward the south side of Áibmoráigi. I followed their fingertip, and I saw a white woolly elk walking toward the south side of the city.

I got to my feet, and I followed the elk, walking the past the Ögonen and following the winding paths through the crumbling stones. Beyond what Indu had shown me when he'd brought me into the First City.

And there at the far southern point, where the bluffs ended against the steep mountain face, there was an arched stone bridge spanning over a steep canyon. The woolly elk paused before the bridge, looking back over its shoulder, the cinnamon-red eyes on me. When it started walking again, I followed it over the bridge.

I didn't look down, because I knew if I did, I wouldn't be

able to take another step. The stone bridge was narrow with no parapets on the side, nothing to prevent me from falling over the edge and down, down, down . . . I took a deep breath and slowly made my way across.

The albino elk was walking faster, not quite trotting, but before I could reach the other side of the bridge, the elk had started to round the mountain. I ran, the bridge shaking underneath me, and I stumbled at the end and fell onto the plateau. The grass and dirt softened my fall, and I got to my feet and ran onward, but I didn't see the woolly anymore.

On this side of the bridge, across the canyon that separated me from the ruins of Áibmoráigi, the air smelled sweeter, and I could hear the sound of rushing water echoing off the cliffside and mountains.

I chased after where the elk had been, but there was no sign of it. Just a wide grassy ledge curving around the mountain. It was angled, with rocks and small boulders hiding in long grass for me to trip over or slip on as I scrambled along.

When I finally rounded the mountain, my bare feet slipping in the mud, I found myself face-to-face with a waterfall. It was tall, with the water coming from a spring far above me, but the way it spread across the rocks, it didn't seem that heavy. There was an ethereal, almost gossamer quality to the water.

If I had to guess, I was about a quarter of the way from the top of the waterfall. The fast-moving water had cut through the land around me, and the pool at the bottom of the falls was hundreds of meters below.

When the coursing water broke over the ledge, it flowed down the mountainside to join the chain of lakes in the valley below. There was nowhere else to go. The elk had disappeared into thin air.

The bridge had connected Áibmoráigi with a bumpy path winding around a mountain ending in a broad plateau jutting out from sheer mountainface so that it seemed more like an island floating in the sky. It curved around the mountain, and it ended when the waterfall cut through it.

I stepped back, trying to see if there was anything I had missed, and that's when I really saw how familiar and beautiful the waterfall looked. I had never seen this one before, but I had seen another like it, in the faded pages of Mr. Tulin's old nature magazines. *Catarata velo de la novia* in Peru, which roughly translated to the Bridal Veil Waterfall in English, had gotten its name because when you looked at it from the right angle, the falling water made a silhouette like a woman standing in her bridal veils.

And that's what I saw now, but not a woman in her bridal veils.

"'Remember to find the woman in the long white dress,'" I whispered.

48

Falls

I climbed up the rocks around the waterfall, scanning the cliffside and rushing waters for any sign of an entrance or anything that would lead me to Eliana. I hadn't seen anything so far, so I was trying to get higher for a better vantage point. Or maybe the entrance was at the top of the waterfall. Or maybe even higher, but the peak of the mountain was a sheer journey—many kilometers straight up.

"What are you doing out here, so far from home?"

I whirled around to see her standing behind me. Her skin was shifting—like the Kanin tribes, she'd shown the ability to change her skin to match the environment, much like a chameleon, and even the delicate gown she wore changed, the green grass and gray stone becoming a sheer lavender fabric flowing around her.

This all gave her the effect of materializing out of thin air as she stepped toward me. Her pale green hair was long and free, and she tilted her head as her lips pulled into an odd, pouty smile.

And that's when I realized it wasn't her. The smile wasn't

quite right, and she had a scar on her cheek—a little mark like a tiny hook.

"You're not her," I realized, and her smile widened, revealing her bright teeth. "You're Illaria."

"So I am. I should've known you'd be able to tell the difference. It must be one of those sisterly things," she said.

"You did know about me, then?" I swallowed hard. "You knew that we were sisters."

She sneered at me. "Of course I did, but because I know something doesn't mean I feel the need to tell everyone about it. For example, I know that you're nothing but a disgusting troglodyte, and I would be bappers if I willingly claimed you as part of my family tree.

"Don't look so offended," she snapped at me. "My mother was descended from Kings, and you're *this*."

"*Alai*, did you lure me out here just to make fun of me?" I asked—shouted at her, really. "What is wrong with you?"

"Lured you? I didn't lure you anywhere." Illaria shook her head. "I followed you to make sure you didn't get into any trouble."

"What about the albino elk?"

She instantly perked up. "What albino elk?"

I rubbed my temple. "It doesn't matter. I don't care. Where is Eliana? I want to see her."

"She doesn't want to see you!" Illaria yelled at me. "The only reason she even went to find you is because she was losing her mind. Eliana's always been little off-balance, but after Mama died, she spiraled out of control. Going after you was the final indignity in a long list of disappointing mistakes on her part."

"Why can't I see her?" I demanded.

"Because she's not here, and you can't go where she is." Illaria had had enough and she threw her hands up in the air. "It doesn't matter. You're not going to be allowed to go anywhere anymore."

"What are you talking about?" I stepped back from her, but there wasn't really anywhere to go.

Illaria was standing right in front of me, blocking the way back to the bridge. Behind me, the waterfall cut through the ground, and the plunge pool was too far down for me to land safely, and the rocks around the falls were too slick for me to climb quickly.

"I told Indu not to let you come here. I told him that you were an unruly mistake and that you did not belong here, not with our kind." She stepped toward me, and the skin around her eyes became a dazzling array of reds, shifting out like fire from her eyes.

"But he *needs* his daughters," she said, taking another step toward me. "So few of his have made it to age, and he can't let go of what little he does have, even if they end up like you."

"I don't even want to be here. Just let me go back and get my stuff and I'll be on my way," I said. "I won't ever step foot here again, and I'll stop bothering everyone about Eliana. It's clear that the two of you don't want anything to do with me, and I'm happy to leave you alone."

"Oh, I know you will. I'll make sure of it," she growled with a smile.

This was not heading anywhere good, and I might only have one chance at this, so I knew I had to make it count. I swung at her, but she dodged out of the way, and I dismally remembered how Eliana had been able to hop around our apartment like an Olympic gymnast. And as Illaria dove away from my next swing, I realized that she definitely took after her sister in that regard.

Illaria kicked me, her foot connecting painfully with my abdomen, and I stumbled backward and fell to the ground. My head hung over the edge of the plateau beside the falls, the cold water misting my face, and when she came at me again, I kicked her back with both my feet. She went soaring backward, and I scrambled up away from the edge.

When I was up again, she charged at me. I faked to the left toward the edge, and when she got close, I jerked to the other side. I caught her, and I slammed her back into the solid rock wall surrounding the waterfall, and she let out a pained scream.

"What is your problem?" I shouted at her. "What do you want from me?"

"I want this to be over." She grimaced, and then in a high-pitched scream she shrieked, *"Nohkihit!"*

Pain shot through my skull, my body went limp, and then everything went black.

49

memorialize

The *medica* wasn't the only thing on the floor beneath the living areas in the Älvolk's underground compound. There was also a dungeon, with thick iron bars and cold stone walls. That's what I found out when I woke up, sharing a cell with Dagny. Across from us, locked behind their own bars, were Pan and Elof.

The story they'd been told, after Noomi and Tuva found them, put them in shackles, and dragged them down here, was that Illaria had caught me breaking into someplace where I didn't belong. To restrain me, she'd been forced to knock me unconscious, and now none of us could be trusted, so they'd had to lock us all up.

Dagny recounted the incident while she was sitting on a wooden bunk, and then she mentioned that they had stolen from her. They'd dumped out her backpack when they dropped her here, taken anything of interest, and left her with some of her clothing, a few paper clips, a pen, and scraps of paper.

Apparently they'd done that with Pan as well, but he had gotten the rest of his clothes back. Neither Elof nor I had gotten any of our stuff back at all. Pan had piled up his shirts to make a pillow, and he was sprawled out on the bunk attempting to sleep, while I stood with my face resting against the cold bars, staring down the dark empty hallway.

"So do all your sisters hate you?" Dagny asked.

"It really does seem that way, yep," I agreed tiredly. "It kinda seems like they were right to abandon me as a baby."

"No, Ulla, don't say that," Pan said, apparently ditching his attempt to sleep.

"I didn't mean it like that," Dagny said, her tone soft and apologetic. "Honestly, it sounds like your family is all a bunch of selfish jerks."

"Maybe I'm a jerk," I said with a tired shrug, and I wasn't sure if it was true or what I meant anymore. My head still hurt from whatever had happened with Illaria, and I felt exhausted and sore deep within my bones.

It was hard not to wonder what I might have done to deserve this.

"Ulla," Dagny chastised me. "You're not a jerk, and you know it."

"None of this is as bad as it seems," Elof chimed in, managing to sound a bit more optimistic than the rest of us. "I have a dead man's code in place."

"What's that?" I asked.

"It's a fail-safe. If Patrik in Isarna doesn't hear back from me, I left him with specific instructions to let the Mimirin and the Vittra Kingdom know, and as soon as the Vittra Queen hears her prestigious adviser and scientist is being held hostage, she will work to get us back," Elof explained. "The Vittra might not be able to find our location, but Indu will eventually leave, to trade, to find his daughters, to make more daughters. The Vittra will make him miserable until he releases us."

"The Vittra can always be counted on to make everyone miserable," Dagny muttered.

"No matter what, it seems like I'll have plenty of time to think about whatever the heck I'm going to do when I get out of here," I said with a groan. "I blew my internship, I found my family but they're a nightmare, and I will probably never see Eliana again, which might be for the best because she probably hates me."

"Eliana definitely doesn't hate you," Dagny corrected me. "And we'll get out of here, and we'll figure out what is really going on with you. I don't trust everything I've heard around here, and I don't think you should either."

"That *häxdoktor* told me some interesting things about hemosterin and glimocytes," Elof said. "I think they may know more about blood here than we do back at the Mimirin."

Dagny stopped her doodling to look up at him. "What do you mean?"

"The blood they gave Pan had glimocytes, a more powerful form of leukocytes unique to trolls, and that—in combination with the *dadarud*—is what made him so happy," Elof elaborated.

"I was very happy." Pan smiled wistfully. "I'm still kind of a little happy right now, honestly, even though this situation is objectively really terrible and I feel so bad for everything that you're going through, Ulla."

There was a loud bang at the end of the hall when the door swung open, followed by fast, deliberate footfalls echoing off the walls. The light cast Noomi's long shadow, so I saw that before I saw her stalking toward me.

Her hair was pulled up the same way it had been yesterday, but she'd forgone the makeup, so the staggered scarred lines beside her eyes were far more pronounced than they had been. Her eyes were more noticeable, too, a pale foggy blue below beneath harsh eyebrows.

She was smiling as she approached, which I immediately took to be a bad sign, and then she reached through the bars and thrust a book at me. "I went through your things, and I took this book for a good laugh."

It was Johan's book about Jem-Kruk, and I took it from her tentatively, afraid this was a trick I didn't understand. "I'm glad that invading my privacy and mocking me is so entertaining to you."

"You know this is all elk shit, right?" Noomi sneered at me.

I tried to laugh her off. "It's a fairy tale for kids."

"No, it's all exaggerated to make Jem-Kruk sound like he's some sort of folk hero, but he's not." She shook her head forcefully, making her ponytail sway. "He's a selfish coward, and I easily bested him in hand-to-hand combat."

"What are you talking about? You know Jem-Kruk?" I asked.

"Of course, I do." She scoffed at me like I was an idiot. "He was friends with your mother. He visited with her once before she died, back when Illaria still lived here. And all that stuff about Senka, that sounds inflated to me too. Your mother never seemed that brave."

Dagny came up behind me and asked her, "Are you guys saying that you actually know the characters from this storybook in real life?"

"They aren't storybook characters," she corrected sharply. "They're real."

"No, wait, go back," I said, as my mind replayed what she had been saying. "Senka. Senka from that book is my mother?"

"No, I told you. The Senka from this book is a *caricature* of your mother," Noomi said. "She was rude and not brave at all."

"That doesn't . . ." I stared down at the worn cover. "This book was written a long time ago, and Jem-Kruk is still young. But in the book, it says he's the same age as Senka." I looked up at her. "When were the twins born?"

"I don't know, and I don't care enough to get into it," she replied dismissively, and her smile was slowly returning. "Besides, it's not like you'll remember any of this anyway."

"What are you talking about?" I asked.

"I will say this about you. Your friends work very fast," she said, sounding pained to voice even the briefest of commendations. "Father has already gotten word that he is to return you to your home across the ocean. We will let you leave, because we have to, and because Father can never bear to sacrifice one of his children.

"You will go, but you will not remember any of this," Noomi promised me. "The Ögonen here are very mighty, and they are under Tuva's command. She will harness their power for the *inovotto muitit*. The *inovotto muitit* is absolute agony as the memories are ripped from your mind, and it will make the *leat fámus* seem like a stroll through a meadow."

"Why do you hate me so much?" I asked her emptily. "What did I ever do to you?"

"I hate you because you exist," she said coldly. She tossed my bag into the cell—now empty of so many of my belongings it had become deflated enough to easily fit through the bars—and then she turned and stalked off down the hall.

"Do you still have the pen?" I asked Dagny after I heard the door swing shut again, sounding Noomi's departure. I started digging through my bag right away, tearing through my clothes, but I couldn't find my Moleskine notebook anywhere. "They must've taken it."

"What?"

"They're going to try to make us forget," I said, and then I had another idea. "I need your pen."

"Here." She handed it to me.

I opened the *Jem-Kruk and the Adlrivellir* book to a blank page near the back. I didn't know how much time I had, so I started writing everything I knew I'd want to remember.

Senka is your mother, Indu is your father
Don't Trust Noomi or Illaria
They're Your Sisters but they LIE
Áibmoráigi is on the northwest mountain beyond Lake Sodalen
The Woman in the Long White Dress is the waterfall
Find the waterfall, find Eliana
Jem-Kruk might be a liar
You and Pan kissed (and you both liked it)

When I finished, I handed the pen back to Dagny, and she made her own list in the margins of my book.

With that done, we were left to wait, and hope that we'd done enough. That we had left ourselves enough bread crumbs that we'd know what really happened here no matter what Noomi or Illaria or any of the Älvolk had planned for us.

GLOSSARY

Abisko National Park—a national park in the Arctic Circle in northern Sweden. It is located over an hour's drive away from Kiruna Airport.

Adlrivellir—the name of a legendary troll kingdom.

Áibmoráigi—the oldest troll establishment on earth. It is located somewhere in Scandinavia, but its exact location has been lost since before 1000 CE. Frequently referred to as the "First City."

akutaq—a traditional Inuit food often referred to as "Eskimo ice cream." It is not creamy ice cream as we know it, but a concoction made from reindeer fat or tallow, seal oil, freshly fallen snow or water, fresh berries, and sometimes ground fish. It is whipped together by hand so that it slowly cools into foam.

álfar—the name given to the trolls from the legendary kingdom of Alfheim.

Alfheim—a mythological realm. To humans, the legend is that it is one of the Nine Worlds and home of the Light Elves in Norse mythology. To trolls, the legend is that it is a utopian kingdom hidden across the Lost Bridge of Dimma.

Älvolk—a legendary group of monk-like trolls, who guard the Lost Bridge of Dimma, along with many troll secrets and artifacts.

angakkuq—an Inuit word that roughly translates to "shaman" or "witch."

ärtsoppa—a Scandinavian soup made of yellow peas, carrots, and onions. Traditional versions have ham, but vegetarian trolls skip that.

Attack on Oslinna—a surprise military attack by the Vittra on the small Trylle village of Oslinna, Wyoming, during the War for the Princess. It left the city destroyed since January 2010.

attempted assassination of Chancellor Iver—the attempt on the life of the Kanin Chancellor Iver Aven by the Queen's guard Konstantin Black in January 2010. It was an attack unrelated to the War for the Princess. It was eventually tied to Viktor Dålig and his coup against the Kanin monarchy that lasted over a decade and ended in the Invasion of Doldastam.

Aurenian Ballroom—a grand ballroom in the Mimirin named after the old Vittra King Auren.

Battle for the Bridge—a legendary battle over the Lost Bridge of Dimma that took place in Áibmoráigi over a thousand years ago. In old myths, it is known as the Vígríðabifröst.

Bay of Bothnia—the northernmost part of the Gulf of Bothnia, which is in turn the northern part of the Baltic Sea. The bay today is fed by several large rivers and is relatively unaffected by tides, so it has low salinity. It freezes each year for up to six months.

Bedtime Stories for Trolls of All Ages—a children's book of troll fables and stories. It contains an origin story about how all the tribes separated.

beetroot salad—a common Scandinavian dish. It is traditionally made with diced beetroots, apples, vinegar, herbs, olive oil, red onions, yogurt, and lemon zest.

blodseider magick—a type of taboo occult practice in extremist troll sects. The practice of *seiðr* is believed to be a form of magic relating to both the telling and shaping of the future.

bullhead kabob—a common meal in Fulaträsk, made with the swamp fish bullheads and peppers. It is described as salty and chewy.

Candida viridi—a fungal infection that afflicts trolls, similar to *Candida auris* in humans. The differences are that *C. viridi* is hearty enough to thrive in cold temperatures and that it leaves a greenish tint to the skin of the affected individuals. The fungus causes invasive candidiasis infections in the bloodstream, the central nervous system, and internal organs. With modern medicine it is easily curable, but without proper treatment it is often deadly. Troll historians believe that *C. viridi* is what caused the Green Death (Grændöden) in the thirteenth century, which wiped out most of the trolls that remained in Scandinavia.

Catacombs of Fables—a mazelike vault in the basement of the Mimirin that houses many of the fictional stories of the past, so as not to confuse fact with fiction.

chadron—a thistle in Louisiana, semi-common in meals and in foraging.

changeling—a child secretly exchanged for another. For trolls, it's an ancient practice, with elite royal families leaving their babies in place of wealthy human babies. The humans unknowingly raise the troll baby, ensuring that the troll will have the best chance of success, with fine education, top health care, and rights to tremendous wealth. When they are of age, they are retrieved by trolls known as trackers, and the changelings are brought back to live with their tribes in their kingdom. The Trylle and the Kanin are the only two tribes that still widely practice changelings.

chromosomes—DNA molecules with part or all of the genetic material of an organism.

Churchill, Manitoba—a small human town in Canada. One must stop in Churchill if venturing to either Doldastam, Manitoba, or Iqaluit, Nunavut, and it may be the easiest way to get to Iskyla, Nunavut, as well.

cloudberry—an herb native to alpine and arctic regions, producing amber-colored edible fruit similar to the raspberry or blackberry. It is commonly used in Scandinavian pies and jams.

Dålig Revolt—the uprising that took place after the unmarried Kanin King Elliot Strinne died unexpectedly in 1999 without a clear heir. The Chancellor appointed Elliot's cousin Evert Strinne to the throne, overlooking Elliot's sister Sybilla and her three daughters. Sybilla and her husband, Viktor Dålig, contested Evert's appointment, and they staged a revolt that left four men dead. The Dålig family was exiled.

docent—a member of the teaching staff immediately below professorial rank. In the U.S., it is often a volunteer position, but it can be paid or done in exchange for room and board. At the Mimirin, docents are paid a minimal stipend in addition to room and board.

dödstämpel—a form of martial arts practiced by trolls. The name means "death punch" in Swedish.

dökkt rúgbraud—a Scandinavian dark rye bread.

Doldastam, Manitoba—the capital and largest city of the Kanin kingdom, located in Manitoba, Canada, near Hudson Bay. The Kanin royal family lives in the palace there, and the city is surrounded by a stone wall. The population is a little over twelve thousand as of 2019.

Eftershom, Montana—a small Trylle village located in the mountains near Missoula. It is nestled in the convergence of several (real) mountain ranges in western Montana. The terrain is notoriously rough and the winters are brutal. When it was originally settled by the Trylle, a Markis asked "Why do we stop here?" And the leader answered, "Eftersom vi har gått tillräckligt långt," which roughly translates to, "Because we have gone far enough."

ekkálfar—an old term used for "troll."

eldvatten—a very strong alcohol made by the Omte. The name literally translates to "firewater." It is also known as Omte moonshine, and it is used in Omte sangria.

ex nihilo nihil fit—a Latin phrase meaning "nothing comes from nothing." It is the motto of the Mimirin.

First City, the—see *Áibmoráigi*.

Förening, Minnesota—the capital and largest city of the Trylle kingdom. It is a compound in the bluffs along the Mississippi River in Minnesota where the palace is located.

Forsa River—the river that runs through Merellä. It is a wide stream that slices the city in half and meets the ocean. The name means "rushing stream."

Frey—a mythological figure. To humans, he is known as the legendary Norse deity of virility and fair weather. To trolls, he is a troll from Alfheim who stayed behind to help rebuild their kingdom after the Battle for the Bridge. He is a prominent figure in the Älvolk cult, the Freyarian Älvolk.

Freyarian Älvolk—the followers of the Älvolk who began following the more extreme teachings of Frey. See *Frey*.

Fulaträsk, Louisiana—the capital city of the Omte, spread out in the trees and swamps of the Atchafalaya Basin in Louisiana.

gädda—the Swedish name for pike. See: *northern pike*.

geitvaktmann—a goat watchman, similar to a shepherd or a peurojen.

giant woolly elk—a name that trolls have given the line of Irish elk they breed. See *Irish elk*.

gräddtårta—a Swedish cream-layer cake. Common during Midsommar.

Grændöden—a plague. See: *Green Death*.

Green Death, the—a mass death of Scandinavian trolls that took place in the thirteeth century. Troll historians believe that it was caused by an outbreak of *C. viridi*.

häxdoktor—a witch doctor or shaman.

Heimskaga—a collection of ancient troll history, all written by the same troll historian, Hilde Nilsdotter. The name is an anglicization of the Norse words *heim* and *saga*, meaning "the world's saga."

Hilde Nilsdotter—the Scandinavian historian and author of the *Heimskaga*. She was born a Marksinna in 1190 in Sweden. Her husband was a troll ambassador, and they moved to Doldastam in 1211, shortly after their marriage. She used her travels to compile the folklore and histories of her kind, before her death in 1254. She had two children who lived until adulthood: Knut and Norri, the latter of which has lineage that can be traced down to the most recent Kanin dynasty, Strinne, up to and including Linus Berling.

hnefatafl—a family of ancient Nordic and Celtic strategy board games played on a checkered or latticed game board with two armies of uneven numbers.

hobgoblin—an ugly troll that stands no more than three feet tall, known to be born only into the Vittra tribes. Hobgoblins are slow-witted, possess a supernatural strength, and have slimy skin with a pimply complexion.

host family—the family that a changeling is left with. They are chosen based on their ranking in human society, with their wealth being the primary consideration. The higher-ranked the member of troll society, the more powerful and affluent the host family their changeling is left with.

Hudson Bay—a large bay in Canada. Doldastam is located on the Manitoba side, with Iqaluit across the bay on the Nunavut side.

Information Styrelse—a committee in charge of information (similar to a board of education) in the Mimirin. These boards are subordinate only to their members and the Korva, and they preside over the Mästares and the teaching staff (including docents). The name comes from the Swedish word *styrelse*, meaning "board of directors." The word *information* is the same in both Swedish and English. Each of these boards has thirteen members.

Inhemsk Project—an effort undertaken by the Mimirin in Merellä to help trolls of mixed blood find their place in the troll world. Though it is primarily run by the Vittra, it is open to trolls from any of the five tribes. The main purpose is to combat the dwindling populations of the trolls (due both to issues like infertility among the Vittra and Skojare, as well as changelings choosing to live among the humans or being exiled because of their mixed race). The effort also seeks to reconnect trolls with their heritage and pass along history and culture.

inovotto muitit—an incantation meaning "never remember." The Älvolk use it to erase memories.

Invasion of Doldastam—the final battle in the Kanin Civil War that ended the war in May 2014. The Dålig supporters were led by Viktor and Karmin Dålig allied with the Kanin guards and the Omte, and the Strinne supporters were led by Bryn Aven and Mikko Biâelse allied with the Skojare, Trylle, Vittra, and many of the Kanin townsfolk. The Strinne supporters were victorious in the Invasion of Doldastam, and the invasion ended with the traitors being executed and Linus Berling coronated as the King of the Kanin.

Iqaluit, Nunavut—the capital city of Canada's northernmost province. It has a large Inuit population, but most residents can speak English. Despite being the largest city in Nunavut, it has a population of only around seven thousand. Nunavut has no roads connecting the towns to one another, and it is only accessible by plane, usually flying in from Winnipeg or Churchill in Manitoba.

Irish elk—a species of deer believed to be extinct; also known as the giant deer. It is believed to be one of the largest species of deer, but humans hunted them to extinction in the wild thousands of years ago. The Vittra have been secretly breeding and raising them, and they are known as "giant woolly elk" or "woollies." They stand about 2.1 meters tall at the shoulders, carrying the largest antlers of any known cervid, and they can weigh over fifteen hundred pounds.

irytakki—a language only spoken in Alfheim.

Isarna, Sweden—an island and village in the Kalix archipelago in the Bay of Bothnia in Sweden. It is a Trylle/Skojare co-op, and the largest—and essentially only—troll settlement in Scandinavia and is accessible only by ferry or boat. The name means "islands of ice." The nearest human settlement is Nikkala, on mainland Sweden.

Iskyla, Nunavut—a small Kanin village, it is one of the northernmost troll communities in the world. Some Inuit humans also live there. It has become a dumping ground for unwanted babies. The name translates to "ice." In 2014, Iskyla had a population of 878.

Jakob W. Rells University of Parapsychology and Medicine—a university in Seattle, Washington. Rells University is renowned for paranormal and scientific studies, sometimes referred to as the Harvard of parapsychology. It was established by renowned telekinetic expert and medical doctor Jakob W. Rells in 1889. Rells presented as human, but he is suspected to have been from the Trylle kingdom.

Kanin—one of the most powerful of the five troll tribes. They are considered quiet and dogmatic. They are known for their ability to blend in, and, like chameleons, their skin can change color to help them blend in to their surroundings.

Like the Trylle, they still practice changelings, but not nearly as frequently. Only one in ten of their offspring are left as changelings. The Kanin are also the oldest tribe of trolls, having been the original troll tribe before the brothers Norund the Younger and Jorund the Elder fought about moving south in circa 1200 CE. Norund stayed in the north, strengthening the Kanin in Doldastam, while his brother went south and established the Vittra in Ondarike.

Kalix Skärgård—a group of 792 Swedish islands in the north part of the Bay of Bothnia. *Skärgård* literally means "archipelago" or "string of islands" in Swedish. A few of the islands have small permanent populations, but most are used only for recreation in the summer months. They are icebound during the winter.

Karelian Piiraka—a Finnish rye pastry. Rye-crusted, handheld pies with rice porridge as the most common filling, but a mix of root vegetables as filling is a frequent variation.

kasteren axe—a small hatchet with curved blades, similar to an ulu knife, and a long, slender handle. Used in the game of *økkspill*. The name means "thrower."

Kebnekaise—the highest mountain in Sweden. The Kebnekaise massif, which is part of the Scandinavian Mountains, has two main peaks, of which the southern, glaciated one is highest at 2,097.5 meters (6,882 feet) above sea level as of August 2014. The mountain is in Swedish Lapland, about 150 kilometers (93 miles) north of the Arctic Circle.

klampiveleska—an *álfar* term for spouse or life partner; the literal translation is "the one you fondly choose to be joined with."

Korva—a title for the Mimirin dean. The name means "crown." The Korva is the highest position in the Mimirin.

Lake Sodalen—an elongated mountain lake in the valley of the Kiruna municipality in the Swedish Lapland. In summer, boat traffic runs on the lake. The name means "valley lake."

leat fámus—an incantation meaning "to be open."

Lost Bridge of Dimma—a legendary bridge in troll mythology—akin to the city of Atlantis or the Hanging Gardens of Babylon—that is watched over by the Älvolk. The bridge was alleged to have connected the ancient troll city Áibmoráigi to the utopian kingdom of Alfheim, and it was believed to have collapsed before the end of the Viking Age (circa 1000 CE). The bridge was lost and the First City of Áibmoráigi was destroyed during the Battle for the Bridge, also known as Vígríðabifröst.

lysa—a telekinetic ability related to astral projection that allows one troll to psychically enter another troll's thoughts through a vision, usually a dream.

mänsklig—often shortened to *mänks*. The literal translation for the word *mänsklig* is "human," but it has come to describe the human child that is taken when the Trylle offspring is left behind in the changeling tradition.

Markis—a title of male royalty in troll society. Similar to the title of Duke, it's given to trolls with superior bloodlines and their correlating telekinetic abilities. Markis have a higher ranking than the average troll, but are beneath the King and Queen. The hierarchy of troll society is as follows: King/Queen; Prince/Princess; Markis/Marksinna; Högdragen; troll citizens; trackers; *mänsklig*; host families; humans (not raised in troll society).

The Markis and the Shadow—a troll reinterpretation of the Danish fairy tale *Skyggen* (in English, *The Shadow*).

Markis Ansvarig—a position of authority in troll communities, similar to a mayor or chieftain. Literal translation is "Markis-in-charge." It is a position used in cities without any major royals, like King/Queen or Prince/Princess. The female equivalent would be Marksinna Ansvariga.

Marksinna—a title of female royalty in troll society. The female equivalent of the Markis.

Mästare—the title given to prestigious department heads at the Mimirin.

Merellä, Oregon—a large, affluent citadel in Oregon. It is technically under the Vittra rule, but many trolls from tribes all over live there. It is virtually a metropolis compared to most troll towns and villages, and it is essentially a college town built around the Mimirin institution and library. The name means "by the sea." It is one of the oldest cities in North America, having been colonized after the trolls came over with the Vikings. Trolls first arrived in North America in early 1000 CE, and the trolls began moving west to get away from the violence of the Vikings. They settled Merellä around 1400 CE. It remains hidden with powerful cloaking spells by the Ögonen.

Midsommar—a trollized version of the festival "Midsommarafton" or "Midsummer's Eve." It is a summer festival, celebrating the end of the long winter, with flowers, greenery, and maypoles.

Mimirin, the—the great institution and library that holds much of the history of the trolls, located in the city of Merellä. The full official name is "Mimirin Talo," which means "House of Mimir," a reference to Mimir, the Norse god of knowledge and remembering. The Vittra were inspired by the Museum in Alexandria to build the Mimirin hundreds of years ago.

Mörkaston, Nevada—a Vittra city located near the Ruby Dome in northeastern Nevada. The name is an anglicized version of *mörkaste höjden*, which means "darkest point."

nettle—a stinging herbaceous plant common in Scandinavia. Nettles lose their sting when cooked and can be used in lieu of spinach or any other leafy green. Nettles can also be used dried and brewed as a tea.

Norra av Nord—a restaurant on Lake Sodalen in Sweden. The name means "Norra of the North" in Swedish, after its owner Norra.

northern pike—a species of carnivorous fish common in the brackish and fresh waters of the Northern Hemisphere, including the U.S. and Sweden. Pike can grow to a relatively large size, with European versions being the largest. Known as northerns and pike in Minnesota, and *gädda* in Sweden.

Ögonen—the trollian guardians who use their powerful psychokinesis to hide the city of Merellä from humans. They are not considered to be part of any tribe and are almost considered to be something of another species. Their name means "eyes." They are described as sinewy and nearly seven feet tall. They are covered in leathery, ocher skin, but it's so thin it's slightly transparent. They are androgynous, with very humanoid dark brown eyes.

ogre—ogres are similar to hobgoblins, except they are giant, most standing over seven feet tall, with superior strength. They are dim-witted and aggressive, and they are known only to the Omte tribes.

Öhaus—the proper name given to the town hall of Isarna. The name means "island house."

økkspill—a game similar to darts. The name literally means "axe games." It involves a board with three bull's-eyes—in white, black, and gold, respectively—and five kasteren axes.

Omte—one of the smaller troll kingdoms, only slightly more populous than the Skojare. Omte trolls are known to be rude and somewhat ill-tempered. They still practice changelings but pick lower class families than the Trylle and Kanin. Unlike the other tribes, the Omte tend to be less attractive in appearance. The Omte split off from the Vittra tribe in circa 1280 CE, when Dag felt like the Vittra favored the smaller hobgoblins and more conventionally attractive "humanoid" trolls. He took the ogres and established the tribe in Fula-träsk. Since 1280 CE, they have had forty monarchs—much more than any other tribe. The high turnover rate among Omte monarchs is due to their violent lifestyle, compromised immune systems, and lower intelligence. They are currently in the Torian Dynasty, with the widowed Queen Regent Bodil Elak ruling until her son Crown Prince Furston Elak comes of age in 2028.

Ondarike, Colorado—the capital city of the Vittra. The Queen and the majority of the powerful Vittra live within the palace there. It is located in northern Colorado, near Walden in the mountains.

Oslinna, Wyoming—a Trylle village that was decimated by the Vittra in 2010, but it has been slowly rebuilding. It is near Gillette, Wyoming.

Ottawa, Manitoba—a city in eastern Manitoba. It is the second most populous city in Manitoba.

Överste—a position in the Kanin military. In times of war, the Överste is the officer in charge of commanding the soldiers. The Överste does not decide any battle plans, but instead receives orders from the King or the Chancellor.

persuasion—a form of psychokinesis that is a mild form of mind control. The ability to cause another person to act a certain way based on thoughts.

peurojen—the one in charge of the giant woolly elk, similar to a shepherd.

precognition—a form of psychokinesis that is knowledge of something before its occurrence, especially by extrasensory perception.

psionic—referring to the practical use of psychic powers or paranormal phenomena.

psionic stun gun (PSG)—a weapon similar to a Taser or stun gun, but instead of electricity, it runs on psionic power.

psychokinesis—a blanket term for the production or control of motion, especially in inanimate and remote objects, purportedly by the exercise of psychic powers. This can include mind control, precognition, telekinesis, biological healing, teleportation, and transmutation.

Rektor—the Kanin in charge of trackers. The Rektor works with new recruits, helps with placement, and generally keeps the trackers organized and functioning.

rose hip soup—a soup common in Sweden, with its deep rosy color and sweet-tart tang. Rose hips, which ripen long after the rose blooms have faded, can be dried to enjoy all year and serve as an important source of vitamin C in northern countries.

Sámi—the indigenous peoples of the Arctic Circle in Scandinavia. They have lived in arctic and subarctic regions for over 3,500 years. Also known as Sami, Saami, Fenni, Laplanders, or Lapps. They have historically had an appearance similar to Inuit and other First Nation peoples.

semla—a Scandinavian sweet roll made of wheat bread, whipped cream, and almond paste. It is similar to a cream puff.

Sintvann, North Carolina—an Omte city located in the Great Dismal Swamp in North Carolina. The name means "angry waters."

Skojare—the aquatic tribe of trolls that is nearly extinct. They require large amounts of fresh water to survive, and one-third of their population possess gills and are able to breathe underwater. Once plentiful, only about five thousand Skojare are left on the entire planet. In circa 1300 CE, Aun the Blue broke off from the Kanin tribe, heading south from Doldastam for a warmer water source. He took all the gilled trolls with him and established the Skojare in Storvatten. They have had twenty-four monarchs since 1300 CE, and they are currently in the Rolfian Dynasty, with King Mikko Rune. His daughter, the Crown Princess Lisbet "Libby" Biâelse, is next in line for the throne.

Storvatten, Ontario—the capital and largest city of the Skojare, it is home to the palace and the Skojare royal family. It is situated on Lake Superior, not too far from Thunder Bay, Ontario, with a population of over fifteen hundred in 2019.

Sverige—the name for Sweden in Swedish.

thrimavolk (or Þrimavolk)—a secret group of female warriors belonging to the Älvolk. The thrimavolk are theoretically the female counterpoint to the Älvolk, and they are all the daughters of Älvolk.

Tonåren—in the Skojare society, a time when teenagers seek to explore the human world and escape the isolation of Storvatten. Most teens return home within a few weeks. Similar to Rumspringa.

Tower of Avanor—the tower in the Mimirin where the lineage and ancestry records are stored.

tracker—a member of troll society who is specifically trained to track down changelings and bring them home. Trackers have no paranormal abilities, other than the affinity to tune in to their particular changeling. They are able to sense danger to their charge and can determine the distance between them. The lowest form of troll society, other than *mänsklig*.

Tralla horse—a powerful draft horse, larger than a Shire horse or a Clydesdale, originating in Scandinavia, and only known to be bred among the Kanin. Once used as a workhorse because they can handle the cold and snow, now they are usually used for show, such as in parades or during celebrations.

triskelion—a symbol consisting of three lines radiating from a center.

troglecology—a branch of biology in the Mimirin devoted to studying the relationships between trolls and the environment around them and with each other. It is derived from the words *troglodyte* (Latin for "troll") and *ecology* (the branch of biology dealing with the relationships of organisms with their environment and with each other).

trolls of mixed blood (TOMB)—any troll that has parents that are not of the same tribe. This includes both full-TOMBs (both parents are trolls) and half-TOMBs (one parent is a troll, one parent is human). By using People First Language, it is more inclusive and socially acceptable compared to *half-breed*, *half-blood*, or *halvblud*. There are fifteen distinct types of TOMBs (ten full-TOMBs, five half-TOMBs). They are as follows:

- KanHu (Kanin & Human)
- KanOm (Kanin & Omte)
- OmHu (Omte & Human)
- OmTry (Omte & Trylle)
- Omttra (Omte & Vittra)
- SkoHu (Skojare & Human)
- Skomte (Skojare & Omte)
- Skonin (Skojare & Kanin)
- SkoTry (Skojare & Trylle)
- TryHu (Trylle & Human)
- Trynin (Trylle & Kanin)
- VittHu (Vittra & Human)
- Vittjare (Vittra & Skojare)
- VittKa (Vittra & Kanin)
- Vittrylle (Vittra & Trylle)

Trylle—the beautiful trolls with powers of psychokinesis and for whom the practice of changelings is a cornerstone of their society. Like all trolls, they are ill-tempered and cunning, and often selfish. They were once plentiful, but their numbers and abilities are fading, though they are still one of the largest tribes of trolls. They are considered peaceful. The Trylle became a tribe in in 1510 CE, when Aldaril became fed up with the inept Kanin King Harald. He went south, taking many wealthy nobles with him, and established the Trylle in Förening along the Mississippi River. They have had twenty-one monarchs since 1510 CE, and they are currently in the Mógilian Dynasty, with Queen Wendy Staad. Her son, Crown Prince Oliver Staad, is next in line for the throne.

tupilaq—an Inuit word meaning "witch" or "shaman."

Ugly Vulture, the—a roughneck Omte bar in their capital city, Fulaträsk.

ullaakuut—an Inuit word that means "good morning."

valknut—a symbol sometimes known as the "warrior knot." It consists of three interlocked triangles, and it's frequently seen on Norse artifacts.

veloma—an álfar term for boy-/girlfriend or significant other; the literal translation is "the one you fondly choose to be with."

Viliätten—House of Vili, the oldest troll dynasty. See *Vilings Dynasty*.

Vilinga Saga—the document that explains the lineage of the troll monarchy that Ulla is archiving. The opening lines of the saga are as follows: "*One war-king called Vili; with his House of Vilings, went to the Western Lands, to conquer all that they would find.*"

Vilings Dynasty—the oldest dynasty in troll history. It is the only dynasty of the united kingdom of trolls. It ran from circa 770 CE with Vili in Áibmoráigi, Scandinavia, and ended with the feuding brothers Jorund the Elder of the Vittra in North America and Norund the Younger of the Kanin in the already established Doldastam, in circa 1200 CE. In circa 1040 CE, Asa the Cold and many of the trolls fled from Scandinavia out of fear of the war on paganism. They sailed with Vikings over to North America and relocated the troll capital from Áibmoráigi to Doldastam.

Vittra—a more violent faction of trolls whose powers lie in physical strength and longevity, although some mild psychokinesis is not unheard-of. They also suffer from idiopathic infertility, with increased frequency in the past century. While Vittra are generally beautiful in appearance, more than fifty percent of their offspring are born as hobgoblins, and a quarter of their attractive populations are born with dwarfism. The Vittra are one of the oldest tribes, having been the first one to split off from the Kanin in circa 1200 CE, when the feuding brothers Norund the Younger and Jorund the Elder disagreed about staying in the north. Jorund went south, establishing the Vittra in Ondarike. He took all of the strong, less attractive trolls with him, leading to the eventual creation of the ogres and hobgoblins. In circa 1280 CE, Dag broke off from the Vittra, fearing they were favoring the hobgoblins and more attractive "humanoid" trolls. He led the ogres down to Fulaträsk and established the Omte. Despite being the second oldest tribe, the Vittra have had the fewest monarchs, in large part due to their supernatural longevity. They have had twenty-one monarchs since their establishment in circa 1200 CE, and they are currently in the Sarafina Dynasty with Queen Sara Elsing.

War for the Princess—a 2009–2010 violent conflict between the Vittra and the Trylle over their shared heir, then Crown Princess Wendy Luella Dahl. Wendy chose to be with the Trylle, and after her coronation as Queen, the Trylle attacked the Vittra and defeated them with the execution of their King, Oren Elsing.

woollies—another name for the "giant woolly elk." See *Irish elk*.

ABOUT THE AUTHOR

Mariah Paaverud with Chimera

AMANDA HOCKING is the author of more than twenty young adult novels, including the *New York Times* bestselling Trylle Trilogy and Kanin Chronicles. Her love of pop culture and all things paranormal influence her writing. She spends her time in Minnesota, taking care of her menagerie of pets and working on her next book.

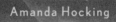